NOT
A BRAVE NEW WORLD

LIZETTE

FOR ALBERT

NOT
A BRAVE NEW WORLD

PAUL K LYONS

A TRILOGY IN THREE WIVES

BOOK THREE

LIZETTE

PIKLE
PUBLISHING

The *Not a Brave New World* trilogy
– *Gillian, Diana* and *Lizette* –
Pikle Publishing, 2014

First published in hardback as
Kip Fenn – Reflections
Pikle Publishing, 2004

* * *

ISBN 978-0954827038

NOT
A BRAVE NEW WORLD

LIZETTE

PROLOGUE

I've told of my early life in the first of these three volumes of Reflections, how I married Gillian, for no good reason, how we messed up our own lives and those of our two children, Crystal and Bronze; and I've explained how my career in the civil service was nearly brought to an abrupt end by a hugely embarrassing weakness that should never have been made public. A switch in departments, and then to working for a United Nations agency, the International Fund for Sustainable Development (IFSD) in The Hague, suited me well.

And so to volume two, and how, in the Netherlands, I met Diana – a theatre designer – who had enough radiance, social and cultural, for the both of us. We had a child together – Guido – and what a joy he was, and is. He was but four years old when I lost Crystal to her demons. A few days later – like some crass compensation from the gods – a fully-grown man, Arturo, turned up, claiming to be my son.

More by luck than judgement or ambition, I rose through the IFSD ranks, toiling away with many thousand others trying to tackle imbalances across the world, and to increase aid from richer to poorer nations. Time and time again, well-off governments were forced – by growing social turmoil instigated through the First Tuesday Movement – to the negotiating table to offer more aid, and three times they agreed huge incremental increases. Yet, it all proved too little too late to attenuate Al Zahir's infernal zeal or to stop him leading Muslims everywhere into Jihad war against the rich Christian world.

I only mention this history because I blame the war for many things, not least my losing Diana, and also, eventually – for this I've yet to tell – exposing the limits of my professional ability. And, although my planned deathday here at Willow Calm Lodge is not far off now, Dr Lipson's pill menu is still keeping me sharp and pain-free so I have time to tell of more pleasant memories, my love affair with Lizette, and our son Jay, for example, as well as the intriguing ventures that kept me busy, far from retirement, through to my late 80s.

PART ONE

Lizette, Bronze and Resignation

The Photograph

'I was (said fixedly)'

The Clone [an extract]

'...
I am (said hesitantly)
I am (said confusedly)
I am (said doubtfully)
I am (said disbelievingly)
I am not
I am not (said hesitantly)
I am not (said confusedly)
I am not (said doubtfully)
I am not (said disbelievingly)
I am
I am (said hesitantly)
...'

The Retiree

'I am (said tiredly)
I was (said resignedly)
I was (said regretfully)
I was (said questioningly)
I am (said amazedly)'

I AM Poems by Kolin Delvreux (2065)

CHAPTER 1

LOOKING AT A PHOTOGRAPH OF GARIBALDI

I have a photograph of Giuseppi Garibaldi on my screen. It was taken in 1860. Two hundred years later, I saw an actual albumen print, made from a glass negative, at an exhibition in Paris. Naturally, I bought the catalogue so that I could copy all the images onto Neil (the name I give to my digital memory store).

This particular photo is a three-quarters portrait, set in an oval cameo style. Garibaldi must have been about 50 at the time. His body, posed with left hand on hip and elbow pointing out, is subtly framed by the slight shadow lines of a jamb and window frame behind. He has a beautiful soft face: a large forehead with receding hairline, hooded eyes intently looking towards the camera, and a thick tidy greying beard. He wears light trousers, a dark shirt (which, because he was famous for wearing a red shirt, the imagination sees in colour), and a neckerchief. Hanging down across his shirt, there is a simple chain attached to something heavy in his shirt pocket, presumably a pocket watch. And, in the only acknowledgement of a military or leadership role, the right hand grasps a sword, held by a harness to his belt, which takes a near vertical line down in front of his legs.

When I first glance at this picture, I focus initially on Garibaldi's face, drawn in by the intent gaze, in which I see not only concentration but seriousness, wariness, curiosity; but also a warmness in the visage as a whole. After some moments, my eye eases down the line of shiny buttons on his shirt towards his hand and the hilt of the sword, and then along the edge of the sword to reach the bottom curve of the oval, before moving back up again to take in more detail, the nonchalant elbow, the sagging pocket, the neckerchief, and the exquisite way the whole portrait has been emphasised by the vertical and horizontal lines behind.

But it is not only the aesthetic qualities that make this one of my favourite photographs. Despite leaving any serious interest in history behind in the class and lecture rooms of youth, I have always had a soft spot for Garibaldi. This is thanks to Flip, aka Philip Liphook, my school history teacher, who was a devout European. Frustrated by the strictures of a course focused on British history, every now and then he would randomly slip into a lesson information about his favourite continental characters. He had a lot of time for Luther I recall, Peter the Great and El Cid, and for the people who built the European Union, such as Robert Schumann and, a hero of his, Jacques Delors. For some reason, I also remember Portugal's Marquis of Pombal, and the Dutch leaders Lamoraal Count of Egmond and his contemporary William of Orange.

Horace, my schoolmate and debating partner, and I had a particular reason to take up Flip's attachment to Garibaldi.

Once, and only once in my time at Witley Academic, Flip organised a debating contest between our history department and that of Charterhouse, another eminent public school in west Surrey. It was an important occasion, held in the Great Hall, with hundreds of students in attendance. There were three debates for different age groups. We were in the middle group, but this was before Jeff Zimmerman joined us, and when Horace and I were Hip and Kip.

I am meandering, reflecting on events that should have been recorded earlier in my story. And yet, lying here, so many years later, I continue to be startled by how strong, how potent these early memories remain. It is as though I can touch the rapture of those times, especially in the debating victories I shared with Horace, and the volleyball wins I shared with Alfred.

Our particular motion read, 'Garibaldi was a great European', and we were given the task of defending it. We thought we had drawn the lucky straw since it would be far easier to argue that 'he was a great European' than 'he was not a great European', but we soon realised this interpretation of the motion focused too much on the adjective 'great' and not enough on the noun 'European'. The other side would be able to argue he was a great Italian hero, thus putting the onus on us to explain why he mattered beyond the Italian nation state.

I should refresh my patchy knowledge (half-remembered from Flip's teaching and Pacciotti's great Hollywood bio-flick with Vincent Mallow as Garibaldi) from *Encyclopaedia Universal.*

In May 1860, Garibaldi landed in Sicily, then ruled by the king of Naples, with a volunteer force clad in bright red shirts and known as the 'one thousand'. By the end of June, he had conquered the island and set up a provisional government. He then crossed to the Italian mainland and, by taking Naples itself, paved the way for the establishment of a kingdom of Italy with Victor Emmanuel as king. Garibaldi, the encyclopaedia says, was a great patriot, a truly honest man, and one possessed of great political and military skills which he devoted to the nationalist cause.

Prior to the debate, I came up with the concept that nationalism had to be an essential precursor to internationalism, or, in this instance, Europeanism, although Flip must surely have helped me with this. Horace delivered the arguments we developed from that idea with stunning panache. Flip's two other teams lost to Charterhouse, but we were victorious and, very properly, the toast of Witley Academic for a day or two.

Chance took Gustave Le Gray, one of the great artistic photographers of the 19th century, to Sicily in 1860. His business in Paris was failing and so he decided to join the author Alexander Dumas on an expedition, aboard his luxurious ship *Emma*, to Egypt. They stopped in Sicily where Dumas became involved in Garibaldi's cause, to the extent of fetching him arms; and where Le Gray took stunning pictures of Palermo in the aftermath of Garibaldi's conquest, including several of barricaded streets. Dumas records in his book, *On board the Emma*, the following exchange with Garibaldi (as reproduced in the Paris exhibition catalogue, English language edition).

Garibaldi: 'Do you have a photographer with you?'

Dumas: 'The best photographer in Paris – Le Gray.'

Garibaldi: 'Well then, let him photograph our ruins. It is only right that Europe should know what is happening here: 2,800 shells rained down in a single day.'

Dumas: 'We shall photograph all this, and you too, in the middle.'

Garibaldi: 'Why do you want to photograph me?'

Dumas: 'Well, I have only seen you as a general; and, really, you do not look like yourself, I would prefer you in your own clothes.'

Garibaldi: 'Do what you like with me. As soon as I saw you, I knew I would be one of your victims.'

And Dumas goes on to record in the same book, how Le Gray spent days making 'magnificent photographs' of the ruins of Palermo and how he (Dumas) planned to send them to Paris 'for exhibition'.

Which leads me back, conveniently, to the spring of 2060, and the exhibition at the Musée d'Orsay in Paris where I first saw the portrait of Garibaldi in an original print, and other magnificent Le Gray originals; and to Lizette.

CHAPTER 2

IN WHICH I FALL FOR LIZETTE COMPLETELY

I met Lizette during a dinner with Pete, my old university friend, and his wife Clarity at their cottage in Chapel Chorlton in 2053.

We did meet again, I don't remember exactly when since I seem to have no email correspondence that would help me pinpoint that second encounter. It was definitely after I had separated from Diana; and Clarity's daughter Joan was six or seven. I remember I was taken for a day trip to the Peak District, which included a walk along Dove Dale (or Eagle Dale in George Elliot's *Adam Bede*, a favourite of Clarity's), a kitsch well-dressing fair at Youlgreave, and afternoon tea with Lizette at her house near Leek. I recall only that she was very welcoming, served an excellent cake using figs from a crooked tree that curled round the corner of a stone outhouse, and was curious about my work.

During 2059, Lizette changed jobs, moving from Keele University to the European University in Brussels. She then contacted me in The Hague, where I'd been living for many years, slowly progressing in my UN career at the International Fund for Sustainable Development (IFSD), to suggest we have dinner the next time I was in Brussels. I felt flattered, but faltered in my response, or lack of.

Several months later, in early 2060, Clarity wrote to congratulate me on my unexpected appointment as director-general of the IFSD, and to pass on details about Pete's achievements or Joan's progress, as she did sometimes. She also urged me to get in touch with her friend, Lizette, who was not finding Brussels easy. Thus, one very cold February Tuesday, we met at Fish and Chippy in the St Catherine area of Brussels. The restaurant had been called Jacques in my Euroil days. Unusually, the place was half empty; yet it was still surprisingly animated and the windows were all steamed up.

Lizette Sanderson, I learned, was born in 2018, just four years before my oldest son, Arturo. Her father, Mervyn Sanderson, had been a civil engineer, a builder of bridges. Wendy, her mother, like mine, had been a teacher but one who worked mostly with disadvantaged children. She had two brothers, one older (Samuel) and one younger (Mercurio). In response to her father's various jobs, the family had moved about a lot when she was young with stints in Southern India, Cambodia and the Philippines. But, by 2028, the scale of social unrest around the world, the growth of the First Tuesday Movement, and concerns about the children's education – Samuel was only a year or two away from his 16 exams, and Mercurio was ready to start primary school – led the Sandersons to return permanently to the UK.

The family settled down in Bristol. Lizette did well at school, with high grades in her 18 exams, and won a place to study materials science under Professor Jean Hunter at Nottingham University. By this time, Hunter was already a celebrated scientist, although it would be a further decade before she was awarded a Nobel Prize for chemistry. While a postgraduate student, Lizette married a trainee lawyer named Clint Tuohy. They moved to Stoke-on-Trent. She took up a research/teaching post at Keele University, and Clint joined a law firm in Newcastle-under-Lyme.

That first evening together, in the fish restaurant, Lizette looked attractive but slightly older than her 41 years. Dressed all in black, a polo sweater and jeans, she wore light make-up except for an excess of kohl around the eyes which contrasted too strongly with dyed-blond wavy hair. She smiled often but it was a smile constrained by a small mouth and thin lips which tried to conceal slanting upper teeth. She was not a beauty, she said so herself on numerous occasions, but she was 20 years younger (and nearly 20 centimetres shorter) than me; she was slim, much slimmer than Diana, who was heavily built and expanded over the years; she talked with the sense of a scientist; and she came across as a practical, down-to-earth woman, with lots of warmth. Most important of all, though, she appeared very interested in me.

At her request, we arranged to meet again the following day, for an early supper, so that I could catch the last train back to Holland. This is when I told her about Diana, and when she told me about Clint. He had disappointed her, she said. Having planned to go far in politics, he had settled for petty squabbling as a councillor on the Stoke City Council and a job dealing with wills and property conveyancing. While at Nottingham they had had similar dreams and ideals, she said, but time and reality had driven a wedge between them.

There were other disappointments. The materials science department at Keele University had been impressed by her Jean Hunter association, and been all too willing to allow Lizette to continue the research line taken in her doctorate thesis. But it had proved to be a dead end, she confided. She was unsure whether this was because of the limitations of her tools, having been unable to attract sufficient funding for state-of-the-art equipment, or because Hunter, with many neophytes at Nottingham, had ruthlessly guided her towards a line of investigation she wanted closed rather than one with real potential.

In the first year of the Jihad War, Lizette took stock of her life and found it wanting. She left Clint, and moved to the house near Leek which she shared with another woman, an administrator at Keele University, called Rhoda Jackmann-Ives. To fill up the non-working part of her life, Lizette took to gardening – 'a mild antidote to chemistry' – and short-term sex affairs, as encouraged by the also recently-divorced Rhoda. And she set about considering how she might escape, perhaps to revisit the exotic places of her childhood. It had taken years to make a move, for one reason or another, and then, when she did, it was no further than Brussels. She had proved herself no less lacking in initiative than her ex-husband, she concluded rather dejectedly.

I told her she was talking nonsense, and that she had been very courageous to come to Brussels. Notwithstanding difficult early days at the European University I predicted that her Brussels life would improve. I must have remarked that

Guido, my son and only child with Diana, had thought of taking a degree there, and then rambled on about missing him and how I planned shortly to go to Paris to see him. Which led to Lizette saying how much she wanted to visit Paris again, and to a suggestion – I'm convinced it came from her, though she denied this in the years to come – that she join me for the weekend.

So, in March 2060, we rendezvoused in the French capital. Arriving late Friday night, we took separate rooms in a high-class pension in the Montmartre area. Part of the Saturday I spent with Guido, while Lizette went sightseeing. She returned with a chalk portrait of herself. That night we slept in the same bed, un-memorably, I'm happy to report (given my long-term sexual insecurity), because Lizette did not want to make love.

The next morning we caught the metro to Concorde and strolled, arm-in-arm, through the Jardin Des Tuileries, along the Seine, across the Royal Bridge to the Musée d'Orsay to wonder at the photographs of Le Gray, and the Garibaldi portrait in particular. This was the start of an affair and a friendship that would last, with ups and downs, the rest of our lives.

A first 'down' occurred all too soon. Two weeks later Lizette came to The Hague to stay with me for a weekend. After showing her round the city during the day, I had thought we would eat out somewhere special. But with Amsterdam planned for the Sunday, we both decided to stay in on the Saturday evening. In any case, it became apparent, Lizette wanted a serious talk about our relationship, which was better conducted in the privacy of my home than in a restaurant.

After our successful weekend in Paris, a series of intimate emails, and a pleasurable day together in The Hague it was clear that something was troubling her. She asked a lot of questions about my children, all of which I had mentioned but, until then, without much explanation. Then she wanted to go to the bedroom and make love, as if to reinforce the bond we had already established without sex. But I was unable to perform. Perhaps I was intimidated by her tales of promiscuity. Lizette thought I simply did not find her attractive. Later, I learned that her affairs had not served to reinforce her self-esteem, which had been the idea, but to undermine it. Thus, in the moment, in the bedroom we (I can use the plural pronoun because we discussed it later) were suddenly caught by a shock wave of alienation, a complete loss of confidence in each other and in our relationship. It was as though a spotlight, that had the power to illuminate self-awareness, had suddenly caught us in the wrong place at the wrong time with the wrong person.

In order to overcome my own feelings of inadequacy, I blundered into various apologies and half explanations. I also tried to reassure Lizette that I found her attractive. She appeared entirely unconcerned by what I had to say. We redressed and returned to the main room with its large window and the night cityscape view. And then, standing by that window, with a mug of Ceylon tea in hand she told me she was 14 weeks pregnant and that she could not, would not have an abortion. Sheepishly, hesitantly and anxiously, she looked over towards me to see how I was taking the news. I waited, without thinking about the confession, to hear the rest. I feared the news would get worse, and she would reveal an involvement elsewhere. She turned to look out across the city's lights.

'I don't think I can tell you who the father is.'

'That helps,' I said. 'That's very helpful.' She put the mug down on the coffee table, and returned to the window hugging herself.

'You sod. This isn't easy Kip. I'm here. I'm telling you. I'm trying to tell you.' She continued to face away from me.

'Maybe you could explain why you can't say who the father is?' My tone was sarcastic, edging towards irritable, I suppose, as I began to take in the full meaning of what she had told me. At this, she spun round defiantly.

'I called you four months ago, more than four months ago. You promised to contact me. Why now, why after so long?'

She turned back round to face the darkness of the window and the night beyond. 'Why don't you think you can tell me who the father is?' I asked the question more softly, more genuinely this time round. I waited. I had been standing too, but now I flopped down on the sofa, weary.

'Is it going to matter? I mean do you still want to go to Amsterdam tomorrow? Will you want to see me again?'

'Not if you're involved with someone else, no, I don't believe I could deal with that.' She swivelled round sharply again.

'No, of course not, of course I'm not seeing anyone else, how could you think that? It was a mistake. A stupid mistake.'

I am recalling the dialogue as best I can, condensing maybe, or improvising. But, from Jay's point of view, this is the worst that was said. And knowing how much both Lizette and I have loved and cared for him, he has no hang-up about his conception being 'a stupid mistake'. Indeed, ever since he's known this snippet of family history – which came a dozen years after being old enough to appreciate that I was not his genetic father – he's employed it mercilessly for the sake of argument or humour. So I've no compunction about mentioning it here.

From my point of view, Lizette had eliminated the worst possibility, but there remained two reasons for the enigmatic silence: either she did not know who the father was because, after arriving in Brussels, she had continued to sleep around, making me one of a sequence, and one yet to be consummated; or, she did not want to tell me, which, in a different way, signalled danger.

'You haven't answered my question, is it going to matter to us?'

'I don't know, Lizette. How can I know. I like you. I like you very much. But I don't know. Only time will tell.'

'Thank you.' Then she came over to the sofa and sat down next to me, linking her arm through mine.

'When we walked through that garden in Paris, past the magnolias and the witch-hazels, it felt good. Holding on to your arm, I felt warm and happy and safe – though I knew already I was pregnant.' She paused and pressed my arm tighter through her own. 'I went back to England for Christmas, to see Ma and Pa, then to Chapel Chorlton for a few days, and then to Leek for New Year's Eve. I part-own the house and use a tiny bedroom to store stuff. Rhoda had a party, as she does, to which she invited Clint. Oh this is so complicated. You need to know that after Clint and I separated, Clint and Rhoda had an affair. No, even that's not the full truth. They slept together once while we were still married and living together, although we had separate bedrooms by then. I didn't mind, it helped with the decision to split up, and, besides, Rhoda had asked my permission, although Clint never knew that.

I rented for a while before moving to Leek, and that's when Rhoda and Clint screwed around some more together. When they gave up, they stayed friends, as I did with both of them. You'd have to know Clint to understand. In public he's professional and competent, but in private he's a child, needy and compulsive, always wanting to be liked and promising to make up for any shortcomings tomorrow. At the same time, he nags for favours, often for company, and especially for sex. He has no self-respect in this regard. But he's lovable. I loved him for years; but I grew tired of it all.

We got back together once, in 2057. I was very depressed, and he had suddenly been discarded by his second wife. I had Rhoda screaming in one ear about how it had taken me five years to get him out of my system, and I was screaming at myself in the other ear. Yet I let him plead me round to giving it another try. He was so desperate to get back together, he said, and he had changed.'

She stopped talking for a few seconds. 'You must know how stupid we women can be. Three months I fooled myself into thinking I might have exaggerated our earlier marriage problems, and that I would never find a man who loved me as well as Clint. And then I woke up, again, and told him enough was enough. I felt guilty, and more depressed than ever, for a year or more.'

Another, longer pause. 'A whisky would be nice. I'm still trying to tell you. I'll get there. But it would help if you could talk a bit, about Gillian and Diana, and, well, how you managed in the bedroom department. I mean four children, it doesn't sound like you had much of a problem to be honest.'

I laughed, poured us some alcohol, and did as she asked. But, as before, I felt as if she were far away, not paying much attention. I wondered if she was using the time to sort out how she was going to tell the rest of her own story.

'I'd like to blame Clint. I'd like to say I had too much to drink on New Year's Eve, and he seduced me with flattery and neediness. But that's not true. I hope you appreciate this, you sod, I hardly know you, and here I am baring my soul. I decided consciously, early, to let him come on to me. But this wasn't a weak decision, as in the past, but a strong one. You have to know I felt that I'd escaped, that I was a new person, and that there was no danger any more of going backwards. But I'd been nearly six months in Brussels without a fuck, and I wanted it easy. And ... shit ... even that's not the whole truth. I'm trying here Kip. I'm really trying.' She held out her glass for a refill, and waited for me to return to the sofa so as to snuggle into me tighter than before.

'The truth is ... I'd given up hoping for a real relationship. Rhoda hadn't forewarned me Clint was coming. When I saw him there that evening, I decided not only to let him come on to me, but to throw caution to the wind, throw the dice, and see if I could get pregnant. So, you see, it's my ex-husband's child. And, before you ask, no, I haven't told him yet. And, yes, of course I should.'

She felt so tiny, I tightened my embrace around her shoulders, and awkwardly kissed the hair on the side of her head. She was crying, so she didn't turn to kiss me back. Instead she slid down so that she was nearly horizontal across the sofa and her head was in my lap. I used one hand to brush aside her hair slightly, and the other to stroke her cheek with the back of my hand, and then the back of a knuckle to wipe away her mascara-streaked tears. Her eyes were closed. For a few moments we remained very still, suspended in time.

I wasn't thinking about her or her story, I was simply enjoying our closeness. Then Lizette slowly wiggled her head slightly, rubbing an ear into my crutch, and, on sensing my arousal, continued. Deftly, she turned over on her stomach, undid my trouser belt and fly, and gave me the kind of lip service I thought only prostitutes performed in cars. Afterwards, I worried, thanks to years with Diana, about Lizette's pleasure, but she did not want to make love as such, and confessed to being glad that we had not had intercourse earlier.

'You'll need some space, Kip, to decide what to do with me. It's not only me, it's me and a child, and, now that I've managed to tell it all to you, I don't want there to be any misapprehensions. If we're right for each other, and I hope we are, there'll be plenty of time for affection, tenderness and other pleasant things.'

Affection, tenderness and other pleasant things. I've always remembered her saying this. I do not know if she invented the phrase spontaneously, or had culled it from a book, but if she hadn't already won me over with her genuineness and honesty, then this idea that a life together could be full of affection, tenderness and other pleasant things won me over completely.

CHAPTER 3
IN WHICH I STRUGGLE AS DIRECTOR-GENERAL

Chintz, my favourite nurse here at Willow Calm Lodge, came in a few minutes ago, bringing with her a bowl of fruit sponge-balls. I was crying. She had never seen me crying before. I told her I was thinking about Lizette, the last love of my life. After all I've gone through in writing these Reflections, revisiting the emotions connected with Melissa, for example, or Gillian or Crystal, it seems so strange that I should be brought to tears by this simple memory. Chintz asked to see some photographs of Lizette, so I promised to search one out, but I'll do it later. For now, I need to press on and record a difficult period professionally.

***

At the time, I did not consider the Peter Principle (which states that employees tend to be promoted beyond their level of competence) might apply to me and my own promotion to director-general of the International Fund for Sustainable Development (IFSD). In retrospect, though, I came to see, as much as one can, the truth behind my appointment. I read and heard a range of opinions at the time; there are some articles stored on Neil, but I can't be bothered to seek them out or re-examine them now. Most commentators focused on the fact that, as a career UN official, I was an unexpected choice, and that only two years earlier the previous British government had made a half-hearted effort to oust me.

It's true that, by this stage, the director-general of the IFSD did not have as much power over his agency as earlier chiefs had done, nor as much as other agency chief executives. Although the IFSD had suffered along with the whole UN system during the Jihad War, it had re-emerged at the turn of the decade – in consequence of the Singapore Peace Treaty – as the funnel through which the largest portion of development aid would continue to flow. Many an ex-diplomat, or ex-minister, or even ex-prime minister from a smaller country coveted the job, and there were plenty of secretary generals, presidents, director-generals and executive directors of other agencies that wished for elevation.

As with all such high-level appointments, mine followed a huge amount of behind-the-scenes bargaining much of which I never knew about. With all the irrelevant positions and manoeuvres filtered out, it came down to this: there was no consensus on three or four prime candidates, but there was an unholy alliance of IFSD members willing to support Britain's proposal to place me in the position. Why unholy? Because half of them, having witnessed my commitment and achievements as director in the early years of the war, believed I was the man to defend and promote the Fund through thick and thin; and the other half wished to attenuate the Fund's effectiveness by appointing someone they believed would be ineffective in the top job. At Singapore, the Western powers may have been forced to agree to further share their wealth, but that did not stop a number of them employing a range of tactics (including, apparently, supporting my appointment) to slow down implementation of the decisions. How they could predict that I would not manage well in the job is beyond me, yet they were right.

I collected a good team of advisers, that was the easy part. I'll mention three in my cabinet. I took Tommy because he wanted to stay with me, and his insight into the never-ending political problems of India and Central Asia was invaluable. I persuaded the much younger Chidi Naiambana that I could not do without his expertise on sub-Sahara Africa, and that two or three years with me would assist, not hinder, his own promotion prospects. (It didn't. Many years later he made it to director-general himself.). And, thanks to Tommy's ear-to-the-ground, I unearthed Eduardo Villalonga, a brilliant Bolivian lawyer languishing in an IFSD backwater where he'd been closeted after falling out with a vindictive supervisor years earlier.

There was MarySue, my English secretary who dealt directly with my other personal staff. I had 'inherited' her from Pravit Krishnamurty when I took over as director of the Future Policy Division, and, apart from three extended breaks to nurture two children and a sick husband, she had stayed with me ever since. What she lacked in humour and tact, she more than made up for in efficiency and loyalty.

As director I had remained in touch, just, with the nuts and bolts of the division's work (the planning, the programming, the projects). I felt, rightly or wrongly, that I could see, albeit dimly, the end result of my negotiations, actions and decisions. But this was not the case as director-general. Consequently – I can only say this in retrospect obviously – I spent too much effort and time trying to control and influence the directors (about nine in all), who were not so much below me in the hierarchy but to my side. As a director I had not understood this intrinsically, I had simply enjoyed my autonomy and fought, usually with success, against any interference. Mostly, though, the IFSD's earlier director-generals had been of the hands-off variety. I was a hands-on chief. At best, I might have helped guide the weaker or more inexperienced directors, at worst I certainly drew other more experienced directors into unnecessary conflicts, thereby absorbing too much of their valuable time. I do not wish to dwell on these failures, but I will give one example, pared down to its basic components.

Liu Xiangjun, a crusty, tallish Chinese man about ten years younger than me, had taken over my job as environment director. He had held a similar high-level position in the World Bank but, earlier in his career, had been an academic (a professor of sustainable development at Harbin University), an environmental policy planner, and, for a short time a deputy ambassador in Hungary. By 2061, two years after the Singapore Peace Treaty, I had become frustrated at how slowly the IFSD was returning to normal operations. As the chief executive, I felt I should be able to do something about this. Barely a day went by when I didn't try to devise ways of speeding up our activities. It came to my attention that Liu's department appeared less dynamic than most others. Instead of focusing on the restart of many important projects which had been stalled by the war, using the special streamlined procedures I had instigated, he had decided to revisit and re-evaluate each one. By insisting on fresh contract and approval procedures for every project, he was adding a minimum of one year to their implementation timetables.

Did I pick on Liu because, as his predecessor, I had been in charge of developing these particular programmes and projects? Lizette thought this might be the case; as did Liu who told me as much in private when I was making a last informal attempt to push him along. Then I issued an Information Note to the relevant directors, which everyone knew was targeted at Liu, ordering work to continue with minimum delay on all stalled projects and programmes.

Since I had played a formal card, it should have been the end of the matter, but Liu decided to challenge my authority publicly. He wrote an unprecedented Information Note Response and distributed it to the other directors. Foolishly, I would not let the matter drop; and, shamefully, I made use of one of his deputies, my ex-assistant, Ninel Horeva, in order to accumulate ammunition for further assaults.

Ninel had coveted the environment director job herself and then, having failed to win it, resented her new chief. She helped select and exaggerate various lethargic practices in the Environment Division which I then used to question Liu's competence. Meanwhile, though, he presented the results of a study, contracted months earlier, presenting the dangers and inefficiencies of restarting projects without a full reassessment. He was right. I had been blind to the extent of the problems caused by, for example, the loss of local staff and expertise, damaged or stolen equipment, and the unavailability of original contractors.

The spat only wounded me, but it did for Ninel. Liu got shot of her as soon as he could, and I was in no position to interfere. She chose to leave the UN system altogether and work as a lobbyist, with a huge salary, for a large Russian consultancy organisation.

Instead of interfering downwards, I should have been doing more hobnobbing sideways with other UN agencies, and upwards with the Secretary General's staff and the General Assembly members, and more moving around the globe promoting the public face of the IFSD. And, if I had wanted to make the IFSD more efficient, I should have done it by a careful reorganisation of its structure and determined efforts to make life easier for the directors, not by trying to do their jobs for them.

CHAPTER 4
IN WHICH I RECALL ZOE BERGMANN'S THEORIES

Would I have been a better director-general if I had taken over at a less demanding time? I like to think that the odds were stacked heavily against anyone managing to guide the IFSD through that particular five year period.

The Jihad War was only recently over. The Singapore Peace Treaty promised to deliver more worldwide equality than mankind had ever known and a long-lasting peace, though there were many doubters on this latter pledge. It also increased the UN's power, under carefully circumscribed conditions, to pull together an intervention army, and to intervene within sovereign states or to control border conflicts.

But the Jihad War had cost many lives, resulting in devastated families; and it had cost many trillions of dollars and euros, which had left most of the developed nations suffering their deepest recession of the century. Recovery was expected. Nevertheless, European and US middle-class citizens, however sympathetic with the plight of those less well off, were resentful about having to pay higher taxes, initially for the war, and then for increased overseas development aid. The UN's authority and position in the world had been preserved and enhanced by the Treaty, but there was a considerable downside in terms of public support and understanding of its work. This public support did not recover in the short term, and when the UN was torn apart again a few years later by the Second Jihad War, it plummeted further. Today, thirty years later, I am pleased to say, the UN has fully re-established itself. I hope it will go from strength to strength in the 22nd century.

Indeed, I am inclined to believe there is some truth in Zoe Bergmann's simple and powerful theory that we will only ever be able to rid war from the face of the earth when the United Nations, or similar, can establish a governing body with the biggest and most powerful army in the world. She says it may take a 100 or 500 years, but history shows a slow, if uneven, progression towards such an objective.

Bergmann grew up in Vienna when the First Tuesday Movement, at least in Europe, was at its most idealistic. Her Jewish parents, both artists, brought her up on a diet of pacificism and FTM marches, and had a perfect right to expect her to develop traditional left-of-centre views. But, as a teenager, she rebelled and turned against them. She rejected a place at Linz University to join the then nascent European army at one of its bases near Trieste. For four years she trained as a soldier, and then as an officer, but all the while studying in her spare time. She waited – so her autobiography says – for a taste of combat, which came when the UN asked the army to help resolve a civil war – the Jamaica Skirmish – before leaving military service and winning a place at Heidelberg University to read history contexts and international politics.

It was only in the 60s, during the war, that Bergmann became a darling, as they used to say, of the English media, which often set her up against Gregory, who I have referred to several times in these volumes. They were both essentially historians, among the best of their generation, and they were both roughly the same age, but the similarities stopped there. She was quiet, controlled and forceful in the way she answered questions or argued in media/public debate; he was often loud, outrageous and long-winded. Whereas Bergmann's theories were the tips of icebergs of her research, it was not unknown for Gregory to make up a theory while on a live broadcast, and then spend six months putting together the research to back it up. Which is not to say that his intellect wasn't razor sharp, or that he wasn't an important social commentator.

In short, Bergmann based her theory on the mechanism known as 'survival of the fittest', initially employed by Charles Darwin to explain the drivers for evolution, but since adapted and used to understand other phenomena. However, although there had been attempts to weave Darwinian ideas and politics together, she was the first to do so coherently and to back it up with such a large amount of evidence, drawn from geo-historical analyses, that Darwin himself would have approved.

She argues that for millennia, certainly since before *Homo sapiens* developed agriculture and civilisations, man, as opposed to woman, has been more disposed genetically to be aggressive. Early on, man needed to be aggressive to survive, to mate and to ensure his genes were passed on to the next generation. If he wasn't aggressive enough, then his genes didn't survive. In other words, and to put the survival of the fittest model the right way round, to be here today, a man's or woman's distant male ancestors are likely to have been aggressive. (This is a gross generalisation – the theory at its most rudimentary – but I only wish to mention the basic idea.)

In the period leading up to civilisation, to larger societies and to nation states, aggressive genes remained extremely useful for individual survival, wealth accumulation and mate choice. But these same genes meant that certain individual men in these societies accumulated far more power than most others, to the point of becoming rulers; and then, in continuing to express their aggressive genes, these rulers sought to extend their wealth and territory by taking over the wealth and territory of other rulers. Thus, Bergmann's theory goes, the powerful 'survival of the fittest' mechanism explains the tendency for aggressive people to rise into positions of power. But more than that, it explains why only strong societies survived, since weak ones were over-run by strong neighbours. Precisely the same principles have continued to apply up to recent times, she says, noting in one of her books that even in the 100 years after Hitler and Stalin, during the golden age of oil and chips, there were more than 500 wars, whether civil, border or international.

Despite these statistics, Bergmann says, the settlement and security of sovereign states, the integration of regions, the rapid growth of trade and multinational companies, and the growing importance of international organisations all meant that it did become more difficult during the golden era for aggressive out-of-control leaders to maintain their power bases. Moreover, democracy as a political system combined with the widespread use of democratic principles was so successful during recent prosperous times that many (intellectuals, politicians, ordinary citizens) thought it – democracy – would be able to overcome the aggressive gene effect and man's historical tendency to war. Not so, says Bergmann.

It has taken me far too long to arrive at this point, and it would have been quicker to use a summary from *Encyclopaedia Universal*.

Bergmann's key argument is this. She says the usefulness of the genes which dispose man to be aggressive lose their usefulness within stable democratic social systems based on equality and liberty, while other genes which express themselves in softer more feminine characteristics, and especially through women, tend to become more widely accepted, thereby influencing the society as a whole. This softening of one society as a whole, ultimately makes it vulnerable to another society which has not allowed itself to mature democratically (using Bergmann's terminology). By bunching themselves together for the best part of a century most of the rich mature nations ensured, with artful politics, threats and bribery, that the worst ravages of the immature and aggressive nations and groups were focused on each other. But this strategy was never going to work forever, not while a large proportion of the world remained poor, under-developed and without the influence of strong democratic principles. It was inevitable that some new aggressive empire (i.e. the male-dominated Muslim sphere, as led by Al Zahir) would arise and challenge the developed world for its riches.

There can be no end to such a cycle, Bergmann claims, until a world government has sufficient authority to distribute wealth, and until it has a large enough army to act as the world's policeman. Only then can democracy thrive; and only then will the expression and the advantages of man's aggressive gene diminish and fade away.

This was far from a populist theory when presented in the 2070s. It attracted considerable opposition from many different quarters, and Bergmann was mercilessly lampooned in the downmarket media, encouraged by Gregory's cheap ridiculing of her. But she marshalled her research so carefully, and her books were so well documented that the historical and political establishments could not vanquish her ideas, however doggedly they tried. While many intellectuals believed the theory reeked of hopelessness, because they could only see into the short term, I was of the opposite view. I believed her when she claimed mankind was moving forwards, albeit very slowly and jerkily, towards a time when a peaceful world could be possible. I suppose I was predisposed to believe in Bergmann's prediction because the United Nations and its evolution was such an important line of evidence in her argument, and I had spent most of my life working for, and believing in, the UN system.

I tried, on many occasions, to persuade Lizette of these ideas. As with others of her sex, though, she got stuck emotionally on the suggestion that, if societies were strongly influenced or dominated by women and women's ideals, they would be weaker than nations dominated by men. For some reason she would not or could not see beyond this basic principle to the more subtle of Bergmann's points that, given a chance, societies choose to 'mature' by becoming more feminine, and that, ultimately, male aggression and blundering will lose out to female gentleness and wiles.

CHAPTER 5
IN WHICH I REVISIT BRAZIL AND MY FIRST SON

As director-general of the IFSD I did do plenty of globetrotting and hobnobbing with power and money brokers, although, as I've said, not as much as I should have done. Half the time, I felt as though my role was little more than chief public relations officer. Not only did I have to present and promote our work around the world but I had to do so to the IFSD boards, the UN's General Assembly and other institutions.

Life in this regard was not made easy by the fact that, after much negotiation, the world's leaders had decided that Ojoru should be brought out of retirement to take on the role of Secretary General. He was not, though, appointed for his administrative or management abilities, which had once been formidable: it was widely known that, in the later years of his political career in Nigeria and leading the African Union, he had become increasingly autocratic. No, he was chosen because of his geopolitical colour.

Unfortunately, as Secretary General his imperious style had consequences. It led to the upper echelons of many parts of the UN system developing a bloated bureaucracy. Thus, to give one small example, a two-sentence command from one of his many personal advisers calling for a report into the underrepresentation of, say, Gambians in UN staff and contract positions would lead to excessively burdensome administration tasks and a huge waste of resources. Which is not to say that Ojoru was not the man for the job, if anyone could have avoided the Second Jihad War, it might have been him.

Incidentally, my friend Alfred might have been in Ojoru's cabinet at the UN headquarters – giving me a useful listening post in the higher stratosphere – if he hadn't burnt his bridges with the man. When Alfred thought Ojoru was a spent force, in the 2050s, he spoke his mind to the media and to biographers, criticising his former president for behaving 'like a dictator'. Mostly I sensed – largely from letters written in the 2040s – that his criticism was kindled out of a disappointment in Ojoru for having been corrupted by power, and, as a result, not achieveing as much as many, including Alfred himself, had hoped. Alfred also told me later, in confidence, which I am now breaking, about an unbelievable incident during which Ojoru had demanded Alfred lick his shoes.

Travelling was a pain. I had done relatively little of it as a director, choosing, as often as possible, to use the cam-conference facilities to get business done. But the ceremonial (which is how I thought about them) duties of a director-general included many activities which could not be done via a screen: opening new IFSD premises, launching IFSD pro-grammes, singing the praises of the IFSD to the presidents of donor nations or multinationals, and enthusing staff in all four corners of the globe. Very occasionally I looked forward to a trip, such as the one to Brazil in February 62, but this was only because it would give me a chance to catch up with Arturo, and to revisit Rio.

I delegated most of the research and planning for this mission to Eduardo, since it had been his notion originally and since he would be travelling by my side. The main priority was for me to be seen opening a new IFSD building in Brasilia. Further, I was scheduled to attend a series of meetings with the IFSD staff, two Brazilian ministers, a collective group of non-governmental organisations (NGOs), and the regional Latin American Community Organisation (LACO). In addi-tion, Eduardo planned for me to fly to La Paz so that I could personally launch a multimillion programme for the Andean countries aimed at reviving traditional craft skills, particularly weaving. The concept for the programme had been tried and tested in other regions of the world, and had proved highly successful in terms of employment, local community integra-tion, and attracting tourism. Eduardo had convinced me that my visit to La Paz would go a long way to reviving the IFSD's reputation in the area, and would serve to persuade a reluc-tant Bolivian government to promote the schemes.

About a week before we were due to leave, I received a communication from Ojoru's office suggesting I cancel the La

Paz extension to my trip. When I asked Eduardo for an explanation, he shrugged his shoulders. I requested Chidi, who had the best line into Ojoru's cabinet, to find out more. Later the same day, he came to my office, his fingers wiggling more than usual. There was a human rights issue, he said, which another UN agency was trying to deal with behind the scenes, under much pressure from Amnesty International, and it had caught the ear of one of Ojoru's advisers.

Eduardo argued strenuously that it would do more harm than good to cancel the meeting, and went so far as to accuse Ojoru's adviser, a Peruvian, of trying to sabotage my visit simply because my itinerary did not include Lima. I weighed up all the information I had been given, and struck La Paz off the agenda. Unfortunately, this decision seriously undermined my relationship with Eduardo – although, because he chaperoned me on the tour with good humour and professionalism, I did not realise it at the time.

Of all the IFSD offices I ever visited the one in Brasilia, designed by a Petrópolis School architect, was the most striking. South America had been largely untouched by the physical devastation of the Jihad War. It had suffered an economic downturn, caused by the general global economic recession, but not as badly as elsewhere. More IFSD projects had continued uninterrupted in this continent than in any other region of the world – although not many given the general disintegration of UN decision-making structures.

Brazil's great leader, Neco Corazón, Neco the Prosperous, planned to redevelop and rebuild the derelict aeroplane of Brasilia: originally, in the 20th century, the capital city had been socially planned and engineered in the shape of an aircraft. Neco never managed to bring the scheme to fruition during his own term of office, and it had to wait more than 20 more years to be realised. The new IFSD building formed part of a redevelopment in the Jardim Botanico sector. It was twenty stories tall, slightly concave on all five sides, with lime-green and lemon-yellow glass panelling and IFSD logos etched into each of the wavy solar window-hoods.

My discourse, given on a large raised terrace overlooking the botanical gardens themselves, was well received. Eduardo had culled parts of it from presentations given on similar occasions. Other speeches were given by the mayor of Brasilia, the government's foreign minister, and the LACO executive director. When the speeches were finished, it was my task to smash the magnum of Brazilian champagne against the Harkness Cylinder. I'd done this enough times before to know the form, but I rarely knew in advance exactly what each Cylinder would deliver. On this occasion, it was scores of self-inflating green and yellow balloons, three self-inflating tethered flags (the IFSD, Brazil, and LACO), and remote triggers for day-time fireworks to sparkle above the rising balloons, and for samba music to start up. There were whoops of joy from the crowd of invitees and IFSD employees, and then, as had become customary with the use of Harkness Cylinders, I presented the unbroken magnum to one of the lower-ranking employees who worked in the building.

There was nothing remarkable about the occasion, except that my son Arturo was in the audience. Arturo was my oldest son, although I didn't even know he existed until his sudden manifestation into my life in 2043. While taking a year out of my degree studies, I had travelled in Brazil and hooked up for a week or two with a good-time girl called Conceição. More than two decades later, Arturo had found me in The Hague, and a DNA test had proved my paternity.

Previously, by email, I had suggested to Arturo that we meet in Rio, because I would have more free time there. But he lived and worked in Goiânia, which was much nearer to Brasilia than Rio. So, I had asked Eduardo to organise a special pass for him to be admitted to the IFSD function. Only after the balloons went up did I catch sight of him at the back of the terrace, smiling widely and raising a glass towards me.

We did not speak more than a couple of words together through the buffet lunch, such was Eduardo's zeal in introducing me to as many notables as possible. But, for half an hour, between the official end of the building launch event and my first meeting of the afternoon, I was able to sit alone with Arturo in a peaceful library room – used only for meetings, but lined with books that had been placed for wall decoration. For a few minutes I let Arturo flatter me, about my appearance and my IFSD performance. He asked about Lizette and Jay, who was a walking talking 20 month toddler by this time. And then, without missing a beat, he said it must be odd to be a father and a grandfather at the same time, to have a son almost the same age as a granddaughter.

'What granddaughter?'

'Alicia, naturalmente.' He was smiling. Sometimes with Arturo you could find yourself smiling back without knowing why, even on the camphone, but this was not one of those occasions.

'Arturo, who is she? Who is Alicia?' I began to suspect he must have a newly-discovered daughter from a past relationship. Like father, like son.

'What you think about cloning?' His English had deteriorated from when he lived in London, but his grin was no less supercilious.

'Are you going to tell me about Alicia?'

'You tell me about cloning, your opinion.'

Despite questions by email, and shortish conversations by camphone at Christmas or on his birthday or mine, I knew next to nothing about Arturo's life, other than that he had married Edna, a cute-looking, black woman from Fortaleza in 2055, and that his own success had grown with that of the company, O Futoro, that employed him. I should have known about O Futoro, but I didn't.

'No.' My free minutes were ticking away. 'Stop playing games and tell me about Alicia.'

'OK, but remember I try to warn you. OK. She is my daughter. She is cloned from me. Edna was infertile. She agreed. She is four years old.' Cloning female daughters from male parents, using two different sperm to gather the X chromosomes, was demonstrated successfully in the 20s, and the technique had gone commercial in the 40s. But, even in the 50s, it was considered a more risky procedure than same sex cloning.

'FOUR!'

'Yes. If you want, we go tonight to Goiânia, to my house, and you meet her. But not Edna. She is gone away. We can go in my plane. It's easy, one hour. I bring you back late tonight or early morning.'

CHAPTER 6

IN WHICH I MEET MY CLONED GRANDDAUGHTER

I read, in one of Gregory's books, that there were many similarities between the tone and extent of the political and moral debate about abortion in the 20th century and the debate on cloning in the 21st century. The content, though, was very different.

At the international level, the Europe Union, the US and most other Catholic and Muslim nations negotiated, during the 2010s and 2020s, very basic objectives through a UN Convention on the Limitations of Human Cloning (and, in time, this did lead to the broad-ranging Agency for Genetic and Cloning Techniques). But some very large countries, including Brazil, China and Russia refused to accept the harmonised objectives, and instead nurtured social welfare and commercial cloning industries.

The European Union and the US went their own separate, but similar, ways, developing far more detailed rules than those at the UN level. In practice, these outlawed human cloning, except in very exceptional circumstances, until such a time as it could be proved that the techniques led to a risk of infant mortality no greater than under normal birth conditions. As a requirement of the same rules, the risk rates and policy were to be re-examined by a UN study once a decade.

Experience accumulated in the countries with cloning industries and this helped the pro-cloning lobby elsewhere not only to gather and present real scientific evidence for the decadal reviews, but to put forward scientific, humanitarian and commercial justifications for a legitimate development of their own cloning activities. Nevertheless, by the 50s and 60s, the pro-cloning lobby in Europe and the US had failed to make much headway. One reason for this was the strong link created, by many anti-cloning politicians and religious leaders, between cloning and the suicide epidemic in the 40s.

According to Gregory, a statistically higher proportion of suicides in some countries were early clones from the 20s, although, overall, the numbers were comparatively low.

Moreover, he pointed out that millions had been affected psychologically by the very idea of cloning, and that while some of these people had harnessed their anxieties into passionate campaigning, others had found it undermined the value of life and their belief systems, whether religious or moral, to the point of mental implosion. It's also worth remembering that Pope Maria spoke strongly against cloning in her first Christmas Day address in 2052.

Personally, I was completely opposed to cloning, as were the majority of Europeans. I could not be moved by the stories of couples that had lost their only child in the war or as a result of tragic accidents, or of young women who had been unable to conceive because they were victims of crimes. I understood all too well that the world was full of tragedy, but, for me, it was a question of priorities. Even as a young man, I never approved of the billions of dollars and euros that were spent on cloning research or on other medical techniques designed to improve, ever more incrementally, the well-being of rich Western peoples, while poverty, inadequate drainage and water supplies, and impoverished inoculation programmes in many parts of the world meant that the life-expectancy gap between the US and, say, Sudan continued to increase not decrease. In this belief, I was much influenced by Triti Madan, the Indian professor who had delivered such a powerful lecture to the London School of Economics when I was but a young and hopeful student.

Arturo was waiting for me with a taxi at around seven. It took less than 30 minutes to drive to the airport, past many colourful and luminescent Petrópolis School buildings, to board Arturo's Amazonia, a six-seater silvered light-jet. It was fuelled, I knew, with the aviation biofuel Vivido, one of Brazil's most important export success stories of the previous 30 years or so.

During the flight, I questioned my son, initially about his work, and then about his reasons for cloning himself to create (how horrible that verb sounds in this context, even today) Alicia. He told me that O Futuro manufactured medical equipment, including the sophisticated devices used for animal and human cloning. Moreover, it owned a subsidiary, in Goiânia, which operated at the high end of the human cloning market. It did good business, mostly for rich Americans and Brazilians who had failed to conceive through normal channels or simply wanted to avoid the trauma of childbirth. Since concluding his degree at Imperial College (the degree I had funded soon after his entrance into my life), Arturo had worked for O Futuro in developing the commercial human cloning business. He had kept this information from me, he said, because he suspected I would not approve. I did not.

Arturo lived in a large modern villa, complete with a swimming pool, stables and a field for two dappled horses. Several staff were present on our arrival. One showed me to a room so I could shower and put on a new shirt Arturo had provided for me, another brought us caiparinhas, and yet another discussed, with Arturo, the meal we would have later.

After rejoining Arturo on the marble terrace overlooking the pool, a woman named Luz, who looked as though she had stepped out of a men's lifestyle magazine, brought Alicia to meet me. There was no doubting she looked like Arturo, in a babyish, girlish sort of way, and however much Arturo had rigged her genes, she was still my granddaughter, and I was predisposed, if not pre-programmed, to want to love her.

This was the awful dilemma about human cloning: an individual, or indeed a nation, could oppose the idea, but once a cloned individual existed nothing other than normal decent human emotions, or laws, could be deemed appropriate in dealing with that individual. Moreover, for most of us, it was hard to keep up any serious level of chastisement against those who had cloned themselves because ultimately this would reflect on the innocent children. Today, there are still those who are violently prejudiced against cloned individuals and their parents, but, thankfully, they are dying out – literally, since most of them are old.

I have a camclip of the two us together taken by Luz and sent to me by Arturo a few days later. Here it is now, on my screen. It starts with a view of tiny Alicia, wearing dark jeans, a red tank top and long pink hair, leading giant me by the hand along a broad marble hallway to her bedroom, which is strawberry coloured and servant-tidy. From there, the camera follows us to Alicia's toy room, complete with an English style doll's house, dozens of dolls and a sophisticated console for the wallscreen, and then through a side door to an enclosed paddock where a shiny grey pony is galloping around. Alicia is jumping around shaking her head, her pink hair flying from side to side. She is shouting (in Portuguese): 'He is my Angel. I want to ride. Can I ride?' The camera swings round towards Arturo, as if looking for an answer to Alicia's request. Arturo puts a smile on for the camera, and tells Alicia it is time for bed.

I had forgotten, until seeing this clip again, how Arturo looked then: tall, very erect and admirably slim, smartly dressed in perfectly pressed trousers and shirt, both in creamy silk or silkette. On both wrists he wore chunky loose gold bracelets; a large gold medallion hung around his neck. Most striking of all, he had dyed yellowy-golden hair, short and curly, eyebrows and lashes. On the IFSD building terrace he had stood out, as if the sun shone for him alone, which, I guess, is why I had noticed him at the back of the large crowd.

I did ask what had happened to Alicia's mother, Edna, suspecting she might never have agreed to the cloning and had left because of that. But Arturo reiterated – and I had no reason to disbelieve him – that she was unable to have children. So then I asked how they had decided which one of them should be the clone parent, and which procedure they should follow. It was as though I had pulled a gun on him. The warmth in his face was dismissed in an instant, giving way to a powerful vicious look I'd not seen before.

'It was my way, naturalmente; I did not want Alicia to have the same problems. The ones Edna had. And, it was my company, my work. It had to be my way.'

'Then it must have been tough for Edna, being a step-mother.' I struggled to comprehend the implications of Alicia having been cloned. Although friends and colleagues had talked about the cloning experiences of people they knew, I'd never come up against the reality of cloning, gene-to-gene as it were.

'The truth is she died of a drug overdose, the day before Alicia's first birthday.'

'Poor her. Poor Alicia. You've kept a lot from me.' It was a stupid thing to say in the circumstances.

Arturo apologised for not flying back with me to Brasilia. We embraced stiffly next to his jet on the runway of a private airstrip not far from his villa. He promised he would send a copy of the camclip and that he would contact me the next time he was in Europe.

I thought about Arturo and Alicia on the journey back to Brasilia. Arturo's villa had been fitted out with expensive decor and furbishings but it was all superficial allure, reeking only of money and vanity. I had always thought, or hoped, there was more to my son than had appeared on the surface. As a younger man, his charm had seemed to give him substance, but in middle-age it hung on him like the loose gold bracelets around his arms. I realised that I had come to despise him. It was not solely because of what he did for a job, or what he had done, because, in the context of a life spent working for a company such as O Futuro, a desire to clone his own child did not seem so outrageous. It was because of who he had become.

As for the sweet lively Alicia, I had the pleasant memory of her miniature hand in mine, leading me confidently through the house, eager to show off her doll's house and pony. Yet it was impossible not to wonder what would become of the child, so motherless and spoilt.

It was not until I was back in the hotel, at about one in the morning, that I checked through the day's messages. A whole 12 hours earlier, Anna Mastepanov had requested I call her immediately. She answered on the first ring as if she had been holding the receiver in her hand. I tried to apologise for not having replied earlier, but she was distraught and speaking fast. Alan, my uncle, had suffered a massive coronary the previous night, gone into a coma, and had died during the late morning. There was nothing that could be done for him.

I offered to switch on the cam, to allow us to be more personal, more intimate, but she declined. Instead, she talked without stopping for several minutes, faster and with a more pronounced accent than I remember. She told me how he had been so well in recent weeks, how they had spent a month over Christmas on Corfu – from where, I realised, I had received my last ever communication from him – with some friends, and how the 'damn bloody cold' had killed him on their return. She said that he had talked so often about me, it was as though I were a regular visitor to their home. But this was too much for me to bear. I had to stop her flow and apologise for never having visited in person, and, bizarrely, I found myself trying to make excuses for this, as if there could be any. My outburst had the effect of calming Anna down. She tried to explain that this was not my fault at all, but hers because she should have persuaded Alan not to be so shy of pressing me to come.

'He loved you, like his own son.'

'Did he? I loved him like a father too. I only wish ... I only wish ...'

'It's fine. He lived well. He did good things. He was a precious, precious man. Now we must warm ourselves with his memory.'

It was Anna who eventually brought the conversation round to practicalities. She told me when the funeral was likely to take place, and insisted, knowing where I was, that I should not interrupt my important mission nor fly halfway round the world. I considered what she had said for a few seconds, and then agreed. It would feel so wrong, I told her, to make such an effort to go there now he's dead, when I never made a tenth of the effort when he was alive. I said I would write, and asked that a few of my words be read at the funeral.

I slept fitfully that night, disturbed less by his death – he was, after all, in his 90s – than by my own self-pity and self-anger at never having made the journey to St Petersburg. The next morning, over breakfast, I told Eduardo the news. He offered me his condolences, but was anxious to know whether he would need to cancel or re-arrange any of our forthcoming meetings. When I reassured him that I had no plans to cancel any appointments, a sharp memory suddenly shot into my consciousness. It was of the email I had received, in 2021 during my student holiday to Brazil, which informed me about the death of my grandmother, Alan's mother, Eileen. What I recalled so vividly was how the news of her death had struck me with fear: fear that I would be summoned home and my Brazilian adventure would be curtailed before it had begun.

***

Jay and Vince took me out to the garden yesterday, Saturday, the first time for many weeks. Not to the rose garden, for it was busy with too many children visitors, but to what Flora refers to as the 'twut' (as in two hut) garden. It has been such a wet summer, but the fuchsias, which remind me of Lizette, are in good colour – 'dripping crimsons, purples, violets', she would say. The hibiscus plants are also doing well. There are so many scattered through the gardens, I suspect there must have been a gardener in generations past who had a passion for them.

Vince is walking again, and full of praise for something called the Alexander Technique which he is employing as a way of restoring order to his body. He wanted to explain in detail but Jay, who has been following the evolution of this chapter I am writing now with some concern, had another agenda.

To begin with, he told me that Guido and Mireille would be making a rare return visit to Holland from Ecuador in late October – no news could have brought me more joy – and that, therefore, Vince and he had decided to take a two week holiday overlapping the same period. Then, using Vince as an unwitting adjudicator, he asked why, in my Reflections, I had fast forwarded to 2062 skipping entirely over his own birth. Even though he knows full well I'm not following a strict chronology, I can understand why he jumped to that conclusion: in our discussions of the last few days, I've been preparing myself to press even further ahead and tackle the events of 2064.

I reassured Jay he was not being left out, to murmurings of approval from Vince: 'Better not, or you'll have me to deal with.' I do like Vince, but where was this loyalty six months ago? How could I leave Jay out? He's my anchor. Without him I would have drifted away many moons ago, leaving not a whit, not a jot, not a single reflection. But yes, I do need to go back a couple of years.

CHAPTER 7

IN WHICH JAY IS BORN, AND ANNA VISITS

While I struggled with the elevated role at the IFSD, my relationship with Lizette flowered. We met most weekends, when I was not away, mostly in The Hague, since she had more time for the travel. Occasionally I trained to Brussels and we went from there to a high-class hotel in Ghent or Leuven to pamper ourselves during an overnight stay.

We spoke every night on the camphone. At Lizette's suggestion, we both installed camphone facilities in the bedroom so we could chat from our beds. As we became more relaxed with this system, so we began to natter while preparing for bed. Thus, by accident, or Lizette's wiliness, we developed a pattern of pleasuring ourselves voyeuristically. To an outsider, this might seem a one-sided arrangement, to my advantage, but Lizette enjoyed pleasing me and watching my pleasure. Moreover, she had her own ways of achieving sexual satisfaction while on the camphone. Best of all, though, our virtual sex enhanced the real thing at weekends. Now that I am in the late afternoon chapters of these volumes, misconstruing the old cliché, I may not stray again to matters intimate, but this is one happy ending: sex in my sixties and early seventies was the best I ever had. Thank you Lizette – with apologies to Jay for saying a little more than he called for.

In July 2060, when the European University semester finished, Lizette came to live in my apartment on Van Hogenhouckstraat for six weeks before returning to England. Then she went to the Midlands to see her friends and undertake some emotional negotiations with Clint, and from there to her Ma and Pa in Weston-super-Mare. She gave birth to Jay in a local hospital, and, having taken maternity leave, remained for the rest of the year at her parent's spacious bungalow.

It was during that winter, when baby Jay was first taking in the bright lights of the world, that the lights went dark for his GrandPa. Having suffered from a form of muscular dystrophy for many years, Mervyn Sanderson finally expired from pneumonia.

Only later did I learn that Lizette had, many years earlier, organised a genetic profile for herself and Clint so as to ensure any children they bore would not inherit her father's disease or any other testable genetic weakness. This knowledge, it transpired, was another factor in Lizette's semi-conscious decision to have a pot-luck fuck with Clint.

Because of various complications, not least the baby and the dying father, I only met up with Lizette twice during this period. Once when I flew to Bristol and we stayed in a hotel there for two nights, and once in Brussels when she needed to check on her apartment and carry out some administrative duties. She was rather upset on this occasion, because, despite special payment to the building concierge, he had let her tub fuchsias, decorating the glassed-in balcony overlooking Parc de Cinquantenaire, dry out and die.

Soon after settling in at the bungalow in Weston-super-Mare, though, she had a private camphone installed in her room, so we were able to talk as regularly as before; and I was able to monitor the baby's progress. In January 2061, she returned to Brussels, found an excellent creche for Jay, and resumed her life, and pattern with me, albeit one more constrained than previously.

The three-way relationship worked surprisingly well. Lizette was eager to put my paternal experience to good use, and to balance it against her own maternal – and, to my mind, overprotective – instincts. I adored Jay as if he were my own child, which was fortunate because Lizette had decided that it would be better for him if Clint played no part in his life. We had many discussions about this, especially in the context of my suggestion that we form a co-op for Jay. I proposed that we should find some way of including Clint. Lizette could not be persuaded. She knew, she said, he did not want a child, and that he would make a lousy father.

We also thought about Lizette's brothers and Rhoda for the co-op and rejected them too. Mercurio was, apparently, feckless, and had embedded himself with the Notek movement, and Samuel was too caught up in his own family and work. Rhoda, Lizette argued, would only be a bad influence. In the end, we agreed to form the Jay co-op ourselves, just the two of us, and we went so far as to use the Dutch legal framework for co-ops, which had proved itself relatively stable. This required us getting Clint's written approval, but Lizette had no trouble in obtaining it.

During 2062, Lizette made regular weekend trips to Weston-super-Mare because of her mother's deteriorating health, and, whenever I was available, she would come first to The Hague to drop Jay off before flying to Bristol. I have very fond memories of wheeling him in his chair through Westbroek Park to the playground, and reading the Sunday papers while watching his antics on the clambering frames and tussle-jumpers. Towards the end of that year, Lizette's mother stepped over the edge, deliberately, to follow her husband to a better place.

It was not until 2063 that Lizette, Jay and I, in our personal life together, had a trouble-free year. We took a substantial joint holiday during the summer, to a gîte near Poitiers in France; but little stands out from those weeks, except a feeling of relief at leaving work behind, and an equally strong sentiment that serendipity had brought me Lizette. Two events that same year, though, are worth recording.

In the spring, Anna Mastepanov came to visit for three days. She was on her way to Brussels, Paris and London to commune (I can't think what other word to use) with people important to Alan. The week before her arrival, a large trunk of Alan's things were delivered to my apartment. There were all the papers, storage disks and personal items he had specified for me in his will, plus a number of mementoes that Anna wanted me to have. She was a lovely lady, older than me in years, but younger in spirit, full of bright but controlled enthusiasms. We spent most of one day going through the papers and items. Inspired by these, Anna talked at length about his passions, achievements and friendships, and about their life together. And, on the second day, we looked at the many photos and camclips on her personal digital memory store, accessed through the net. There were surprises.

For more than 30 years, Alan had donated a minimum of 10% of his income to a health clinic in a small town in Bangladesh. He had visited it often, and knew many of the people there. Anna, too, had been on three visits and was full of stories about the lives of the characters in the camclips and about how the clinic had served not only the town's health but its economic well-being.

At one moment, Anna saw me drifting away in my thoughts, looking wistful, and asked me why. This was the difference between Alan and me, I said. He had helped on the ground, with people, real people, getting his hands dirty, spending his own money, risking his own life, sacrificing his own time. And I thought, but did not say, that he had done and lived while I had only done and lived by proxy. Anna cut short my maudlin self-pity to tell me that Alan's view was the complete reverse.

'It's easy to help, he used to say, but few can help – like Kip does – when it comes to the big picture. He was very proud of you,' she said. 'I would hate for you to forget that for one minute.'

Another surprise was that Alan had an adopted son, a Czech man called Karel. There were photographs, but no camclips, of Alan together with a woman called Tamara (who I had met once in Brussels) and Karel as a child, and of Karel alone at different ages through to adulthood. Anna knew little of Karel's history. Tamara, it seems, had been very keen on adopting a deprived child, but then, soon after the adoption, she had fallen out with Alan and run away. He had never had any contact with either of them since then, except that occasionally a photograph would arrive by email. Subsequently, I searched all through Alan's records and his few personal jottings but there was no correspondence to or from Tamara – which shows he must have carefully edited his files in good time before dying – and no explanation of why he had never told me or my mother about Karel. On our third day together, Anna and I strolled around the city. We talked about Diana, Guido and Lizette; and then, tearfully, she left to continue her pilgrimage of sorts. She was heading for Paris next, to see Monique.

CHAPTER 8

IN WHICH I SPEAK AT THE WORLD VOLLEYBALL FINALS

If I were to trawl through my own papers, I might find other events that year more worth recording that the short trip I made to the world volleyball finals in Munich. Fortunately, these are only my Reflections, and I've long since demonstrated that I have no intention of documenting my life or the world around in any rigorous way.

One morning, in autumn 2062, MarySue called through to tell me that she had a very strange person on the line. He insisted on talking to me personally, MarySue said, but refused to say what about. He said his name was Sanfry and that it was personal and important. There was something about the name Sanfry which rang a bell, and so, against my better judgement, I told MarySue to put him through. As soon as I heard the word volleyball, I remembered who he was. Alfred had kept me informed of his progress over the years: starting with the Nigerian team aged 17, he had become its captain at 20 and led it to a world championship triumph in the early 40s. Now, as president of the World Volleyball Association (WVA), he was calling to ask if I would present the trophy to the winning team at the world cup finals in May 2063. Because such an event was beyond my usual public appearance portfolio, I hesitated slightly. But then, when Sanfry explained the details of another duty I was to perform at the same time, I accepted the invitation with alacrity.

Alfred. Alfred. Alfred. To my shame, I had forgotten about my old schoolfriend recently. I spoke to Chidi as soon as I had finished the conversation with Sanfry. He had no recent news either, so I asked MarySue to track him down.

On the phone, I heard the voice of a resigned man. I learned how resentful he was of Ojoru, how his wife Fayola had left him for a richer man, and how his son, Fela, had become a banker, 'a greedy man'. I discovered that he was working in public relations for an agricultural exporter, biding his time until he could afford to retire and go to live on Zanzibar. He had bought a plot of land there many years previously, and wanted to build a house. Later the same day I talked to Chidi again. Within a month, we had created a place for Alfred as a special adviser in the IFSD's Abuja office, not I hasten to add out of charity, but because we knew he could be an excellent interface between The Hague and Abuja offices, and between the IFSD and the Nigerian administration.

I did not see Alfred in person until the Munich volleyball finals – I had exacted a commitment from him to go, and promised to pay all expenses. I sent him a return plane ticket, with an option to travel on from Munich to The Hague for a few extra days (which he did not use). I persuaded another of my old volleyball buds, Peter de Roo, into accompanying me for the weekend. It turned out to be a fantastic trip. Alfred knew many of the people there, but even Peter and I, long-since aliens to the volleyball scene, found several long-forgotten buds from the summer contests of our student days. We watched four matches, two semi-finals on the Saturday, and, on the Sunday, a youth cup final between the US and Brazil, and the world cup final between Nigeria and Russia.

I sat with Sanfry and all the high officials of the volleyball association, while Peter and Alfred sat a few rows behind in seats that Sanfry had secured for them. During the youth match, Sanfry talked throughout; he wanted to explain his personal debt to Alfred, and then to reaffirm how much he had done for Nigerian volleyball over the years. After I had awarded the trophy to the winning youth team, and its members had left the arena, I was due to deliver a short speech and hand over a WVA annual award for services to volleyball. Earlier, I had arranged with a technician to use the big overhead screens to show a camclip I'd given him access to. I began by asking the 10,000 audience to humour me for a minute. The technician launched the clip, and I spoke over the top of it.

'Fifty years ago, Italy beat Croatia in a European cup quarter-final that was held in Guildford near my home town in England. It was universally acknowledged to be one of the most exciting games of volleyball you could ever wish to see.

Croatia went on beat Spain in the final, and then to reach the finals of the world championship two years later.'

The camclip froze, and my 13 year old (grainy) self filled the screens. I paused for effect. My heart was thumping so loud I feared the microphone would pick it up. I had grown used to public speaking, but this was personal, not work, and I had not adequately discounted for the difference.

'This is me, ladies and gentlemen. And you can see, by my showing it today, how proud I am of my appearance as a ball-boy at that famous match. It was the day that volleyball entered my soul.' (Chidi thought 'soul' was more appropriate than my suggestion of 'heart'. I should say that Chidi assisted me in drafting the speech, which was kind of him for it was not official business. He had a gift for speech-writing, and knew how to enliven my dull drafts, to spice them up, while keeping to a style that suited my way of speaking.)

'I was so fired up by those European championships that, not many weeks later, while waiting in the queue in the school canteen, I waylaid a boy I didn't know.' I stopped to turn and look at Alfred to see if he had understood where this was going. It had been Sanfry's decision to keep the award a secret.

'Perhaps things have changed but, in my day, talking to someone you didn't know, from a different year was taboo. And the only reason I spoke to this boy was his height. I knew he would be perfect for our volleyball team. We soon became good friends. He went on to captain our team and lead our school to its greatest sporting triumphs. I may be exaggerating, but then who cares about football or athletics.' I was worried about this line, but Chidi, who knew nothing about volleyball, understood what specialist audiences enjoy. It drew a great applause, and I was glad we kept it in. I went on to list Alfred's achievements in Nigeria, and Nigeria's achievements in the world, not only in terms of success on court, but in terms of encouraging other developing nations to nurture their sporting talent. I then closed with the following words.

'Forgive me if I have drawn a straight line from my recruiting efforts in the school canteen to the presentation of this award today, but you all know the achievements are his, and that I have been but a bedazzled bystander. And I cannot end without saying, in all honesty, that I would not be here today, presenting this award, were it not for a lifetime of this man's friendship and support. So you can understand why I am overjoyed to present the 2063 WVA award for services to volleyball to my great and dear friend Alfred Ajose.'

Alfred made his way down from behind us and manoeuvred himself onto the walkway in front of where I was standing. I didn't shake his hand as I had done with the captains of the youth teams. Instead, we instinctively slapped palms in our accustomed manner, to the delight of the crowd; and only then did I pick up the trophy and present him with it. He turned and bowed elegantly to the crowd receiving a huge ovation, and returned to his seat. No sooner had I sat down, emotionally drained, than the presenter came on the loudspeakers to introduce the teams for the world cup final. Sanfry chattered throughout the game, probably to divert himself from the pain of seeing Russia defeat Nigeria by three sets to none. I didn't mind the dull match because it left Alfred's award as the climax of the day.

CHAPTER 9

IN WHICH I AM KIDNAPPED

Now I should move on from this high point to a very low one. In September 2064, during a routine visit to Belfast, I was kidnapped. It was the second most physically dramatic episode of my life, second only to Cyclone Kip. Though in reality it was all a bit of a farce, the episode would lead to my resignation from the IFSD. The timing could not have been worse – to mimic one of the media's most beloved expressions – as I was due to be in Paris a few days later for the wedding of my son Guido, and his childhood sweetheart, Mireille.

I had arrived by jet without any delays in Ireland's second city, installed myself at the O'Hilton, and completed two separate meetings with ministers and their officials, one of which included lunch. My schedule then allowed me a free half an hour in the hotel room to make calls. From there I was due to find my way alone, my assistant having gone on ahead, to the adjacent O'Hilton Conference Centre to deliver a keynote speech to an important gathering of international environmental NGOs, many of whom worked with the IFSD all over the world.

While on the phone to MarySue, there was a knock on my door. A waiter presented me with a tray containing a teapot, cup, milk and biscuits. I protested mildly that I hadn't ordered anything but thanked him as he left. I know I finished my call, drank the tea, and looked at the text of my speech. After that I recall nothing, nothing at all. I learned later, from the police, that I had been given an illegal mental anaesthesia drug, and that two captors had walked me out through the back staircase and the hotel's rear entrance, while successfully using beaked caps to hide their faces from the surveillance cams. Apart from the rest, which I am about to record as succinctly as possible, it was terrifying to experience one of these hypnosis drugs for myself: to realise that I could have been persuaded to do anything, while appearing compos mentis, and yet remember nothing.

I recall waking, feeling very groggy, and finding myself in a shoddily furnished basement room with one high window of frosted wired glass, a table, chairs and a heater. I didn't know if it was the same day or the next morning. My watch, phonepad, identicard and cashcards had all been removed from my suit pockets. I was lying on a threadbare sofa with one hand cuffed to a metal backplate. My head hurt. Water and biscuits were in reach on a rectangular plastic-wood table. I desperately needed the toilet. I assumed I had been taken hostage, but had no idea why or by whom. Why would anyone kidnap me, and in Ireland, such an un-turbulent place? I shouted out for help. No one came. I drank some water, and the ache in my head eased. I thought about my conference speech and felt sure I must have been missed; then I thought about Guido and his wedding on Saturday; then I debated whether I was desperate enough to urinate through a gap in the cushions onto the floor behind the sofa; and then I remembered the tracer in my ear.

Whoever had kidnapped me, they were not professionals or else they would have made allowances for the possibility of a tracer. They could have put me in a deep bunker, or dressed me in a metal fabric jump suit with metallic ear pads (earlobes being the most common location for tracers), or questioned me and cut the tracer out without causing a serious wound. Being taken hostage was a chronic risk for all those travelling into the less stable parts of the world. Mostly rich businessmen and politicians were snatched and ransomed, but there had been two top UN officials abducted in the 50s. As a consequence around 300 key UN staff were offered tracer implants. I became one of the chosen when I took over as the IFSD's director-general. Each tracer had a unique code and could be identified through special equipment, controlled by a carefully vetted commercial company, based on the Galileo satellite system. (Such tracers were also widely used for other purposes, by police and prison services, for example, to keep track of undesirables, and by ethologists to monitor animal migrations.)

I tried to calculate what should have happened. When I failed to show for the conference presentation, my assistant would have returned to the hotel, checked with the management, checked my room, and then called MarySue. Not finding any note or message as to my whereabouts, the Irish police would have been contacted, and they would have begun an enquiry within, I calculated, two hours of my disappearance. That would have been at about 4pm.

Meantime MarySue would have gone to my desk to find an envelope she knew was there to be opened in such an emergency. She would have called the special UN elite security group, which in turn would have contacted the upper echelon of the Irish police. That would have taken at most another 90 minutes, say two hours. I was, therefore, fairly sure that by 6pm somebody somewhere should have known where I was.

I shouted again. This time the door opened and a tallish man came in. He was carrying a gun, and wearing a black hood with large eye holes, a bomber jacket and scruffy jeans. A youthful male voice asked me what I wanted, and I said I was desperate for the toilet. He went out of the room for a few moments, and, when he returned, unlocked the cuff, and led me a few steps through the door to a filthy smelly bathroom, where I was able to relieve myself. He then escorted me back. I tried asking questions but was told to 'shut up'. I was re-shackled to the sofa, this time by both wrists.

The youth left the room, but two minutes later was back again. He put a blindfold around my head, and then another person entered. This new person, another man but with a croaky false voice, told me the plan. I was to make the calls necessary to ensure that one million euros were transferred from the IFSD to a given private account – by midnight. I laughed. I laughed, and was slapped vigorously across the face. It was shocking. The second man shouted angrily 'leave him'. My face stung. I could not remember being hit since I was a child. I felt very, very vulnerable. I decided to measure my words, and my laughter.

'I laughed because I can no more get one million euros from the IFSD than I can one hundred,' I said with a controlled voice having filtered out the anger and the fear. 'It doesn't work that way. We have hundreds of financial staff, a financial director, a budget committee, an oversight committee, an auditor, bankers, financial control procedures etc, I never see a cent.'

'You could if you had to. Call the financial director. Tell him it's an emergency. Do it. Do it now.'

'I can't. The financial director would laugh at me. He'd say it was a joke, and if I insisted he would call security. He would know something was wrong.'

'What the fuck now?' the young man asked the other. It was a farce I realised.

'Shut up, I'm thinking.' This time the second voice was less strange, less disguised. I recognised it. Bronze!

'I can get you an absolute maximum of 10,000 euros of my own money, now, on the phone. I can transfer it wherever you want, but you have to promise to let me go immediately and get out of here now.'

But it was not enough for my stupid, idiot son.

'One hundred thousand euros and it's a deal. You go free and unharmed. No negotiating. If you refuse, we hurt you, until you agree.'

'I can't do it. The bank has rules and I'm limited to how much I can withdraw by phone in any one day.'

'Fuck you, you're lying.' This was the first man again. They questioned and threatened me several more times, and then I lost patience.

'Look Bronze, I know it's you. This is ridiculous ...'
The youth interrupted.
'Fuck me, how does he know who you are?'
I told him.
'Fuck. This is weird.' I could feel him trying to come to terms with this. Bronze too was stunned to realise that I'd twigged his identity. The two of them then engaged in a loud argument.

When, after a few minutes, I heard a very loud knocking from the floor above, I shouted over the top of them.

'This is ridiculous. The police know where I am. I have a tracer.'

'What's that?' the youth screeched. I explained. This sent him into an excess of fury and expletives, until he crashed an ornament to the ground, and raced out of the room. He was caught, I was informed later, exiting from the back of the house.

CHAPTER 10

IN WHICH I BARELY RECOGNISE MY SECOND SON

Bronze left the room too for a few minutes, and I heard that he was communicating with someone far off, but not what was being said. He came back, and took my blindfold off. I barely recognised my son. I had only seen him three or four times in the last ten years (his choice not mine), and since the last occasion, he had put on much weight, clearly evident through his heavy overcoat, and let his hair grow long and unkempt. He looked ill, with a yellow tint to the skin on his face, and dark rings around his eyes.

'I told them I'd kill you if they came in.' He showed me a gun, presumably the one the youth had brandished earlier, now in the pocket of his coat.

'Why did you do that?'

'Shut up.'

'Let me walk out freely now before this gets out of hand.'

'It's too late. We stole a car, and the gun, and we injured a hotel porter who tried to stop us.'

'Nevertheless, it'll go much better for you, if you let me loose now.'

'I can't do that.'

'Why?'

'Shut up.'

He did let me go, but not for half an hour, during which time he bared his soul, in a quite extraordinary way, as if he were in a priest's confessional. Initially, he remained silent. I asked him to remove the cuffs so that I could sit comfortably. I promised I wouldn't leave until he said I could.

'Bronze, why are you doing this?' I asked. The question caused him pain, visibly so, and led, a few seconds later, to a wheezing fit, followed by a confession. I cannot pretend to remember his words sufficiently well, all jumbled up as they were, to reconstruct the monologue, as I have for the dialogue above. But the gist of what he told me in a nebulous way was this. He was tired of serving the New Crusaders, giving his all and getting nothing back any more. The organisation repeatedly promised he would be sent out on a crusade, a mission to set up a Christian church in Iran or Tunisia or Tajikistan – he very much wanted to go to Tajikistan. Whenever he questioned the duration of his self-paid training or asked the leadership about the schedule for his mission, he was told there were no funds at present. And yet he had witnessed hundreds of crusades, planned and implemented, many of them by recruits who had joined the New Crusaders years later than him.

Tired of being passed over, and, presumably, exploited, but that's my word, he decided to raise his own funds for his own crusade. He acquired sketchy details of my trip to Dublin from an exchange of emails which had begun with my invitation to Guido's wedding. The kidnap plan was hatched with a young friend he had recently recruited to the church, and who had underworld connections. I discovered later these 'connections' were the youth's father, from whom the gun had been stolen.

As his soliloquy continued, punctuated by frequent bouts of wheezing and half choking on his medical throat spray, I came to understand how much Bronze was burning up with bitterness. He felt bitter towards god for not dealing him a better hand; towards the church and his work colleagues for not acknowledging his self-sacrifice; and towards his mother, whom he saw as infrequently as me, for never having loved him. He even savaged himself for messing up friendships. I thought I was being left off the list. I could hear the police loudspeakers penetrating the basement room asking for a response. There was frequent rapping on the outside of the room's one window. Telephones chimed in the distance. In his last few minutes alone with me, he admitted, finally, to hating me. He cited my having left Crystal and him alone with their mother, and my failure, like hers, to love him properly.

I came to realise that for most of his life he had dismissed the relationship with his father as unimportant and irrelevant, but that recent developments had steered his psyche towards identifying me as being at the root of his problems. One of these developments, no doubt, was my involvement with Jay, about whom I'd written often. More immediately, my obvious delight at Guido's forthcoming wedding may have sent Bronze over the edge.

I feared the police would make an inappropriate armed break-in, so I walked over to Bronze, put my arm around his shoulder, took the gun, shepherded him out of the room, and up a set of stairs. At the same time, I shouted, as loud as I could, that we were coming out.

Outside, a street of sad-looking terraced houses – in a town, it turned out, called Birr, central Ireland – was full of police vehicles, ambulances, and armed police wearing protective suits. Bronze was arrested and taken away in a police van. I was driven to Dublin, with a high-ranking policeman called Tyrone Lopping, in an un-marked police car. On the way, I called my assistant and MarySue.

There were so many varied ramifications of this ridiculous episode, I will not try to pin them all down, nor do I wish to dwell on them.

As it was in my interests and those of the security services to avoid any publicity, I discussed with Lopping how this could be done. But it couldn't. He could vouch for the police under his command, he said, but not for the ambulance crews, other sundry officers or the bystanders. Furthermore, there were reporters at the NGO conference that would be making enquiries. Then I asked another question: would it be possible to keep it quiet about Bronze being my son, since he had taken Gillian's name, Tilson, not mine?

By midnight, having been subject to two hours of close questioning, and having called everyone I needed to, including Gillian and Lizette, I was back in my hotel room watching the breaking news on my kidnap and release. For about 24 hours I lived in hope that the relationship between Bronze and me would not become public. It broke on the second day, I don't know how or why. My office and private phones were inundated with calls. I gave my journalist friend Bobby Jespersen a detailed exclusive and asked her to make clear that I would never be talking about the matter again in public. She was most comfortable with political reporting, and usually steered clear of human interest stories, so I hoped she would not delve too deeply into my personal history. Accepting the interpretation I gave her, and in sympathy with it, she was happy to portray Bronze as a cult victim rather than someone with criminal intent.

Neither Bronze nor his partner in crime were given bail by the Irish authorities, even though I employed an expensive lawyer. I did not attend the trial six months later. They both pleaded guilty and were sentenced to ten years incarceration. After a year at Mountjoy Prison in Dublin, Bronze was transferred to Highdown Prison in south London, which made life a lot simpler for Gillian who, surprisingly, visited often and acted like a caring mother.

I visited rarely, once every two or three months. It was a trial of duty. Bronze and I never re-established, or should I say established, any worthwhile relationship. During my hour-long stays we talked of trivial things, about prison life, about Gillian, and about his efforts to convert fellow inmates. He never asked about Guido or Jay, and I never mentioned them. He died in 2066 from a punctured lung sustained during a vicious fight. His assailant, a convicted killer, was later found guilty of Bronze's murder.

Until he took me hostage, Bronze had been so distant, so minor a part of my life, that I had successfully shunted him beyond my emotional horizons. I had stopped thinking about him, except for occasional emails and very intermittent encounters, and I had almost stopped caring for him. So, in one way, his desperate ploy worked, for afterwards, barely a day went by when I didn't wonder about him, when I didn't have to cope with feelings of guilt and inadequacy. I would think of him when I was in the lift, or on the toilet, or waiting at the station for Lizette and Jay to arrive, or in the middle of a meeting.

And, without doubt, he not only wiped the shine off my happiness the following Saturday, but stripped the veneer too.

CHAPTER 11

IN WHICH MY THIRD SON'S MARRIAGE IS AN EVENT

I had no involvement in the preparations for the wedding. Didier and Helene Rocard, a wealthy couple long since, insisted on paying for everything; and any parental involvement on Guido's side was handled by his mother, Diana. My only job was to liaise with Guido's half-brothers. With Bronze I must have tried too hard, but with Arturo I did not try at all. Guido had no particular interest in Arturo, especially after I'd informed him about the Alicia situation, and so I took responsibility for not sending him an invitation.

There was a huge row between Mireille and her parents over the shape and style of the wedding. I know this because Guido kept me fully informed thinking he might need me to intervene. Guido, obviously, sided with his wife-to-be, but Diana aligned herself with the Rocard parents.

The problem arose because Didier wanted to 'produce' a wedding, a theatrical event, which Diana would design. I've no doubt it was a generous, loving offer from both of them. Mireille was as plugged into the theatre world as her parents and Guido, and, at first, the idea did tempt her. But when Didier began talking about possible themes and ideas, Mireille's toes caught a chill. Guido advised her to talk to her father immediately, but she prevaricated, unsure of what was right, and afraid of disappointing him.

To cut a complicated story short, Mireille left it far too long before deciding. By which time, Diana and Didier had launched various initiatives, not least negotiations for a venue. They were not prepared, therefore, to drop the whole thing because of Mireille's cold feet. They tried to talk her round, to bribe her, to threaten her. The more they argued, the more Mireille realised, to Guido's relief, that all she wanted was a simple quiet church wedding. It was only later that I discovered how close Guido and Mireille came to running off to marry in Corsica. According to Guido, their decision, a year or so later, to go to live and work in Ecuador had much to do with Mireille needing distance from her father.

The Rocards may have called it a simple quiet church wedding, but few others would have done. The church – scouted and bought for the day by Didier – was opulent with gold and silver ornamentation. Diana had ensured it was further adorned with the wildest, most exotic flowers you could imagine. And then, as if that was not already enough colour and splendour, there were 150 or more friends and family most of them theatrical and dressed up to the hat. Rudy de la Roo, the best man, and Guido stood at the head of the aisles on one side, with a portly cleric who was heavily made-up as if more concerned about the camrecording than his appearance in the flesh. Guido wore a brushed silver knee-length jacket, and silver-white trousers. He looked like a prince; but an image of fat Bronze with unkempt hair and a wheezing cough would not let me go.

While we waited for Mireille and Didier to enter the church and walk down the aisle together, a choir sang quietly, and an elaborate organ was played by someone I could not see. Lizette, Jay and I all sat in the same pew as Diana and her partner, Karl, various introductions having been made earlier outside the church. Opposite, on the other side of the aisle, sat Helene and Mireille's sister Veronique with her partner Yves Lafont, the then famous footballer-poet.

Behind us, the other two members of the Guido co-op, Peter (Rudy's father) and Dominique sat with their respective partners Livia and Waltar and various very adult-looking offspring. There was also Arnout, a fidgety five year old, Rudy's son, and Peter and Livia's first grandson, who later, at the reception, linked up with Jay for mischievous expeditions.

If these had been Guido's Reflections, Rudy, a gifted saxophonist, would have filled many pages. He and Guido had played a lot together as children, on and around Peter's barge; and, as students, they had employed our barge *Ginquin* to take their girlfriends (Mireille in Guido's case) on holidays through the Dutch and German waterway systems.

I might have been thinking about Karl, having never met him before that day, or wondering what Diana and Lizette were making of each other, but I wasn't. I was thinking of Bronze. Mireille, when she arrived, looked ravishing, in a tight cat-suit made of the same brushed silver as Guido's jacket and a long flowing white muslin train. Together, Mireille and Guido belonged in some yet to-be-written futuristic fairy tale with an enchanting beginning and, I hoped, a happy ending. Bronze, for his sins and mine, belonged in a prison.

Didier had apparently compromised with Mireille over the wedding service. In return, Mireille and Guido had let Didier and Helene have their wish with respect to the reception. It was the biggest social function the Rocards had hosted since the ball in 2049 to celebrate a milestone in the fortunes of their puppet artwork company. I thought – ungenerously and unkindly – the wedding reception was no more than another Rocard promotion. Guido confessed to knowing only a fraction of the people present, and not being interested in any of them.

I tried to remain at a dining table, quietly talking with Lizette, Peter and Livia, or catching up with Dominique's news. Yet we were constantly interrupted. I was the father of the bridegroom, which meant Mireille and Diana kept trying to drag me off to be introduced to every Tom, Dick and Hamlet. More than that, though, I had become something of a celebrity in the last few days, first with the kidnap, then with the revelation that it was my 'other son' who had done the kidnapping.

People were naturally curious, and, given the world in which they inhabited, their curiosity was not tempered by any care or respect for my feelings. I am being unfair. Both Didier and Helene were very likable characters, and they had produced two very eligible daughters. I was glad for Guido. He had made an excellent match. But, by then, I had become easily irritated by those in the theatre and art world.

Thinking back, I believe this was a consequence of my relationship with Lizette. We talked often about my work, and more generally about politics, science, culture. Life had been different with Diana. Yes, she was brilliant, but she had only been able to maintain that brilliance, like many artists, by focusing exclusively on her own world. I had followed her there, onto the stage, as it were, as an observer, a friend, a patron, but by the time of our son's wedding I had already drawn far away, and was no longer so easily taken in by the scenery and spotlights. Not then, but now, I wonder whether I resented in some way Guido's decision to follow Diana into her world.

CHAPTER 12

IN WHICH I RESIGN FROM THE UNITED NATIONS

That year, 2064, was 'one helluva year' for me (as Betty Arklington famously said of 2051 before losing the US Presidency to Steve Tarbuck). Not only did I lose Bronze and Guido, in different ways, but I lost my job too.

As I have tried to indicate, I neither enjoyed being director-general nor was I very good at it. I had unintentionally alienated several of the directors, I had shirked my duties as an ambassador, and, worst of all, in response to the Singapore Peace Treaty and subsequent agreements, I was failing to make the institution respond effectively and efficiently to its renewed and extended responsibilities.

Personally, I do not think this latter failure was even half my fault. The UN's General Assembly had been much inflated – puffed-up in fact – by the terms of the Peace Treaty, but elsewhere in the UN system, which included many agencies large and small, problems of policy, politics, diplomacy had been hindering actual operations. The world and its nations and their disputes were taking a long time to recover from the Jihad War. Some thought this was natural, others that the underlying tensions had not gone away and were ready to resurface at any time. Our experience in the IFSD gave weight to the latter opinion. We blamed our problems on the distrust between nations, between Muslim and Christian, African and Asian, southern and northern Europe, and Europe and the US. And the difficulties did not ease. Unfortunately for me personally, some smaller UN agencies recovered more quickly than the IFSD, and thus our apparent stagnancy began to attract close scrutiny. Then came the incident in Dublin, and a twenty-fold increase in requests for interviews with, and profiles of, me personally, every rejected one of which was a potential nail in my professional coffin.

In early November, Eduardo Villalonga asked for a private interview. Since the Brasilia trip, our professional relationship had stalled, I would say. I had no reason to fault his work or his advice, but it only ever went so far, he never put himself out for me, nor did he inspire me with confidence. In short, I expected more from the members of my cabinet than he gave. This said, it was a shock to hear him threaten me with resignation. He had followed the media as closely as I had. He had taken his own soundings, and read his own runes. If I did not resign within two weeks, he said, he would. Eduardo, himself, could not have brought me down, but his private threat was clear evidence of my soon-to-be untenable position.

I took Tommy – my most loyal of assistants who had so effectively helped me hold on to my job as environment director some seven years earlier – for lunch at Lake Toba restaurant. I wanted to break it to him gently that I was not prepared to fight this time round. I had no more to offer, and it would not be fair to start a battle I did not think I could win. The very fact that my own son had caused a major security alert for the Irish authorities and for the UN system was sufficient reason in itself to resign. I tried to explain how I had hoped the media frenzy would die down quickly, or that there would have been some measure of support for my position forthcoming, at the very least, from British heavyweights. Now it was obvious such backing would not come voluntarily, it was time to go. Tommy tried to hide the relief but it showed on his face. Faithful Tommy. He never was any good at hiding his feelings. He had, it transpired, spared me the worst of his bush telegraph intelligence.

Although the UN's chroniclers have judged my last years harshly, thankfully none have gone so far as to blame me personally for the Second Jihad War. This may sound like a fanciful notion yet there are radical historians who believe the second conflict was caused, not by the rich-poor divide, or the Muslim-Christian divide or by Al Zahir's power-crazy ambitions to become Islam's second most important prophet after Mohammed, but by the United Nations and its leaders, not least Ojoru. A better organised, a better functioning, a better led UN, they say, could have averted the war. Dreamers, every last one of them.

There was another reason for my deciding to resign which I did not reveal to Tommy. I can be certain I am not inventing this now, in retrospect, because, at the time, I had an argument with Lizette over the matter. The simple truth is that I saw – and feared – war coming again, and I did not want to be there when it arrived. Lizette refused to believe I could act so selfishly, or that I would capitulate simply because I saw a tough road ahead. Perhaps she sensed echoes of her stamina-less husband Clint, or perhaps – this is another ungenerous thought – she did not want to lose status (she certainly enjoyed being taken to official functions).

Because she had not witnessed the full extent of my commitment to the IFSD and its objectives during the early 50s, I searched out a few favourable press clippings. I also recounted the story of how Tommy and I had campaigned to preserve my position when I was still only a director. Above all, I stressed, I would not have considered resigning then but for the daggers that were already unsheathed and being sharpened.

Officially, I cited old age and ill-health as the reasons for my resignation. I was granted a grand retirement party, at which several long-standing colleagues delivered kind words about my contribution to the IFSD. I have a vivid recollection, which unfortunately has tainted my memory of that party, of Eduardo being unctuous, a side of him I had never observed before. I received many cards and messages of goodwill, including one from Pravit Krishnamurty (who was to die within the year): 'It is not so bad in the grandstand, my friend, you can twiddle your thumbs, shake your fists, and shout "bloody fools" out loud.'

Lizette's flat was too cramped to accommodate me for more than a few days at a time. I tried to think about my future, but I refused to discuss this with colleagues and well-wishers who contacted me with offers and half offers and rumours of offers. I told them I needed time. Neither the thought of staying put in The Hague, or moving to a place in Brussels appealed much to me.

I spent some time with my antique photograph collection, then, after ensuring I had high quality prints of my favourites and copies of them all on Neil, I put the whole lot up for sale at Swann's. The auction did not take place until the late spring in 2065, months after I had left the Netherlands. I cajoled Lizette into taking a day off, arranging a friend to collect Jay from school, and travelling to Amsterdam so that I would not be alone when my treasured possessions went under the hammer. My photographs, quaintly sub-titled in the catalogue 'The collection of a gentleman', took less than 20 minutes to sell. Lizette, who had only seen individual items, was humorously outraged to discover that a good third of the collection was erotica.

Over Christmas/New Year the three of us floated around England. We stayed with Samuel and his family, then we opted to use a London hotel for two nights so that I could catch up with Horace, the Turnbulls and others, and visit Bronze, and then we ended up at Rhoda's house for my birthday, with a New Year's Eve celebration at the Sampsons in Chapel Chorlton. It was during these travels, feeling very rootless, that I decided I would return to England and buy a house somewhere near where I had grown up, in Surrey. This caused friction with Lizette, who was troubled by my decision to move further away from, not closer to, her. I sold the eco-roof apartment on Van Hogenhouckstraat, and shipped a small volume of furniture and a large number of books and papers into storage at Guildford. By the spring I was spending several days a fortnight being shown around a bewildering array of Surrey properties. I had no real idea of what I wanted, and so would store up a handful of possibilities and wait for when Lizette could join me to trail round them again.

In-between times at Lizette's flat and in Guildford, I visited friends. Oddly, I saw more of Peter and Livia after having left the Netherlands than I had in my last years living there. Both of them had done well in their respective, and unusually straight-lined, careers, allowing them to take early retirement.

Livia, after extended maternity breaks and several unpaid sabbaticals, had eventually become a director of the company she joined not long after arriving in the Netherlands. Peter himself had served his country well, choosing to remain an energy research and policy analyst, focusing for many years on the development of the hydrogen economy. He was one of the key scientists who had helped the Netherlands remain one of the greenest and pollution-leanest nations in the world.

Since retirement, Peter and Livia had moved out of Amsterdam to a rural retreat, not far from Leiden or Alphen aan de Rijn, near where they still moored a barge. Livia was finally fulfilling a lifetime ambition by designing clothes for her old company; while Peter was opting to take on the occasional freelance consultancy work for commercial firms to bolster their retirement funds.

Guido and Mireille had moved into a pad near Pigalle, characterful but tiny (bought outright by Didier as a wedding present), and, although they were both always very busy, I was invariably made welcome.

Horace's house in Southampton was too far from the Godalming/Guildford area to be a good base for my house hunting, but, nevertheless, I went there often to talk politics, politics and more politics. Nothing much else interested my old friend. Once politics had been his only mistress, now, past his prime, he was one of her many vassals.

In June, I found a property in Tilford, a pretty village with a slanting cricket green, east of Farnham. Built of brick in the 1930s with part tile-hung elevations, and a mature vine pinned to a solid trellis across one half, Taunton House was one of the prettiest properties I'd been shown. It had a huge lounge with sunlight streaming in on one side in the morning and the other in the afternoon, four bedrooms (one in the attic), and a refurbished kitchen. The energy and waste systems were all ultra-modern. The electrics and electronics had been recently upgraded, and the decorations were first class. Even the half acre garden, with its two oaks, had been loved, with shrubs a plenty, fruit trees, and a vegetable plot behind a low stone wall. This was it. I had been looking and prevaricating too long.

In order to win Lizette over, I employed old negotiating tricks: I under-promoted the house so as to let her find its charms for herself; and, I set it up against other properties which had no charms. The strategy worked better than I had hoped. Having long since resigned herself to my resolve to buy in England, Lizette approved the house with undisguised enthusiasm; and then, during the three months it took to buy, she decided to terminate her contract with the European University and, until such time as she found her next job, to live with me in Tilford.

EXTRACTS FROM CORRESPONDENCE

Alan Hapgood to Kip Fenn

January 2062

We've escaped the bitter cold of St Petersburg for a rare holiday. Anna has a cousin called Akilina here in Corfu, in Kerkira, near a village called Velonades. The name Akilina means eagle, and the lady does have a broad generous wing-span, but there's nothing remotely predatory about her. She owns an estate villa, and runs a large olive tree plantation. They are beautiful trees, the olives. Have you ever been here? I mean with time for yourself, not with your IFSD collar on; I remember you going to Rhodes once ...

When you first see the ancient gnarled trees – single-trunked but also, so unusually, double and triple-trunked – layered down the hillside, they draw you in, into a darker and darker stillness, into an Escher-like maze; it's as though they are woods that might be haunted with Tarquinade's ghouls or Narnia's evil spirits. They say that old men become children again, and I wonder if that is true. If we could but return to the simple world of our childhood imaginations, where truth and courage and loyalty could see us through the darkness to the peace and truth beyond.

Akilina is busy now, at this time of year, with her workers collecting up olives from the ground nets. They use the olives primarily for local power generators, but about 10% go to a restored traditional mill run by (not very hard-line) Noteks to produce eating oil. And very flavoursome it is too. But Akilina gets less than half her income from the olives, the rest comes in subsidy from the island government to maintain the groves. Officially, the subsidies are payments for farmers to be ready and willing to providing emergency irrigation when necessary, so as to preserve the island's environmental heritage. Unofficially, as everyone knows and Akilina certainly acknowledges, the olive groves are subsidised because they draw tourists to the island.

Anna (whose love I do not deserve – I confess this to you only) is out sightseeing, and I am meant to be writing a few letters. Yet I am caught with the image of the forest, as the poet Robert Frost said, 'mysterious, dark and deep', and I find myself thinking back to my early days, childhood days playing hide-and-seek with Julie (and always winning), and to your childhood (reading you the *Realm of Tarquinade* – do you remember it?) and to your teenage years in Godalming, those special times we spent together.

I'll be back in St Petersburg by the middle of January. It would be good to see you this year or next!

Keep in touch.

Kip Fenn to Anna Mastepanov

February 2062

No news could have saddened or touched me more profoundly than that of Alan's death. He was not only an uncle to me, but a brother and, at times, a father. And more than that, a wonderful friend.

Your sorrow must be great also – to lose such a friend, such a partner in life – but I've no doubt he's left you with a store of memories which will sustain you through this difficult time.

When I was but a toddler, Alan gave me a cuddly toy panda. I called it Karshula. I was about 15 when Alan asked me – I've no idea why – what had happened to it. I didn't know and didn't care. I relived this exchange in a dream 40 years later. I saw Alan's face, as it was then impressively open and optimistic, stonily refusing to laugh at my natural adolescent insouciance for all things childish. That dream came after a post-conference day trip from Hong Kong to Chengdu to visit the panda research and cloning centre. During our walk through the Panda Park, Karshula had come to mind, and, absurdly (for I was with other high officials talking about some big funding project or other), I caught myself thinking back, trying to remember what had become of it. That same day after the visit but before the dream, I emailed my mother

Julie to ask if she could remember. The next morning, after the dream, she emailed me back – I was in a transfer lounge at Hong Kong airport – to say Karshula had gone to a kindergarten in St Albans, before our move to Guildford. I had thrown it out of the window once and left it to rot in the garden, and my mother had rescued it. Yet more absurdly, I recall being thankful that I had asked this question while my mother was alive (she died later that same year). Alan would want to know – I never bothered to tell him while he was alive – that Karshula had found a good home.

I tell this silly story only because it gives an idea of how firmly Alan is embedded in my life, in me. Although he was often overseas, I always felt he was there, round the corner, at every stage of my life, ready with a kind word, generous with advice and contacts, regularly sending me books, and, best of all letters, richly embroidered with stories of his friends and his environmental endeavours.

One period stands out, though, when I was in my young teens. He lived in England, then, near my mother and me. My own father, Tom, had gone away – or so it seemed – and Alan had come in his stead, to spend hours chatting about politics, and history, and religion, world events and, inevitably, green issues. At the time, I considered there was nothing unusual about this, but, knowing more about teenagers now than I did then, I realise how very patient he must have been. And kind, and wise, and generous ...

In his last letter to me, only a few weeks ago, he said this: 'If we could but return to the simple world of our childhood imaginations, where truth and courage and loyalty could see us through the darkness to the peace and truth beyond.' I am sure that Alan is there now, somewhere, basking in peace and truth, for no man other deserves to be there if not him.

With love and sorrow.

PART TWO

Jay, War and the Grey Years

'Once or twice a year a mighty wind in the Out-There blows up a sand-fog which lasts several days, and then I peer, trance-like, into the swirling depths and imagine. I imagine that when it falls still there will be green pastures and fields with sheep and cows, and hedges and trees as far as the eye can see. And perhaps a river with stepping stones. Or else I imagine there will be a mountain scene with a hamlet in the foreground and a forest of pine trees in the background. These are pictures from the story books of the Long-Ago. It's hard to accept that once such scenes were common in our world, before the greyness in the sky, before the great and terrible drought, and before the Domes. But when the sand-fog settles, there is only sand in the Out-There, sand and more sand.

Beyond by Lucretia Quant (2018)

CHAPTER 13
IN WHICH BEGINS THE SECOND JIHAD WAR

Despite a self-imposed deadline of completing this book by the year's end, I stopped writing for a week in order to read over material stored on Neil, to refresh my memory on the traumatic events of the late 60s and early 70s, and to talk with Jay. He does remember being aware of the Second Jihad War through his primary school years, but has no clear recollections of it. By contrast, he has vivid memories of images, taken by aerohover cameras and imaging satellites, of the eruption of Toba. And he has no difficulty in identifying the Grey Years as coinciding with his early years at the Witley Academy of Excellence (my old school Witley Academic, long since renamed) – the classroom never quite warm, the swimming pool unheated, and his hands and feet often frozen during sports or while waiting for the school bus on winter mornings.

Now that Jay has entered the story, so to speak, he is more self-interested than before, so we talk at length about his childhood, his mother, his friends, his activities. Unfortunately, this means that his advice about what to include and what not to include in these Reflections is not as objective as it has been.

But it is thanks to Jay that I have decided to elaborate on my reasons for resigning from the IFSD. When I explained about my fear of the onset of war, and my remembered conversation with Lizette, he quizzed me.

'I don't understand why you didn't want to be there when the war arrived? I don't feel you've explained this well enough. From what you've said, Ma thought the same.'

I closed my eyes, and thought about how to answer him. I could have said: I was tired, I'd had enough, and I had no stomach to fight to keep my job, when the job itself, already a nightmare, was going to get worse; and besides, as I have already explained, I would certainly have been pushed out if I'd not resigned. But I didn't. There was more to it. There was more to the reason why I would have been ousted, and consequently why I resigned before that could happen. And so, despite Jay's sudden protestations that I was looking weary and should sleep, I told him.

Perhaps, while composing earlier chapters I forgot – maybe the pills are not working as effectively as before – or perhaps I deliberately skimmed over the truth. In either case, I've decided I should correct the error. The end of these Reflections is in sight, so if I were now to bypass verity – when I've endeavoured to stick to it as carefully and objectively as one person can – I would undermine much of what I've already written.

The messier truth is not that difficult to uncover. I had, throughout my years at the IFSD, consistently tried to ensure that the conditions under which aid was provided were as loose as possible. I am not exactly certain when or why I developed the conviction that this was necessary. Alan influenced me in a general way when I was a schoolboy, but it was Pravit Krishnamurty who probably affected me more directly. I was also much affected by the many ideas and proposals we came across during my early IFSD years in Enterprise 35. Although I had friendly arguments about and around this subject over the years – in the office, meeting halls and zini bars – there was no recognition by my peers or political masters of my disposition on the issue (I doubt I could have defined it myself), not even when my position as environment director came under threat.

As I hope I made clear earlier, my power as an administrator over policy was never significant, and, at most, my influence to change or direct it was never more than marginal. Nevertheless, as I said, I do believe I had some – as opposed to no – influence. At the policy level, this might have come through the way my team drafted proposals or put forward suggestions for negotiating compromises, or through the informal advice we gave occasionally to representatives of smaller recipient states when we thought they were being outmanoeuvred by the heavyweight donor countries. And, at the programme and project level, we sometimes tried very slightly to de-restrict the conditionality on contract terms to allow the money to be committed or released more quickly and/or to be used more flexibly.

One of the arguments put forward by those who considered it necessary to shackle all aid with the tightest of conditions and contracts was about ensuring that the donated funds were not wilfully misused to support, in any way, the ability of recipient countries to develop police state or military capabilities. Six months before I resigned, the US administration had published a report demonstrating how, in the run-up to the First Jihad War, several member countries of the International Islam Brotherhood for Peace (IIBP) had misappropriated large amounts of UN aid and used it to build up their military structures. The aid may not have been employed directly to buy arms, yet it had helped with the costs of apparently benign but, in fact, military-related training, supplies and infrastructure. In a final section, the report suggested that this trend had recently begun again in earnest. Indeed, it warned, certain countries were exchanging experience on how best to exploit the UN and others. No fingers were pointed at any individual, but the report became highly influential, especially with those in the so-called West who had been reluctant about the Singapore Peace Treaty.

It is certainly possible that this same report undermined my confidence at the time, and thus led me, subconsciously, to give more weight to other reasons for resigning. I certainly took due account of it more consciously when, some years later, I began preparing an important theoretical exercise on the future of the UN about which I will have more to say later. But, even in retrospect, how can we really know the truth of things. Maybe, in some slight way, I did assist those countries which wanted to abuse the aid mechanisms; but then how could this fault in the system be gauged against the benefits a more open/flexible approach brought other countries, whose ability to implement development programmes was significantly improved by not having to follow Western strictures on scrutiny, deadlines and other red tape.

The first unmistakable sign that Al Zahir had only paused for breath, as it were, in order to allow the IIBP countries to regroup, rearm and reconsider objectives, came when a Brazilian journalist, Sé Lobo, was captured in Mozambique, and then escaped. His scoop made headlines around the world. A conflict between Muslims and Christians had been under way in the country for decades. It began as a guerrilla operation by a marginal group of Muslim fanatics, but escalated when they won hold of a northern corner of the country bordering on Lake Malawi. Prior to the First Jihad War, the IIBP had funded the Muslim group modestly and secretly, then, during the war, it had stepped up its backing with air support and troops. When the group had occupied nearly half the country, NATO moved in to help defend the secular (but Christian dominated) government.

The dispute should have been settled by the terms of the Singapore Peace Treaty, which gave both the IIBP and the NATO countries six months to withdraw troops, military advisers and use of their hi-tech satellite eye equipment. Moreover, the Mozambique government had promised to amend the country's constitution to provide more autonomy for Muslim-dominated regions in the north. However, with ongoing guerrilla activity, the government had dragged its heels. This was one of the so-called 'left-over wars'. It was a fundamental part of the Singapore Treaty that neither the IIBP or NATO affiliates should interfere militarily in such conflicts. Sé Lobo discovered that there were hundreds of Syrian and Algerian personnel directing, organising and supplying the Mozambique guerrillas. The government had claimed as much but its claims had fallen on deaf (or closed) ears.

Soon after, in 2066, other left-over wars flared up, as if Lobo's article had been a starting gun. Each one was brought to the United Nations. The most interested Western countries and groupings protested vehemently at violations of UN resolutions implementing the Singapore Treaty but without much consequence.

In a rare interview granted to the Western media, carried by *GlobeOne*, Al Zahir called the violations 'minor infringements', and said they would be dealt with. 'Peace is our aim,' he declared, 'and peace is our destiny.' Al Zahir's position as leader of Iran, the IIBP and Muslims across the globe had strengthened since the First Jihad War. *GlobeOne's* front cover portrait made him appear elderly, thoughtful, benign, and the article itself served to provide, for want of a better description, the Al Zahir appeasers with much fuel.

Fortunately, I was never in a position where I had to make any decision which would lead our armed forces into a battle and to our sons and daughters dying, but if I had of been, I'm sure I too would have opted for appeasement rather than give any excuse to restart the Jihad War. And, if we had not appeased – by allowing Syrian and Algerian troops to multiply in Mozambique without reply, for example – would it have made any difference? I doubt it, not in the long run.

In 2067, things only got worse. The Second Jihad War, the history books say, began in May 2068 and came to an end in 2071, but this is only half the truth. There was already much turmoil under way long before May 2068: the Islamic terrorism and riots in Europe; the rapid escalation of left-over wars where agreements on paper meant nothing in practice; and the emergence of armed Islamic groups in previously peaceful countries and regions, especially in West Africa. And, at the end, there was a cease-fire in 2071 but no settlement until the following April, and this only dealt with very major issues. The fear, poverty and hunger of the Grey Years may have helped bring the war to an end, but it did nothing to assist the peace. Today, three decades later, the Christian-dominated rich nations continue to live in fear that a new Al Zahir will appear one day, unify Muslims everywhere, and set light to the fragile truce now guarded by a stronger, but still very flawed, United Nations.

CHAPTER 14

IN WHICH JAY STARTS TO GROW UP

In Tilford, a quiet corner of sunny Surrey, Lizette, Jay and I were well insulated from the terrors of war. There was a mosque nearby, but the local Muslim population was surprisingly well integrated. Most of the mosque members were loyal British subjects and opposed to Al Zahir's Jihad. One of our near neighbours, Dr Sami Abd al-Jabbaar claimed Pakistani heritage. He was a consultant at Guildford hospital, an official at the local mosque, and regularly featured in the *Surrey News* because of his prize-winning vegetables. Jay played with one of his two boys; and I saw him occasionally whenever we were leaving from, or returning to, our homes on foot at the same time. He never lost an opportunity to condemn the latest terrorist outrage in a European city or IIBP military exercise.

Lizette was fortunate to find a well-paid teaching post at the Farnborough Science University. Jay settled in easily to the middle-sized primary school across the other side of the village. As for me, premature retirement did not suit. For all my adult life I had been faced with busy-ness: people, meetings, papers, deadlines. Now I was spending much of the day alone, in the small office we had had built at the back of Taunton House. For the first and frustrating year in Tilford I attempted to write a book called *The IFSD Years of Expansion* for the same publisher that had handled Alan's work. But I had no will to do the necessary research nor could I find a coherent view or analytical framework to give the book meaning. I had taken no advance, nor signed any contract so, bit by bit, I let the project evaporate.

I took up bowls, which I played once or twice a week, weather permitting. It was refreshing to join in the petty squabbles and friendly (and not-so friendly!) sparring, to swap inane remarks about the terrors of the war or the conflicts on the parish council as if they were of equal importance, and to mull over, for hours afterwards, shots made, both good and bad. I spent much time in the garden, usually under instruction from Lizette.

And, for Lizette, I read countless books on the art of bridge, in all its variants. I managed to better my technique and learn the conventions, but not my ability to memorise and mentally sort cards, which was more important. Thus, I never improved to the point where Lizette wanted to partner me in competitions (did I ever really want to?). In frustration, and because being a mother didn't leave her that much free time, she eventually stopped badgering me and decided to put her hobby aside for a while. For my own pleasure, I would tune in live whenever there was an important auction of 19th century photographs, and watch it through from beginning to end, drooling over the old images on the screen.

Whatever my daily activity, I looked forward to mid-afternoon when I would stroll through the village to the school to collect Jay, and then, on the return, dawdle slowly back across the green, stopping perhaps at the local shop to buy Jay an ice-jet in summer or a sherbet-dinger in winter. There are dozens of episodes I could recall from Jay's early school days, but this one, I am about to recount, stands out as well as any other; it was the first time I realised Jay had his own life, his own secret world.

During the walk home, I would quiz Jay about his day. He was never very attentive to my questions or responsive, and I was lucky if I caught a snippet of information, about the lunch menu, a special lesson, or another child being told off. On occasions we would walk back from the school with other children and their parents. If the weather was clement we might stop at the playground by the river. One time, when Jay's buds had left, and I was pushing him round on the roundabout, I asked who he played with at school. He told me he was a bit sad. A bit sad? I asked him to explain several times but without result. I reported the conversation to Lizette who suggested he himself might not know why he was sad. Then, later, when I was reading him a story in bed, in his attic room, I asked again about being sad at school. This time he was more forthcoming.

'She makes me sit down, and takes off my shoe. And she doesn't give it back. Until later.' With further gentle questioning I discovered that a girl called Lindsay had taken Jay's shoe several times and each time this had resulted in Jay crying.

Lizette and I had assumed Jay was happy and untroubled at school, and so this news – extracted with difficulty – came as a shock. Lizette wanted to approach the school, but I argued we should help Jay deal with the situation on his own. Lizette cautiously gave way. I explained to Jay that Lindsay's actions were definitely wrong, and that if she took his shoe again he should say firmly and loudly 'don't do that', hoping an older friendly child or a teacher might hear. If Lindsay threatened or hurt him, he should tell a teacher. I have no idea if the advice worked or not, for Jay never talked about being sad again, at least not in relation to life at school.

Jay has pointed out (!) that this is a dismal anecdote, and that I should balance it with 'a nice one' from his early school years. I am happy to oblige. On his seventh birthday, in late September 2067, Jay was sent a box of simple magic tricks by Lizette's brother Samuel and his family. One weekday soon after, when the school was closed to pupils for some reason, and Lizette was away all day at work, Jay kept pestering me to show off the tricks. I suggested he save them and put on a performance for Lizette and me that evening. For the rest of the day, he beavered away in his attic room, interrupting me in my office only rarely. Once he came to give me a ticket, complete with seat number, code and tear-off section. When he heard the front door, he raced down the stairs to give Lizette a ticket too.

At the appointed time, we went together to the top of house. On the door to his room he had pinned a sign saying 'Jay's Marvellous Magic Show'; and inside he had arranged two chairs with seat numbers. Jay himself was hiding in the toy cupboard. A mock deep voice said 'take your seats', and then he appeared, cutely dressed wearing a bow tie and a plastic make-it-yourself top hat which had come with the magic tricks box.

This was no static magic show, for the magician needed a member of the audience for each trick, which meant we were both up and down every few minutes choosing a card, closing our eyes, or waving a wand that went limp if we didn't hold it right. We laughed and laughed – except when he lost his props or made a mistake, in which case we pretended not to notice. After each trick we clapped, and Jay bowed. When, at the end, we demanded an encore, and explained what we meant, he looked crestfallen at not having any more magic to give us, until we explained it was perfectly acceptable to do his best trick a second time. We applauded enthusiastically again, signalled for Jay to retire from the stage to his toy cupboard, and then departed the attic-theatre. Ten minutes later, Jay came downstairs looking very miserable.

'I feel very sad. I've worked all day and now it's all over.' Sweet, sweet boy. Lizette cuddled him. She wanted to explain about how enjoyment should be sought from the work itself not the result, and how the best cure for sadness was to start work again on the next thing, but he wouldn't listen.

For a couple of years, our lives were complicated by Clint Tuohy, Lizette's former husband and Jay's genetic father. While Lizette had been in Brussels, Clint had considered Jay out of reach, and had abdicated interest and responsibility. This had suited Lizette and me, and had allowed or encouraged us to form the Jay co-op without him. Once back in England, though, we went on a visit north to see Pete, Clarity and Rhoda, and, during that trip, Lizette took the trouble to call on Clint. Thereafter, her ex-husband began transferring funds to Lizette's bank account for Jay's maintenance and, at the same time, demanding access. Lizette returned the monies, and tried, via camphone, to persuade Clint that, after six years of minimal contact between him and Jay, during which time I had effectively taken over as Jay's father, contact with him would only confuse the child.

Lizette thought she would be able to reason him round, but she was wrong. His interest in Jay grew to the point of a fixation. He turned up in Tilford, one Saturday lunch-time, uninvited. We treated him hospitably. But after showing him round the village, and taking him for a walk along the river with Jay, we expected him to go. He didn't. He wheedled and whined, and begged to stay the night. Lizette wanted to kick him out, but I couldn't agree. In the morning, Lizette found him playing pick-a-stick with Jay in the lounge.

Later, after breakfast and after we had finally got him out of the house, Jay told us that Clint had asked to be called 'Dad'. Lizette was so outraged by Clint's behaviour that she called him immediately, and screamed abuse down the phone while he was driving north.

After that, he turned up regularly, every few months, always uninvited, always unwelcome and always apologetic. He was never allowed to stay the night again, but, if it was possible, we did let him spend a couple of hours with Jay. Between these visits, there were arguments, threats and counter-threats. Clint demanded more regular access, and indicated he would take legal action. Unfortunately, the Dutch co-op laws, which might have given us some protection in the Netherlands, were not valid in Britain. Lizette counter-attacked by suggesting she might send anonymous letters to the local Stoke media about the unacceptable behaviour of one of its upright citizens and councillors. From Clint's side, I should add, we also received streams of apologies, promises and presents. The whole situation was horribly messy. Lizette and I spent far too much time discussing it between ourselves, and Lizette spent yet more time moaning about Clint on the phone or by email to her friends Rhoda and Clarity.

In autumn 2067, Clint vanished from our lives. We learned, from Rhoda, he had formed a new relationship. We assumed it had become convenient for him to forget about Jay. Some years later, when that relationship broke down, Clint again tried to impose himself on us and Jay. He started with phone calls and emails, but when he turned up on our doorstep, we would not let him enter the house or see Jay. Lizette warned him to stay away or she would seek legal advice. Jay can tell his own story about Clint, in his own time, if he can be bothered – I've given him too much space already.

Lizette was a demanding mother, expecting much of her son. This was partly because of her insecurity about the paternal side of Jay's upbringing, in particular Clint's intrusions. But her own background also played a part. From what she told me of 'Pa' and 'Ma' they had been committed parents, never prepared to accept second best. Clearly, the approach had worked with Lizette, and with her elder brother Samuel who had become very successful as an engineer (tidal turbines), but not with the younger brother Mercurio, who, for whatever reason, had opted out of mainstream society. Perhaps, also, the escalating war exaggerated Lizette's disposition in some way.

Whatever the reason, she tended to push Jay academically, providing only occasional effusive praise when he produced excellent work, and criticising him regularly for modest or poor work. At times, when she was being overly harsh or pressing him too far, I tried to intervene, but in this aspect of Jay's upbringing, his education, she would not be swayed by my opinions. Certainly, there was little in my track record to inspire any confidence in me as a parent: during the first year of our time in Tilford, I was still making occasional trips to visit another of my sons in prison.

Instead of intervening I observed quietly how Jay learned tricks – not magic ones – to avoid being assigned harder and harder tasks, or being the target of higher and higher expectations: how to pretend he didn't understand what was being asked of him, how to ask sweetly for help over and over again, and how to underplay his own knowledge or ability. As he grew older, so Lizette became partially wise to these games, which caused plenty of strife during Jay's teenage years. I sincerely believe this had no long-term negative effect on Jay's intelligence (I'm on dangerous ground here), but I suspect it did divert him away from Lizette's beloved science subjects, towards less academic ones such as drawing cartoon characters and designing impossible worlds on the computer, although this was already later on.

CHAPTER 15

IN WHICH GUIDO DECIDES TO GO TO ECUADOR

I say my interest in writing a book on the IFSD petered out, but this was partly because, after about a year in Tilford, I let myself became involved in other, more engaging projects. I agreed to join a team of retired WWF campaigners to take a close analytical look at ten large recent programmes conducted for or with one of the UN agencies, to see if any lessons could be learned, not on the policies themselves, but on the procedures for winning project funds, for collaboration and for implementation. In addition, I took on two non-executive directorships, one for a large environmental consultancy, Greenwell-Plasset, and the other for a subsidiary of Euroil which made and marketed a synthetic aviation fuel, a competitor to Brazil's Vivido.

Greenwell-Plasset paid me only a modest wage which I balanced against the idea that I might have some beneficial influence over their activities. Euroil, though, rewarded me very well and demanded little in return. I had no doubt I was being paid because my name and former position enhanced the company's international credibility, but as long I was not asked to do anything unethical, or vaguely unethical, I didn't mind. In fact, during a preliminary lunch with Euroil people, at the Greensand Retreat – which had been completely refurbished in the Romaine Riche style, and looked and felt more luxurious than ever – I drew such a collection of smug smiles of self-satisfaction when I told them I had once worked for Euroil in Brussels as a young man that I decided there and then to give them a rough ride. I spoke frankly, controversially even, at the meetings I attended, and soon became more trouble than I was worth. When my three year contract expired, no one offered to renew it, and I had no time to ask why.

In April 2068, Guido and Mireille came to stay at Taunton House for a week. They brought presents for Jay and expensive chocolates for Lizette. I joined them on various explorations, to the South Coast to see the old docks in Portsmouth and to promenade in Brighton; and to London to experience some of the best shows I had seen in a very long time. This was at the same time as the IIBP's unexpected missile attack on Rhodes, the one which wiped out a European Army base, and led to the formal start of the Second Jihad War.

On one day, we took Jay out of school and went to Alexandra Palace, which once, 15-20 years earlier, had been the greatest museum on interactive broadcasting history and technology in Europe. Jay and I watched the same 30 minute holographic movie *Jungle Journey* that I'd first seen with Diana and Guido on a trip to London in the late 40s. Guido, who had oversold the place to Mireille, spent most of the day criticising the lack of investment and innovation.

On our return, I received a message from Tommy, who was still at the IFSD, and with whom I corresponded occasionally, informing me that MarySue's son, Conrad, had been killed in Rhodes. She and I sent each other New Year cards, but otherwise had not communicated for ages. I had known Conrad slightly, and MarySue had talked about him often. One time, Guido and I had met MarySue and her son while shopping in Leiden. Conrad was a young teenager at the time, and Guido only seven or eight, but, for a few minutes while MarySue and I chatted, the two boys joined forces to admire the ultra-cycles and cycle paraphernalia in a shop window.

I was under the impression that Guido and Mireille had come visiting for a break, but Guido's mood was not as light as usual, and both of them prevaricated whenever I asked about their plans and projects. After supper one night, Guido took me for a drink and a manly chat in the village pub, the Barley Mow. We bought a bottle of English rosé wine (why do I remember this?). As soon as we had settled down at a corner table, he told me the news he'd been holding back all week, the news he'd come to Tilford to deliver.

'We've decided to go and live in Ecuador, in Quito. There's a theatre there waiting for us. Teatro Sucre. Our names are already etched into the crumbling facade.' He paused, waiting for my reaction, but I didn't say anything. 'We met a man, an entrepreneur, called Felix Rico Montechristo. He was in Paris, he came to our show. Some people call him Felix, others Rico. He's Ecuadorian but his mother was American. His main business is managing celebrities ...' and here Guido listed half a dozen names of footballers and singers who he thought I might recognise but didn't. Then, still trying to build a credibility bridge between Felix and me, he mentioned that he managed the Ecuadorian volleyball team, and in particular, its captain Carlos Mallastro. I did know of Mallastro because he had led the Ecuadorian team to a place in the quarter-finals at the 2063 world cup in Munich, and, only last year, to a semi-final place at the world cup in São Paulo.

'Felix has bought a dilapidated theatre in central Quito, and wants to refurbish it, make it glorious again. He wants us to manage the artistic side. We've accepted. We're leaving at the end of May.'

I knew they had been to Quito some months earlier, but I had no idea the trip was more than a holiday. Mireille had studied European literature and literary traditions at the Sorbonne, but then demeaned herself – this is the assessment of her father, Didier, long before the wedding – by becoming a stage manager. Guido, after completing his degree in Amsterdam, went to Paris, partly to study mime, and partly to be near Mireille. After realising the limits of his acting ability, he reluctantly gravitated towards the same occupation as his mother, theatre design, for which he had a real talent.

A year or so after the wedding, the two of them discovered, to their own surprise, how much they enjoyed working in tandem on the same productions. Subsequently, in-between separate regular paid assignments, they teamed up together to direct and design small-scale adventurous plays with low production costs and in which actors would perform more for love than money.

'How long are you planning to stay?' I asked. Guido drank swiftly, looked away and then back at me.

'Two, three years. We have no fixed plans. But we'll come back, to see you and Mum, of course, and Mireille's parents.'

'It's so far away,' I said. Confusion and sadness must have shown on my face, for Guido went on quickly, wanting to explain.

'And far away from the coming war. It's not that we're afraid, but that we want no part of it. We feel it has nothing to do with us, with our lives.'

'I'm sure many people feel that way in France and in England and all over Europe, but they're not emigrating to another continent. France, Holland, Britain, they remain among the most safe, cultured and sophisticated places on earth.'

'I know. We know. It's not the only reason. It's a great opportunity too. We could never hope to run a whole theatre in Paris, not for years and years, and certainly not without the help of Didier. And to be honest, Mireille is sick of him trying to help her. She falls for his offer of money sometimes, and then is too ashamed to tell me. That's not all, he talks secretly to friends and colleagues in the business, and encourages them somehow to give her work. Then halfway towards a production she finds out, and it's too late to extricate herself. He's suffocating her, us. And Helene is becoming impossible too. She keeps discovering new distant relations, holding dinner parties for each one, and insisting – really insisting – on us being there so she can introduce us. She's uncovered dozens of relations in her own family, Chastrain, and twice as many Rocards, all within a train ride of Paris. Family is so important, she says. She's become obsessed.'

'I didn't know things had got that bad. I haven't had any contact with them, Does your mother see them?'

'Not much, I don't think Karl has time for them any more. They used to get on when they were younger. Now, they're too rich for him. He despises anyone with money. I don't see Mum either.' Guido didn't need to tell me. Several times over the years he had confided that he positively loathed Karl, mostly I think because of his influence over Diana. 'And Karl and Mireille have a mutual aversion to each other.'

'I can't imagine anyone not liking Mireille. She's so pretty and thoughtful. Lizette was delighted with the chocolates ...'

'She won't accept Karl's brusqueness or arrogance without a challenge. He hates her telling him off. I watch Mum put up with the behaviour, but Mireille won't.'

'So you're running away from family as much as from war, I hope that doesn't include me.'

'Mireille adores you, you know that,' he said, pointedly, jokingly, leaving himself out of the response.

'What did your mother say?'

'We haven't told her; she's next.'

'And Mireille's parents?'

'They're last.'

'So I'm the dress rehearsal.'

'It was Mireille's idea. We thought it would give us more confidence if we had your blessing.'

'And was it Mireille's idea that you should talk to me alone, man to man, down the pub?' I didn't wait for him to answer. 'This Felix character worries me. Won't you be completely dependant on him once you're out there? And neither of you speak much Spanish.'

'We've been studying night and day. And Felix is cool, we've discussed this a lot. He's a true patron. He paid for our trip, he's offered us good long-term contracts, and he's shown us a delightful villa we can rent cheaply. He loves our ideas for the theatre. We're going to make it the most important play-house in the country. If we stay in Paris we could work for 20 years and not be noticed and, even if we were, we'd never stop worrying that Didier was pulling strings behind the scenes.'

I gave him my blessing, which is not to say I wasn't sorry about them moving to another continent or concerned about the risky enterprise. To my shame, I suspected Guido and his wife, having been introduced to famous actors and writers during their brief lives, were thinking of this move as a short cut to eminence. I underestimated them both.

CHAPTER 16

IN WHICH I STUDY THE FUTURE OF THE UN

A few months after Mireille and Guido had departed for South America, I became involved in a project – thanks to Horace, or so he claims – which was to preoccupy me for several years.

Horace was one of our most regular visitors, rarely a month went by when he didn't stay over on a Thursday or Friday night; now and then he came on Sundays too. He had found a route through from London to Southampton, passing nearby us, which took him only half an hour longer than on the toll roads, and saved him from paying the high charges. Horace was not a poor man, despite devoting his life to the House of Commons, because he and his brother Tim had successfully developed a smallish property business. Yet he had a compulsive hatred of road tolls. Horace did not oppose them publicly for that would have been no different from opposing taxes in general, but he was often the first critic to appear on the media whenever a hike in tolls was announced, whoever was in government.

I was always happy to see Horace. Lizette tired of him at times. If he was droning on about a topic of the day, usually the war and the policy of the British government towards the latest developments, she promptly told him to change the record or to shut up and let someone else get a word in edge-ways. He never took offence. When she was annoyed by him, though, she would suddenly disappear, to the garden or the bedroom. Then Horace, often glossy after too many drinks, would drift into airing a grievance or rehearsing an argument or statement he was hoping to make in the House, and I would drift too – but into sleep. I should say that Horace was a polite guest, ever considerate, and always ready to take us out to eat. He regularly sent us invitations for events in London (which we rarely accepted). Jay called him Uncle Talk-a-lot, although there's was nothing remotely uncle-ish about him. He had no idea how to converse with Jay.

Sometimes, though, he would bring Tim, his younger brother, who did communicate well with our son. Tim had divorced years ago, and his three children had long since gone their separate ways. He missed seeing them regularly. Tim and Horace were similar in appearance with their medium-height, spectacles, and wispy regenerated hair. But Tim was fatter all round, with a large paunch, puffy cheeks and a second chin. Strangely, it was Tim who was the more active of the two, having played golf and done some sailing in his time. Horace kept surprisingly lean, without ever taking up a sport or controlling his diet. Whenever Tim drew attention to this difference between them, which he did regularly (why, I never understood), Horace claimed, one way or another, that it was mental activity that had kept him thin, thereby implying the opposite was true for his brother. This enraged Tim, who had spent his life far removed from Horace's intellectual world, mostly using his accountancy skills in the service of country estates, and also to run their joint property business.

During one of his stay overs (before I lose the thread of this narrative entirely), Horace mentioned that he had lunched with Matt Fortune during the week. The two politicians had remained friendly since I introduced them to each other in 2057. Matt had retired from Parliament and gone to work part-time for the London branch of the European Institute of Politics and Diplomacy (EIPD), which was one of the most important and respected cross-border think-tanks in Europe. Matt had told Horace about an ambitious study on the future of the United Nations, and that the EIPD was still considering who should administer the project. At this point in the conversation, Horace claimed, he had proposed me. Later, though, Matt said my name was already on a draft short list.

Without knowing it, this was the work I had been waiting for. The EIPD's illustrious 50 year reputation had not been won by shadow boxing with governments or other institutions over issues of the day, or by responding to requests from the European Union, which had provided its funding for many years, to investigate a particular topic, both of which it did regularly, but by involving the highest calibre politicians and diplomats to launch debates on big questions, on the controversial subjects of tomorrow.

Ten days after Horace's visit, I received a call from Matt himself inviting me to the Institute in Cavendish Square. A week later, when I was ensconced in his office, he explained in detail about a major study on the role of the UN once the war was over. It would investigate whether there was a case to start again, with a fresh model. The working hypothesis would be that the UN had served well for 100 years, but that its failure to avoid the First and Second Jihad Wars was a sign of terminal failure. Would it be possible, the EIPD wanted to know, to combine the experience of the UN with that of the European Union – undoubtedly the most successful regional integration model in history – and find a new way forward for the world in the 22nd century. The study was to be called World Union – thinkable or unthinkable?. He briefed me on how it was to be planned and implemented. I listened intently. My role would be that of administrator, organising and overseeing a group of 30 prominent political characters, 'wise men', through from beginning to end (three years in all) and liaising with the EIPD. Yes. I said yes. Matt, genial as ever and with sideburns so bushy and white he could have materialised from a Dickens novel, thanked me profusely.

Initially, during the early stages of the project in autumn 2068, I was obliged to travel to a large number of meetings in Brussels and other European capitals (and to arrange ad hoc Jay-care for the first time since being in Tilford), which was a pain because journeys, whether by train or plane, took two or three times longer than in normal circumstances due to the heightened security arrangements, and security alerts. Once the study proper was under way, I was able to manage it partly from home and partly from the EIPD office in London which provided the necessary secretariat and cam-conferencing facilities.

I organised for our wise men to be provided with a library of background documents. These included the two important, but much over-looked, analyses carried out decades earlier by management consultancies; several documents from my term in the IFSD's Future Policy Division; numerous papers and reports that various UN agencies had produced on their own future; and whatever papers/books we could track down that had already been written on the subject of world government.

The wise men elected Dr Luigi Costa, by dint of his seniority, as their chairman. He had been a prime minister of Italy, and there were only two other ex-prime ministers on the panel, both from countries smaller than Italy. In my opinion, he was not the best man for the job. He had been a pedantic leader, safely honest and bureaucratic, but short on charisma and inspiration. His main claim to posterity came during his first stint as Italian prime minister, in the 40s, when he had been one of the loudest voices in Europe advocating the Next Step and propelling a strong European input towards what became known as the Djakarta Settlement. Certainly, he was one of the most internationally-aware leaders Italy had produced in the 21st century.

More than half of the wise men approached their task with determined objectivity, while the others let politics dictate their opinions. Most of this latter group had held high office, and, although retired from the political front line, retained constituencies – if not with voters then among colleagues within their own parties – which needed servicing to one degree or another. A few of this group, which included Costa, could see no further internationally than the politics of the ongoing war, so every idea they offered, every opinion they put forward, every bit of text they drafted was tainted in some way by their positions on the war. Fortunately, these individuals did not all pull in the same direction; moreover, Costa's position as chairman gave him no extra weight, so long as the others were vigilant enough not to let him exert undue control over their opinions.

It was my job to ensure they were vigilant, and to keep the wise men's thoughts firmly focused on the long term and not on the present or short term. Thus, I often found myself in conflict with Costa. He would ring me up at all times of day and night, demanding to know why I'd distributed this or that document or why I'd drawn conclusions from a meeting or a round-robin of opinions which ignored his position. Other times he called to discuss the most minor of changes to a draft agenda simply to tailor it to his preferred shape. I dealt with him firmly and fairly. When necessary, I reminded him of our respective roles: his was to be a wise man, to think forward, strategically, imaginatively; and mine was to implement a framework in which he and his colleagues could do this to the best of their ability.

For three years, this job kept me lively. It diverted my attention from ruminating too long on daily reports which told of an ever increasing number of military campaigns, bombing raids, destruction, death. I was again in contact with important and interesting characters, many of whom I'd met, or heard of or read about in the media. It felt like a useful task and, therefore by extension, I felt useful. Prior to the EIPD study, Lizette had begun to worry about my lack of employment and so, when I started, she was content to see me busy again, even though it meant I had to travel and be away from home more often. She relished me confiding in her about the clashes between the wise men, whether because of character or policy; and she took my occasional requests for her opinion so seriously that she would think about them for days.

What did we achieve? *World Union – thinkable or unthinkable?* is available on the net, and through any good library, so there's no purpose in my reiterating it in any detail here. Also, as is evident, there is no World Union today, and the United Nations is extant, with much the same basic underlying structure as it has always had. Nevertheless, the aim of the report was to launch a debate, and this it definitely achieved. The European Union, for example, having largely bailed out of the UN in the 70s as a consequence of the Jihad War, deliberated carefully over the ideas in our report. It set up an analysis group and produced several major policy documents. Eventually, though, it lost its nerve – or saw sense, depending on where you stand – and decided to re-support the UN model.

Now, as I dictate – with next century optimism filling the corridors of power – very serious consideration is again being given to major changes in the UN system: a more powerful General Assembly; a complete overhaul of the structure of the agencies to provide greater coherence; better coordination, and clearer lines of accountability towards the General Assembly; and, as we proposed 30 years earlier in the EIPD report, a virtual parliament to provide a degree of democratic control over the General Assembly.

We calculated that a world parliament would need no fewer than 4,000 members, with only one physical plenary session a year hosted by countries in rotation. Otherwise plenary debates and votes could, with the right technology and safeguards, be adequately conducted on the net – we produced a supplementary report on how this could be done. To prepare for virtual plenary sessions, 50-60 special committees could function in a virtual way but with more frequent physical meetings at permanent bases in selected locations.

Crucially, the report suggested, each member of this visionary parliament would be made responsible not only for representing his/her constituency to the parliament, but for representing the objectives and achievements of the parliament to his/her constituency. Any voter who did not know what the world parliament did, the report proposed, should be advised by the UN itself through the media against voting for the incumbent member. I only mention this last point because it was the single good idea (to my mind) that Costa brought to the report. He had suffered during his political career, he told me repeatedly, because he had been unable to transfer his enthusiasm for the objectives of the UN or the European Union to his public, and consequently he had never reaped sufficient applause at home for his achievements internationally. He had always wondered why this was, and how individual citizens could be made more aware of their responsibilities beyond municipal and national boundaries.

CHAPTER 17
IN WHICH I RECALL MORE ABOUT THE WAR

Flora died yesterday. Chintz told me. She came last night when her shift was over. I asked the standard question: was there any suffering, any pain? The answer was no, it's always no. Pain is what I personally fear most. If the doctors and the plumbing and the pills cannot keep the pain away, I'll not be able to sustain the will to hold on and finish this book. Flora's going makes me feel especially vulnerable since, coincidentally, we had both planned to die on the same day.

I too could expire at any time. I might not wake up tomorrow. Conversely, if I feel as well on 31 January as I do today, there'll be pressure – in my head and from Jay – to postpone my deathday. But so long as I have completed these Reflections, I am determined not to falter, not to change my mind. The euthanasia forms I signed require two doctors to agree that my condition is one of 'rapid deterioration'. I only need to stop popping the pills for that to happen. It's what people do, people like me who wish to move deliberately and considerately to their end, people like me who insist on keeping control of the inner light switch until the last.

To cheer ourselves up Chintz and I watched Amy Mistral's classic 60s thriller *Zola's Loop*. Over the years I've experienced all the possible plot sequences, so I let Chintz decide on Zola's timeslip factor at the three choice junctions. She opted for a route which led Zola through a very early film called *The Third Man*, references to which appeared in many Mistral movies. Afterwards, knowing how much Chintz enjoys my gossip, I bragged about having met Mistral and having been present at her infamous *Third Man* centenary party.

And then I rambled on about Babashkin's remake of the same film. Vadim Babashkin, unknown in the early 80s when he made the film, substituted war-torn Karaganda in the final months of the Jihad conflict for Vienna in the aftermath of the 20th century's Second World War. Some thought the film was the arrogant conceit of a young man and overly stylised, others (including myself) that it was a worthy homage.

***

Kazakhstan was indeed torn apart by the Second Jihad War. At the outset, it was generally thought, *Encyclopaedia Universal* explains, that the IIBP's aims in the Europe/Central Asia region were only to install an Islamic Republic in Kazakhstan, and to support Azerbaijan's territorial claims to part of Armenia. The occasional missile attacks from Turkey, Algeria and Libya on military bases in Greece, Spain and Italy respectively were judged to be no more than an attempt to keep the European nations focused on their own territory, and to ensure minimal support for Russia in helping to defend Kazakhstan and Armenia.

The US, having been chastened by its unprofitable and costly involvement in the First Jihad War (not to mention the political lessons of Tarbuck's Gamble), and under the leadership of the mealy-mouthed President Paul Kidderminster, declined to involve itself in any of the main IIBP-instigated conflicts in Europe, Asia or Africa. Kidderminster and most of the US administration believed – or wished to believe – the IIBP's statements of support for the long-standing, but fragile, Palestine-Israel peace treaty, and did not want to pull any trigger that might switch Al Zahir's attention towards Israel.

NATO, which had been through more formations during the 21st century than a zylovex, required its members to help each other under clearly defined and varied conditions. Only in late 2069, when Turkey and the IIBP, after weeks of sustained bombing, invaded Cyprus, then Rhodes, both of which fell easily, and then Crete, did the North Americans finally agree such conditions were met. Their military strength was employed to reinforce the Mediterranean coastal frontiers of Portugal, Spain, Italy, France and Greece. But, while this was happening, Turkish troops moved into eastern Bulgaria, as ever with IIBP campaigns, 'to liberate repressed Muslims' and to bring 'peace for all peoples'.

We had no idea at this point where Al Zahir and the IIBP would stop, or where they could be made to stop. Every day our screens brought frightening images: the extraordinarily flamboyant displays by IIBP nations of their weaponry; hundreds of thousands of Muslim troops, all in disciplined formations reminiscent of Russia and China during the 20th century Cold War, historians said, across North Africa, in north and west Turkey, in Azerbaijan, Uzbekistan, Kyrgyzstan, all ready and willing to die for the Jihad cause, for Allah; and scenes of chaos where IIBP missiles had found their way through the NATO defences, missed their military targets and killed dozens, or in some cases, hundreds of Spanish or Greek citizens. But we heard little or nothing at the time of other major conflicts: in Africa, such as civil war in Nigeria; and in the Far East where there was a massive uprising in the Muslim Xinjing province of China.

Al Zahir, himself, could be seen day after day repeating the same ideas: 'Peace is our aim, peace is our destiny. Christian nations must share wealth with their Muslim brothers'; and (a particular favourite of mine), 'The IFSD is but a petty bribe, a dummy to our mouths – now we demand what is rightfully ours.'

Some commentators began speculating that if Bulgaria and Greece were to fall, the 'IIBP hoards' could trample through the Balkans, and this might give them the confidence to take the Moorish route through Southern Spain; Sicily could fall too, and Sardinia. Many of these same analysts urged, once again as they had done a decade earlier, for NATO to use its superior nuclear and 'ultimate weapon' capability. Yet no single leader across the Christian world came out in favour of such a strategy. The simple, awful truth was that all European airspace could not be guaranteed all of the time, despite NATO's technological superiority, and the IIBP would, one way or the other, be able to deliver nuclear and/or bio-chemical weapons. If he chose to, most Europeans believed, Al Zahir could kill 100,000 if not half a million civilians somewhere – whether in Spain, Portugal, Latvia, Ukraine or Finland – in one strike.

With Europe becoming the focus of the war itself, so political and social strife multiplied across the continent. The media was full of stories about families torn apart by bereavement or injury, or because one sibling had chosen to fight while another campaigned for demilitarisation, or because some members had fled to Australia or Canada and been branded cowards. Violent clashes between peace protesters and those willing to fight for freedom became commonplace, in the workplace, in pubs, in suburban streets, and during weekend protest marches.

Worst of all, though, was the breakdown caused between Christians and Muslims. Distrust spread like a plague, and wherever ignorance and fear took hold, so racism and victimisation followed in its wake. The vast majority of Muslims in Europe, as with the vast majority of Christians, agnostics and atheists were fair minded people who did not want this war or support the actions of the IIBP. But there were a few Muslims that did. Either they felt oppressed or unfairly treated, or else they agreed with Al Zahir's philosophy. The most fanatical ones worked secretly, as terrorists, helping to promote fear and panic in the most unexpected of places; others worked to encourage and finance the peace movements. European governments, depending on their politics and their national situations, reacted differently; but all of them went further than they had in the First Jihad War to monitor Muslim individuals and communities.

CHAPTER 18

IN WHICH I ELABORATE ON VILLAGE MATTERS

Our neighbour Dr Sami Abd al-Jabbaar was a very reasonable man. His paternal grandparents had emigrated from Pakistan to England in the last century. His father had won a scholarship to a good medical university, married a mixed race, English-Indian, girl, and become a successful geriatrician. Sami himself was an orthopaedist, working with the national health service, and had married an English woman, Iona, with no trace of foreign blood.

Despite this history, and despite the fact that he practised, with Iona who had converted, a popular Westernised form of Islam, he was obliged to register at a regional centre set up for the purpose. He had to sign a form affirming his support for the British government and denouncing any connection with Muslim terrorism or illegal propaganda. It was degrading, he told me. Moreover, as he and all Muslims knew, this registration process was an empty gesture, a sop to warmongers and fear-spreaders, since only signed-up members of mosques or other Muslim organisations had to register, and no terrorist or political agitator would let him or herself appear on such lists. Fortunately, for Great Britain, which recovered relatively quickly from the war and the Grey Years, we had more Muslims of Sami's ilk, willing to keep their resentments low key, and ready to work patiently for the good of the community as a whole, than many other countries.

I was fond of Sami, but not of Iona. Lizette had no time for either of them. She judged them smarmy, socially competitive and materialistic. As a consequence, Lizette tried to dampen down Jay's friendship with their son, David, because she thought he was a bad influence. For about a year they were forever scampering around together, but then it was Jay who dropped David, under pressure, I suspected, from his non-Muslim buds at school. In the late summer of 2069, though, two incidents led us to give our neighbours more consideration.

One weekend at the village playground, Lizette witnessed a vicious assault on David by Lindsay, who, by then had moved on from primary school bully to teenage terror. Jay had not come home in time for supper, so Lizette went to find him at the playground down by the river. David was lying on the ground and Lindsay was screaming verbal abuse and lightly kicking him at the same time. Jay and a friend of his were calling – not very urgently – for Lindsay to stop. Two other children were laughing. Lizette intervened immediately, established that David was not hurt, and attempted to censure Lindsay. She ambled away laughing.

Ten days later, Sami came to see me very early on a Saturday morning. He appeared distraught, face unshaven and grim, hair uncombed and shirt sleeves loose. His vegetable and fruit garden had been vandalised in the night. I was still in jamas, but he insisted I come immediately to inspect the damage. Elaborate cane frames for beans and raspberries had been crushed to the ground; various green vegetables had been kicked apart and trampled on; and marrows, pumpkins, aubergines and melons had all been sliced into pieces. He was hoping I might have heard or seen something in the night, but I had not, nor had Lizette or Jay, or any of our other neighbours.

Later the same day, Sami came over to discuss if we thought he should go to the police and/or to the local newspaper. Lizette was adamant that he should certainly go to the police. She argued that if nothing was done, the hooligan would continue with impunity. Sami, though, was cautious. Whether the attack was racist or personal, he did not want it to lead – deliberately or by accident – to any escalation of racial tension in the village. I tended to agree with his approach, and he went away having decided to take no action, other than to spend the rest of the weekend trying to rehabilitate his garden. When Sami had gone, Lizette let the full extent of her anger show, not only against Sami, who she suspected of cowardice, driven by his or Iona's determination not to lose face in public, but against me for giving him moral support.

***

There would be no more to these two anecdotes were it not for a conversation I had with Jay a few days ago.

'Did Sami Abdi ever find out who did it?' Jay asked.

'Dr Abdi. Is that what you called him? Sami Abdi? No, I don't think so. Although the same thing happened again the next year, didn't it. And then, when we lost the sun, he gave up. It was Allah's will.'

'I knew.'

'You knew what?'

'I knew who it was, who messed up Abdi's garden.'

'How? Who was it?'

'She told us herself. It was Lindsay Durring, the primary school bully. She's the one who stole my shoes. She also knifed open my bag once, stole other kid's lunch money, and started a cannabis cabal in the bicycle shed. She wrecked the bowls green too ...'

'I don't remember. Was I away?'

'She used a mechanical device to churn up holes in the grass. We laughed when she boasted about it at school, partly because she was a good entertainer, and it didn't sound that serious – sorry Pa – but most of all because we weren't the victims in this instance. She calmed down a lot for a period, during one school year, the year before the incidents with David and Sami's garden. We had a teacher, I forget his name, who had a lot of time for Lindsay, encouraged her comic side, and listened to her long after others had got tired of her lies and exaggerations. He only stayed a year at Tilford. After that Lindsay went from bad to worse. Later, while at secondary school and during the Grey Years, she burnt down the village hall. It was the night before the Ramadan play. You must remember that.'

'Why didn't you tell us any of this at the time? Especially about Sami's garden?'

'I don't know. I might have been afraid, or I didn't think it was important. She was caught for the village hall arson, and went to a junior prison. The mother and a younger sister moved away. I don't think I ever heard of them again.'

'You should have told us.'

'We thought the whole village knew. Poor old Sami Abdi, I think he loved his vegetables more than his children. David used to tell me he wished he had a father the same as you ...'

'Me?'

'Yes, collecting me from school, reading me bedtime stories, defending me against Ma.' He said it casually, as though he were referring to a third person. I closed my eyes to savour the idea that Jay had thought of me so well, even back then when he was a child.

'I didn't know you set me up as a role model for your friends.'

'I had to as it goes. When you came to collect me from school, they all called you my grandad: "Look Jay, there's your grandad." '

Surely, this was sufficient punishment for relishing a false pleasure, but Jay hadn't finished ruining the moment.

'Lindsay nicknamed you Wrinkle Man.'

'She should see me now.'

CHAPTER 19

IN WHICH TOBA ERUPTS AND WAR ENDS

Lizette did lose her temper at times, not only with Jay when he refused to understand a simple precept from science or maths, or when he dodged out of working, but with me. She and I rarely argued over practical arrangements, as Diana and I had, but over points of principle, politics or morality. The argument over Sami's garden was such a case.

More often than not, it was my laid-back, laissez-faire attitude rather than my actual position that infuriated her, to the point of shouting. I'm not sure I can explain this properly, since it sounds bizarre. I used to say to her that a lifetime of public service meetings was enough to trim the passion off any individual, but this alone could incense her. I think she felt that if she got angry with me, I would get angry back; but, when I didn't, she got angrier still as if any lesser reaction might undermine the justification for her original exaspera-tion. Then I would compromise on the point we had been discussing, and this infuriated her further. During these (short-lived and, I must stress, infrequent) episodes, I was often to be found – apparently – without a backbone.

After we had been in Tilford a few years, there was a period when Lizette's temper shortened significantly and became more personal. I thought the war might be to blame. It had recently veered towards Europe and was thus the subject of daily debate. Yet, Lizette's anger seemed to stem more directly from Jay's less-than-perfect performance at school or my continuing involvement in the EIPD study, which meant I was away and busy far more often than I had been hitherto. I did not say anything or draw attention to the problem; I hoped it would go away. And it did, almost over-night.

I was aware that Lizette was bored with her teaching job, and longed to return to research. I had said we should move if she could find a good position somewhere else in the home counties. She was reluctant, not only because she was happy with our plan to send Jay to the Witley school when he reached 11 and did not want to disrupt our lives, but because she loved Taunton House. I did not, though, make the connection between her job dissatisfaction and her erratic moods.

One day in February 2070 Lizette returned from work, radiantly happy. She had been to the hairdressers in the morning, which invariably lifted her spirits, and she had a bag full of shopping with knick-knacks for Jay and me. She also had an announcement. There was a research/lecturer position falling vacant at Surrey University in Guildford. She would apply for it, she predicted, and she would get it. Our lives improved appreciably from that moment, apart from a tense month when, because of the draconian government cutbacks in public spending, there appeared to be a doubt over funds for the position. Notwithstanding her excitement, it was an awkward move for Lizette, involving a loss of seniority, a cut in pay, and a return to research in an area for which she had no particular expertise.

I cannot claim to appreciate in detail what she did at Guildford, but it was linked to the efficiency of collecting electricity from plastic glass. Lizette's boss, Professor Sidney Jensen, who had spent his entire career devoted to photovoltaics, saw no reason why every window on earth shouldn't produce electricity. It was only a question of cost and efficiency. I knew from my experience at the IFSD that photovoltaic windows were near standard in buildings above a certain size in cities with plenty of sun where electricity supply was expensive. I also knew that, with time and effort, they had become cheaper, more efficient, more reliable and easier to install. But this was a long way from Jensen's dream.

Lizette's role, as I understood it, was to work on the molecular mechanisms by which the photovoltaic film-covered plastic glass created and transmitted electricity in low light conditions. This entailed creating new forms of the photovoltaic film, through micro-biomolecular manipulation, and then testing each one for a range of properties. Promising variants – I usually heard about them – were then given more substantial tests. It sounded laborious, but Lizette enthused about her work, and she soon became very fond of Jensen and her other colleagues. Then, of course, after the Toba explosion, the research became much more important. Jensen's team never made any substantial scientific breakthrough, not while Lizette was there, but it surely contributed to the sum total of knowledge, which itself led (not during the Grey Years alas) to a rapid expansion in the use of, the now generically-named, z-glass.

We – Lizette and I and the people we talked to – took only cursory notice of Toba when it first began to splutter. Not only had there been dire warnings about the volcano for years, but the first big eruption had to compete, news-wise, with the following: NATO's withdrawal from western Crete; a NATO air-raid on Istanbul which resulted in nine aircraft shot down; a mosque explosion in Marseilles killing a group of 35 Muslim schoolchildren; and an Intent missile deliberately aimed at Cathedral Sainte-Marie Majeure in Toulon, on a Sunday morning, killing 200.

There is no doubt that, at this time, in September 2070, the IIBP was still on the attack, winning the war, and Europe was very much on the defensive. The Turks with the help of Iranian, Syrian and Iraqi forces had won substantial territory in eastern Bulgaria and eastern Greece. Constanta, Bucharest, Sofia, Thessaloniki, Malta were all subject to regular attack. Several Greek islands were already under Turkish and/or Egyptian occupation. Russia was finding it equally difficult to help Kazakhstan defend its large land mass, and had all but given up on Armenia. It was also considering a major strategic retreat behind the Caucasus leaving troublesome Georgia to be divided between Turkey and Azerbaijan, or so the media reported. The US had finally entered the war a year earlier and inflicted substantial damage on the aggressive states in several arenas; mostly, though, it had helped stall, but not necessarily prevent, assaults by the North African nations across the Mediterranean.

Most historians thus agree that the Toba eruption saved parts of Europe from a Muslim future. They are divided as to how much territory they believe the IIBP forces could have conquered, and as to how far the ambitions of Al Zahir and the IIBP went; this all depending on the extent to which they believe the writings and retrospective claims of various Islamic leaders at the time. There is no dispute among them, however, that Al Zahir intended from his earliest days in power to win Israel back for the Palestine people, and that his strategy of duping NATO – not Israel itself, which never trusted him – into believing otherwise was all too successful.

Only when it became clear a few days later that upwards of 100,000 people had died immediately and many more were still dying as a result of the initial explosions in the Toba caldera, did we all begin to pay much closer attention to the media reports. The images were terrifying: the isle of Samosir disappearing into the sky as gigantic plumes of rock and rubble and ash (a 30 kilometres high mushroom cloud); the waters of Lake Toba flooding out across thousands of square kilometres of Sumatra, wiping out hundreds of villages and those inhabitants that hadn't managed to escape; and the airfalls destroying property and crops across Sumatra itself and the peninsula of Malaya, and killing unfortunates in cars hit by falling boulders, or caught in collapsing buildings. All that – as is well known – was only the start.

The modern world knew about war, had coped with it throughout its history; nations, societies, and cultures had survived and grown stronger as a result of its terrors and horrors and tragedies. But it knew nothing about a catastrophe on the scale of Toba, a volcanic eruption more powerful than 1,000 class A nuclear bombs, the media said. Humankind had no experience, no relevant history, no cultural memory to draw on. The five months of permanent night in most of Southeast Asia and the Indian subcontinent led to a minimum of 100 million deaths mostly from hunger and disease but also because of the violence that came with an epidemic of robbing, looting and marauding. Some countries managed better than others, depending on the strength of their economic and political alliances with the richer nations.

China, which had made no friends during the First or Second Jihad Wars, and which, because of the prevailing winds, caught the worst of the short-term full darkness, suffered very badly.

Before the full extent of the disaster became apparent, Al Zahir was able to maintain his war in Europe and surrounding areas. But the volcanic aerosols having settled dark night on a fifth of the world's population for several months spread out through the troposphere worldwide, reducing daylight, initially with a haze, then with the equivalent of cloud cover. When signs of determined protest against the costs of the war began to surface in the Muslim countries, the IIBP decided, once again as it had during the first war, to focus all its forces on Israel. It consolidated gains in Europe, and eight of the Brotherhood's nations turned their full air and missile power on the Jews.

Because of the nuclear winter already descending on the world and because it was ready to fight to the death, Israel used three nuclear bombs (two class C and one class B) on Lebanon, Syria and Iraq. Syria responded in kind, destroying Haifa. Muslim troops stormed in from Egypt, Jordan, Syria and Lebanon. The US made a token effort to help Israel, but would not employ its nuclear weapons. In any case, it was heavily occupied in Europe, and becoming preoccupied with its own domestic situation in response to the loss of sunlight.

Opposition to Al Zahir's war continued to grow with massive domestic protests from Rabat to Islamabad: Muslims everywhere were scared, and they wanted their governments to attack problems of crop failure, water contamination and disease, not Christians or Jews any longer.

In December 2071, some 14 months after the Toba eruption, the IIBP finally agreed to a cease-fire and to begin peace negotiations. Four months later, on 15 April 2072 in Colombo, NATO and the IIBP signed a territorial treaty which is no less controversial today than it was then. More than half of Israel (which had already lost land in the First Jihad War) was divided up between Syria, Lebanon, Jordan and Egypt. Turkey took small bites out of southern Bulgarian and eastern Greece. It also retained Cyprus, Rhodes and other sundry islands. Crete became a divided island administered by NATO and the IIBP (and, evidently, has remained divided between independent Crete and Turkish Crete, mirroring what happened to Cyprus in the 20th century). Georgia and Armenia held on to their independence, while Russia, Turkmenistan, Uzbekistan and Kyrgyzstan all accrued territory in Kazakhstan, and an Islamic Republic was installed in what was left of the country.

The future of the United Nations took more than another ten years to resolve – as did sundry other NATO/IIBP-provoked disputes around the world.

Although these tumultuous events of history are common knowledge, it is difficult to make sense of our own lives without some reference to them. On the other hand, given their impact on our world (international and local) and the suffering they caused, it feels wrong to skim over them so lightly. But I continue to try and hold fast to my own Reflections.

CHAPTER 20
IN WHICH I AM APPOINTED TO RUN REACH

Apart from the comfort and joy of having each other, Lizette and I were fortunate in so many ways.

We benefited from being in Europe, which was relatively rich and technologically capable of dealing with the worst of the Grey Years. Further, we were fortunate for being in Great Britain, which was even better equipped than much of Europe to cope with adversity. In line with most countries, we had food rationing for many products, price controls, specific laws against greed (what strife they caused), and strict regulations on vehicle use. But, as a nation of gardeners, we the British – though not Sami – took on the challenge of finding edible plant species and varieties that would grow in chronic low levels of light and mildly acidic rainfall. Almost nothing green and edible grew without artificial light, but the effort helped with morale.

As a nation of hobbyists and enthusiasts, we also found it easier than our European neighbours to re-adapt to traditional do-it-yourself house maintenance – Notek books were never so popular – and to the barter mentality of car boot sales. Even more significantly, our country relied less on solar energy than many others, having invested heavily in tidal and wind energy which maintained a good level of electricity production throughout the Grey Years.

In addition, Lizette and I were both lucky for being employed, meaning we were well paid, enabling us to maintain a reasonable lifestyle, and we had work to keep us occupied. While the relatively modern Farnborough Science University closed down altogether because it was starved of funds, and most of the research programmes at Surrey University were also frozen, Professor Jensen's department, in which Lizette worked, survived.

I too was busy. In spring 2071, I had taken on a new task, overlapping the EIPD study slightly. London was chosen by the European Union to host a new and swiftly-established agency to administer Rapid Emergency Aid for Countries seriously Hurt by climatic disturbance (REACH), and I had been asked to manage it. I presumed my experience and reputation at the IFSD was ample qualification, and my work on the EIPD study had kept me visible. The job sounds more important than it was, otherwise I doubt it would have been offered me.

I should explain what REACH did – though Jay, a couple of days ago, found my explanation convoluted and warned me not to bother.

Soon after the start of the Second Jihad War, the United Nations, which had only partially recovered from the aftermath of the first war, imploded again. By the end of 2068, the European nations had withdrawn a large proportion of their development aid contributions to UN agencies such as the IFSD. Thereafter, and during the war years, these same funds gravitated towards military and defence uses.

However, then came Toba and the darkening of the skies and the consequent humanitarian crises around the world, so most rich countries began to restart modest national aid programmes. The European Union, though, wished to make a more obvious and visible contribution, at least until such a time as new agreements re-legitimised the UN agencies. Thus, it was decided to set up REACH: a temporarily-constituted agency to use funds which might otherwise have been apportioned through the UN, 'for rapid assistance where urgently required in order to save lives'. Initially, and until the cease-fire was agreed, the funds were only to be allocated to projects in areas not affected by the military conflict.

But REACH was given a very tight mandate and an inconsequential budget. The British government donated office space near London Bridge, in Pickle Herring House. My main tasks were administrative, to get the agency functioning, to install procedures quickly and efficiently, to find the necessary staff (80 at its peak), and to ensure the available money was spent, and spent wisely. In a few cases, it was possible to employ people I respected and who had been made redundant by the IFSD. Furthermore, I enquired to see if there was any chance MarySue wanted to go back to work, but the war, the greyness and especially the death of Conrad had drained all the life out of her. I made the mistake of calling by camphone and was shocked to find her looking shrunken, and 20 years older than when I had last seen her.

Mostly, though, I needed to employ experts with experience of managing emergency aid, since I had so little myself. For my deputy, I took on Jean-Michele Olivier, a Belgian recommended by experts in Brussels. He proved to be a wiry, tense and surprisingly vain man. His mother, I learned over time, had been posted to the Belgian embassy in Tunis, where she had been seduced by the owner of her rented apartment. She thought the relationship would last, but, when it didn't, she returned with baby Jean-Michele to Brussels and married a civil servant colleague. When I first met him, Jean-Michele was about 40. He had spent most of his career working with various agencies, in every link of the aid chain, and most recently with Water Aid in Milan. He had divorced an Italian wife and was willing to return to Northern Europe. Being somewhat temperamental, he was easily upset and only worked well (and tirelessly) when he felt he was being appreciated. Some colleagues found him amusing, others intently irritating. Initially – I confess this freely – I wondered if I had made a huge mistake by accepting him on my staff. But the reverse was true: REACH never achieved a great deal, but what it did achieve was largely thanks to his know-how and ingenuity.

Jean-Michele had a real talent for being able to assess potential aid allocations, their realistic value in terms of human lives (both senses of the word), their viability, and potential problems. And, for the important challenges, the ones we believed in, he could imagine and conceive an efficient, often imaginative, pathway through from idea to implementation. When other staff, government liaison officials or enactor agency chiefs occasionally complained to me about his manner, I would sympathise lightly and expound on his abilities, as if he were an artist of some kind, to whom one needed to show tolerance.

I recall my uncle Alan complaining in his letters about prima donna colleagues, and wishing they would all grow up. I don't mind, he used to admit, if they've got something real and tangible to give. Despite his waxed moustache, Jean-Michele had a lot to give, and his heart was in the right place. So long as his vanity was in tact, he would spend 24 hours a day if necessary on the shop floor, so to speak, tying up every last loose end to ensure a consignment of water, food, fuel, medicine or tents would make it through to the planned destination.

Lack of sufficient money aside, prioritising was our biggest headache. Each day we received informal and formal requests for funds. We had adequate procedures but this did not stop European governments trying to bypass the rules, or desperate developing countries pleading for more scraps from Europe's table, or members of our own staff being moved to tears by media reports of disasters-in-the-making and preparing own-initiative plans. I found it easiest, morally and practically, to stick rigorously to the selection rules we had established. Where this left equal choices – which often happened – I relied on Jean-Michele to advise and influence the selection committees.

CHAPTER 21

IN WHICH JEAN-MICHELE IS A REGULAR VISITOR

Jean-Michele became a regular visitor to Taunton House, and would stay over from Saturday to Sunday, although never if Horace was expected – they only met once which was enough for them to establish an instant antipathy.

Initially, Lizette had disliked his pompous demeanour, and, after his first visit, asked me not to invite him again. But I talked about him and his invaluable assistance so often that she grew curious enough to want to give him a second chance. As she warmed to the man, so he became more comfortable in our house and more interested in us and our lives, which in turn led us to appreciate his idiosyncratic company. He was a very handy man to have around the place, as comfortable with electrics and basic electronics as he was with carpentry. He often went out walking on his own, usually across the green-sand heaths which remained attractively covered in heathers and bracken during the Grey Years. Jay, by then well and truly into teenager-hood, found him patronising and comical; but he too changed his opinion in time.

During the last of the lost summers, in 2073, when he was 13, Jay suffered a severe bout of depression. We did not know whether this was a genuine SDD/CDD (seasonal/climate disorder depression) or not. He endured various tests, including those for melatonin and serotonin deficiencies, but the results were inconclusive. The medical establishment had not fully accepted SDD, with critics citing the ability of an individual to affect his or her own neurochemical levels by eating a good meal, sex, sport or watching a movie. In the media, sceptics called it 'scarce-dollar depression'.

Lizette was a sceptic, believing that effort and work and activity was the way out of any depression, especially during the Grey Years when the whole population was chronically depressed. It's my belief, though, that she pressed him too hard on his school work, and then, when the doctor proposed he might have SDD, she became yet more demanding, driving him further into his own personal greyness. She may have been able to browbeat him to working more when he was younger, but as a teenager her efforts were counter-productive.

It was Jean-Michele who rescued Jay. He had heard Lizette moan about Jay's lethargy more than once, and he had remembered Jay talk idly of redecorating his bedroom. One weekend morning, he asked Jay to show him the attic room and to explain what he might wish to do with it. Then they sat down for several hours with paper and pencils and a ruler. By lunch-time, Jay was excitedly showing us a plan to refurbish the room with a custom-made stilted bed and desk space, a larger screen on one wall and Live wallpaper on another. Lizette was stunned by Jay's apparent change in mood, and when Jean-Michele promised that he and Jay would under-take the whole project together without any outside help she offered up no objection.

For the next few months, Jean-Michele came once a month and worked busily with Jay the whole time he was here. In-between visits, Jay regularly emailed his new friend seeking advice on an interim task or putting forward new suggestions. Once the room was finished, Jay claimed it was the most stylish in the house, and possessed real 'Jay-space'. He went so far as to organise an opening ceremony, with a ribbon across the door frame, a bottle of wine, and a short speech thanking Jean-Michele for all his help. The Belgian, beaming from one edge of his moustache to the other, took a slight bow, and magically produced a party-sized Harkness Cylinder. When Jay flicked the coloured crystal apart with a finger, it released a spray of glitter, and a dazzle balloon playing one of Jay's favourite pop songs.

Jean-Michele. There was a touch of the Harkness Cylinder about the man himself.

Jay's imagined or real SDD never returned. Unintention-ally, the way events transpired, we were able to return the good deed. Despite his visits to Taunton House, we knew very little about Jean-Michele. I had never been to his apartment near Clapham Common, nor had he talked much about his private life. It was as if he did not have one. But there was a moment when his guard dropped. We were in the office, both tired and downhearted after failing to secure an increase in our budget allocation from the European Parliament. The other staff had left for the day, and Jean-Michele was moaning about the world in general, and REACH's impoverished budget in particular. Then suddenly, as if struck by a lightning existential crisis, he said it would all be easier to bear if he wasn't so lonely. I asked him what he meant, but he dismissed his own remark and my question as irrelevant. I relayed the comment to Lizette, and she suggested we invite Jean-Michele when other friends were visiting rather than when they were not. Of her friends, though, only Rhoda was single, and Lizette would not have wished Rhoda on her worst enemy.

In October 2073, around the time of Lizette's 55th birthday, Pete and Clarity came to stay for a few days. Pete had retired by this time, and was keeping busy by writing course material. Clarity too had left the university and was working, mostly from home, as a researcher and presenter for the BBC's Kurdistan news network. Their visit was timed to follow on from a conference Clarity was attending in London. At that conference, Clarity befriended a Russian woman called Raisa who worked as a translator for the BBC and others. At Clarity's request, we invited Raisa to join us all – including Jean-Michele – for lunch on the Sunday. By late afternoon, our two single guests appeared to have bonded, and it was no surprise when they then made the necessary calls to alter their pre-arranged rotor transport so as to travel back to London together.

Thereafter, we saw far less of Jean-Michele. When I asked if we would see him at the weekend, he replied saying he was busy. When I asked if he was busy with Raisa, he made a flamboyant hand gesture as if to wave away my question. I could never pin him down, and he continued to keep mum about his personal affairs. It is only because Raisa stayed in touch with Clarity for a few months that we knew the two of them had fallen in love. That Christmas, and at Lizette's insistence, I urged Jean-Michele to bring Raisa to Taunton House but he declined politely.

If I am now focusing too much on the personal, it is because the only way any of us could cope with the mayhem across the world and all around us, was by turning inward, to our own families and friends, for solace.

CHAPTER 22

IN WHICH I SAY GOODBYE TO FRIENDS

Over 500 million people died between 2070 and 2075, from drought, starvation and disease mostly. It is estimated that a further billion died later, prematurely as a direct consequence of the Toba eruption, many from lung cancers and other respiratory diseases caused by the polluted air. The gross national product of the world fell by a third, with much of it reverting to economic standards prevailing one hundred years earlier. Europe and North America suffered proportionately less than most other regions, at least in terms of physical human death and suffering, which is all that really mattered.

Not to Gregory, though. He wrote about the psychological trauma of the rich Christian nations. He suggested there was 'a correctional downshift in expectations of seismic proportions'. Such downshifts are as inevitable as hills on a hike, he said – if I recall the oddly-reversed metaphor correctly – but it is better for an economy (or more accurately for the individuals within that economy) to walk up a steep hill for a short time (short-lived but very deep depression as with war and the Grey Years) and walk down a shallow hill over a long period (sustained growth) than the reverse (a long period of recession with a short boom).

As I say, Lizette and I coped reasonably well with the Grey Years. The same cannot be said for those afflicted with real or imagined acute SDD, Gregory's psychological downshift, or CDCB (circumstance-driven criminal behaviour) many of whom had to be locked up for the safety of the rest of us. The British police force nearly doubled in size during the early 70s, absorbing men and women from the armed forces. The prisons, correctional institutions and cloisters for those with brain dysfunctions were all overcrowded; new ones were created in a hurry, often in unsuitable premises.

Gillian, the mother of our two dead children, was sent to one of these temporary cloisters, and died there. I'm not sure why or how. She had married a second time. Her husband, from whom she had recently separated, tracked me down, and asked if I wanted to go to the funeral. I expressed my sorrow, and apologised for not being available.

If I shed no tears over Gillian, I did over Alfred. One day, in November 2072, I received a warm and informative email from him. A few days later, before I had had a chance to reply, I received another email from his son, Fela, informing me that Alfred had died in a road accident in Zanzibar where he was living by then. A drugged-up gang of youths had stolen a service vehicle and taken a joy-ride; they killed seven pedestrians, including Alfred, before crashing. Since one of them had a gun, the police shot them all.

I phoned Fela. This kind of thing is happening all the time, he said, especially on the east coast islands of Zanzibar, Pemba and Mafia where rich Africans like to retire. It was bad enough during the war years, he added, now it's anarchy. I told him what a great man Alfred was and how much I had loved him. I could hear Fela's voice, on the other end of the line, full of emotion, trying to tell me he wished he had not been such a stubborn child and listened to his father more when he was young.

Fela had disappointed Alfred initially, that was true. He had rejected public service and sought material happiness; but, eventually, he had turned his early banking career to good use by going to work for the West African Development Bank, a benevolent institution set up during the Ojoru years. I told him each man has to find his own way, and that Alfred's pride in him had shone through in all the recent letters to me.

There was no question of me flying to Zanzibar for the funeral, given the cost of, and restrictions on, international movements, but I promised Fela I would take part by camphone if he opted to allow a private broadcast. He didn't; but the service was recorded and I did receive a camclip a few days later. There were only a dozen Zanzibar friends in attendance. It was a sad end which I do not wish to dwell on.

Instead, I prefer to see Alfred on the volleyball court, taking three long elegant strides towards the net, rising high into the air, so high that my imagination see his fingertips touching the gym roof cross-beams, and swinging his arm to hit the ball gracefully yet so forcefully and accurately that the opposing team has no chance of a return. Or else, if I must see him as an older man, I recall the time in Munich when I handed him the trophy, his vigorous black face for a moment serious and then bursting into a smile full of humility and pride and warmth and friendship.

I said goodbye to other friends during the Grey Years. Matt Fortune died of a broken heart, in both senses, not long after his wife succumbed to a cancer. He left one son, Oliver, who has followed Matt's path into politics. MarySue, who like me had returned to England to retire, never fully recovered after the loss of her son. It is likely she was one of the victims of the government's policy on rationing of medical care for the aged.

Incidentally, my increasingly eccentric friend Horace was campaigning against his own party on the issue. He did this despite the fact that most sensible people across the political spectrum recognised the need for public service cutbacks in all but a few areas, such as law and order.

In distant St Petersburg, the cold dark weather sunk into Anna Mastepanov lungs, but not before she had written asking if I would carry on the regular donations to Alan's health clinic in Bangladesh. She made me promise I would go there once. I never did. But Jay has already taken over the responsibility from me. He will, I'm certain, make the trip there next year. He has also promised me, I should add, to seek out a real or email address for Karel, Alan's adopted but estranged son, so as to send him a copy of these volumes.

And I lost the Turnbulls too, although in a different sense. They cashed in their assets and emigrated to Australia, from where they sent me a couple of letters. Then we lost contact.

During the Grey Years, efforts to rehabilitate the United Nations and its constituent parts were doomed to fail. The world and all its nations were in double shock, recovering from the Second Jihad War and the mega global disaster caused by sustained low temperatures and light levels. Even the European Union, which despite more than a century of unsteady progress had remained the world's most successful example of regional integration, became unstable and threatened to fall apart at the seams. It may well have done if the skies had not begun to clear in 2074.

CHAPTER 23

IN WHICH WE FINALLY SEE THE SUN AGAIN

The first time we saw the sun in nearly three years, Lizette's brother, Mercurio, was staying with us in Tilford. Once a year, he would leave his Notek community in Pembrokeshire and do a cycle tour of the south of England, passing by various family and friends. Jay adored his strange, long-haired scruffy-looking uncle, and anticipated his visits with mounting excitement. Lizette was more cautious. She looked forward to seeing him, but anticipated arguments, many of them stemming – this is my personal assessment – from her inability to accept his Notek way of life.

The Notek movement emerged during the 40s in North America then spread to northern Europe. Pop culture histories say the 30s was the decade in which individuals exploded with anger protesting for change, and the 40s was the decade when they began searching inward trying to cope with the hatred and violence they had seen in the 30s and with economic and technological stagnation. The world had appeared on the edge of a dangerous precipice in the mid-30s with the universal excesses of the First Tuesday Movement protests and riots; but it was in the 40s that the deeper and more consequential problems began to evolve, particularly with the intensity of religious activity, both alternative and mainstream, and cults of one form or another, the worst of which, of course, was the Pearly Way.

But there were also many benign cults, including the Noteks, which flourished during the introspective 40s. The not very original name 'Notek' was coined by a Canadian news organisation to describe a group of art students at Vancouver University who were expelled because they refused to work with computer technology and submit their work electronically. They had been inspired by a Californian writer called Chuck Harris who argued that the insidious spread of electronics into every part of our lives had led individuals to feel they were no longer in control. If our cars, our plumbing, our lamps, our toys went wrong, he said, we used to be able to mend them, now we can't – there's a chip in everything, and who knows how to mend a chip. He railed against all aspects of life which involved electronics, but was particularly angry about, and opposed to, the way electronification of the media and communications had created vacuous virtual communities at the expense of physical ones and 'human human relationships'.

Over three decades, many different types of Notek communities sprang up all over the world, not only inspired by Chuck Harris, but drawing on naturalist philosophies stemming back to Lovelock and Vernadsky in the 20th century. Those that tried to impose their alternative standards on others, did not last long. For some reason, perhaps because the British had a tendency towards cultism, Great Britain had – and obviously still does have – a flourishing Notek population. During the 60s and 70s, amid much anguish at local level, Noteks managed to buy into whole hamlets and then villages, and turn them into Notek communities. Old churches were converted into book libraries and meeting rooms, around which the communities revolved.

In time, and not before a national election had been won and lost over the issue, the law found a way of dealing with these communities, allowing them to pay reduced taxes in return for reduced services. As the communities became more widely accepted, so they attracted some important intellectuals; and, there seems no doubt, the laudable Church of Moral Atheism originated within the Notek movement.

More prosaically, among a basket of social innovations, we must thank Noteks for the Mildew – not that I can personally recommend the sinuously wild dance, having never tried it myself. Nowadays, it is not considered an easy life in one of these Notek villages, and some of them only survive through tourism, which is frowned on by the hardliners.

At this time, immediately after the Grey Years, in the mid-70s, there might have been half a million Noteks in Britain, but not all of them lived in communities, and the figures were inflated by those claiming support for Notek ideas but unwilling to give up their phones or screens. It was ironic that many people turned to the Notek philosophy during the Grey Years: while electronics had helped the world become far more resource-efficient than it had been in the 20th century, the sun – an icon of the power of nature for the Noteks – had disappeared.

Although I argued at length with Mercurio about this, I was prepared to acknowledge the Noteks had some beneficial influence on our society. When Lizette joined in these friendly disputes, however she became exasperated at the childish way Mercurio refuted my arguments. He was able to rile her, in a way that her equally lightweight students at Guildford could not (or so she told me). As his older sister, she felt responsible for him in some way. Moreover, she was angry that he had two children, aged ten and four at this time, who she had not met in person. He had never invited us to Pembrokeshire, and he had certainly never cycled with them to Tilford. On top of these frustrations, she also worried – rightly and ultimately wrongly as it turned out – about his influence on Jay.

As the nearest being to a sun worshipper we knew, Mercurio was the right person for the occasion. Although we had no specific information about when the sun might break through, we'd been told the day was not far off. For months, there had been media reports of celebrations across the globe, and in recent weeks there had been a few in northern Europe.

That particular morning there was a cold and very blustery wind, but it was breaking up the cloud cover and giving brief glimpses of clear sky. Mercurio wanted us to bike to nearby Waverley Abbey, a 12th century ruin and beauty spot. I protested against the venture, claiming my arthritic ankle was too painful to cycle, but both Lizette and Jay were so enthused by the idea and refused to go without me, that I finally agreed.

It was only about three kilometres and the pain in my ankle was not that great, especially if I pilled-up and we rode slowly. I expected the place to be deserted, as it always was during winter and cold weather. But there were hundreds of families there, some with picnics, some with flexiscreen camphones and many with what appeared to be umbra-lighters. Jay, who was our only link with the day-to-day fashion and trends of the young, explained they were not umbra-lighters (which no one would need in daylight), but new-fangled umbra-viewers, with transparent filter material specifically for looking safely at the sky and enhancing the cloud shapes and light densities. Jay managed to borrow one from a school-friend for a few minutes, so we all got a chance to see the essence of the sun behind the clouds.

Two hours passed, during which time the crowd numbers trebled, before the shy sun finally gave us a glint. It may have been shrouded in a heavy veil of haze but it was, most definitely, sunshine. We were all on our feet, some standing on the ruined Abbey walls, waving umbra-viewers and hats and scarves and shouting whoops of joy. Mercurio fell to his knees and gave thanks.

With the sunlight, hope returned. People everywhere began to rebuild their lives, their communities, their nations, and their international institutions.

Evidently, I was most interested in the last of these. No one doubted that the world needed a United Nations system, but what kind of system. Most citizens in the richer developed countries opposed the idea of sharing too much of their wealth through a bigger stronger United Nations (as they always had done), but their leaders recognised that a new world order could not go backwards from the best of what it had been before the First and Second Jihad Wars, and that it would have to compensate for the alarmingly uneven death toll of the previous five years. In 2074, when the Islamic countries joined the preliminary conference on the future of the UN, they were still dominated by Al Zahir. His position had been weakened during the Grey Years, yet he had retained sufficient power to hold the IIBP together, and to present aggressive demands. That conference and subsequent ones disintegrated amid chaotic claims and confused counter-claims.

The truth was plain to see: a quarter of the world insisted on doing business through Al Zahir, and the rest of the world, but especially the American and European allies, would not trust any commitment or offer he might make about the future. After all, he had started two world wars and annihilated half of Israel. In Russia and Europe, there were deep resentments over Kazakhstan and the Greek islands respectively. The Catholic world had been told by Pope Maria that Al Zahir was the third modern incarnation of the devil, after Stalin and Hitler.

How strange it is that the Israeli policeman, Noam Livnat, is almost as notorious as Al Zahir himself. The former killing only Al Zahir, two other men and himself, while the latter was responsible for the deaths of hundreds of thousands, and that's without calculating how many fewer people might have died in the Grey Years if five trillion euros and incalculable other resources had not gone up in smoke during the two wars. Historians agree that Al Zahir would eventually have been displaced within the IIBP, but that Livnat's revengeful deed accelerated the UN's rehabilitation by three or possibly five years.

In the year after the assassination, the IIBP splintered into factions and this allowed less tainted, more acceptable Islamic leaders to present themselves at the international negotiating tables.

CHAPTER 24

TINA'S VISIT AND TALK OF SAMBA

Yesterday, Chintz and I watched Flora's funeral on my screen. It didn't take place here, as mine will, but 250 kilometres away at a crematorium in Liverpool. There's a garden there with a family memorial containing the ashes of, among others, her mother, father and one son, the one that played cricket for England. Months ago, she showed me a picture of the stone vault, and expressed impish impatience at the time it was taking her to get there. The chapel room was full, and the traditional Christian service mercifully short. Flora was described as a woman who had lived a very full life, who carried joy around with her wherever she went, and who would be greatly missed by many grandchildren and great grandchildren.

'And by us,' Chintz added sadly. 'She was the life and soul of this place,' and then, thinking this might offend me, continued 'but you're the life and brains of this place ... and my movie master.'

I was far away, trying to imagine the scene at my own funeral a few months hence.

And this morning, as if telepathically understanding that I needed cheering up after yesterday, Tina arrived. She came alone, not wanting to wait until the late afternoon when Jay would be free. Previously I had only seen her in the flesh twice. Once in the 80s, when Lizette and I did a mini-tour of South America, and once about ten years ago when she spent a northern hemisphere summer travelling around Europe. Tall, sultry and sexy, Tina had inherited the looks of her grandmother Conceição – the girl with whom I had had an affair in Brazil more than 80 years ago – and the charm of her father Arturo.

I had warmed to her as a teenager and a young lady, but now I'm disappointed to find her copying too many of her father's superficial characteristics: swathes of make-up, gaudy clothing and an excess of jewellery. Her black hair, once shoulder-length and free, was tightly pinned together with a woven double chignon, and decorated with silver clasps. Also, I found her allure had become more deliberate with age, more sticky if that makes any sense – but maybe this is me being paranoid. It is impossible not to suspect that Jay's endeavours to encourage these doubly-distant relatives are succeeding only because they hope I might favour them in my will. (Jay knows the truth: most of what remains after my excess medical and hospice bills are paid will be his, although Tina, Inti and Maria will receive token endowments.)

Tina's English is adequate, nevertheless talking with her was tiring. She told me about life as a hairdresser in Belo Horizonte, where she lives with a boyfriend she met on a holiday in Rio, and about her aim to become a fully-qualified child nutritionist. She has been studying in night classes for three years and is about to take an exam which will, if she passes, qualify her to work in a health practice. She had little news she wanted to share about her brothers, or her mother Fatima. She became most animated when talking about samba. I knew she was a good dancer, and that this took up a lot of her spare time. But I did not know, until she told me, that she belongs to one of the premier samba groups in Belo Horizonte and is responsible for coordinating the headwear and hair design for the carnival parades. As with all samba groups, Tina said, hers is already preparing for the February 2100 carnival.

'I send you how to watch carnival here on the screen. I will wave for you.'

'How will I know it is you?'

'OK, I will send you picture first, of me, in costume, then you know it is me waving. I wave like this.' She waved, and giggled, and in that moment it was Conceição – my Gabriella – that I saw.

EXTRACTS FROM CORRESPONDENCE

Guido Oostlander-Fenn to Kip Fenn

(freely translated from the Dutch original)

March 2069

After six months, it is still a struggle. We've had to put back the schedule for opening Teatro Sucre until September. Everything, and I mean everything, takes twice as long as expected. This week, finally, I've been able to meet with the upholsterers to finalise the material for the seating. This should have been done before Christmas, but Felix insisted we use a particular company, and for weeks they were too busy, and then Felix wanted to look over the samples but he was away, and then Felix ...

What I actually want to tell you, but I find it so embarrassing is that for three months – sorry if I haven't written since your birthday – Felix has been trying to seduce Mireille. Felix doesn't only adore the theatre, he wants drama around him, everywhere. He started quietly flirting with her and – well you know what she's like – she didn't take it seriously, just rebuffing him tactfully. Then he became more overt, which upset her, because she had to be more obviously resistant. At this point she told me, and said she could deal with it. But he carried on with direct invitations for a quiet dinner, or a weekend at his Salinas villa; and then, when she continued to refuse, he began applying pressure, saying we might have to move out of the house soon, or that the money for the theatre might run out. We needed to be flexible, he kept saying.

I got so angry I wanted to return to France. But Mireille viewed it as no more than a difficulty, one of many we would have to face. I went to confront him, to tell him to leave Mireille alone – I felt so stupid. He laughed at me, and said he only wanted her once, to taste her once. And he asked me why it was such a problem. Didn't we trust each other? Hadn't we had sex with anyone else before? And then Mireille and I discussed it. We discussed her sleeping with him, one time. I mean it happens. You know it happens. You must know how it feels. Sorry to be so direct. It makes it a lot easier knowing how happy you are with Lizette. I hope you don't mind. But it was different with Mum, I suppose, because she wanted Karl. And then we (Mireille too) thought that, with half the world engaged in war, we were being so stupid, childish. We should have known from the beginning there would be a cost, that fairy godfathers don't exist. I bet you knew, I bet you thought Felix Montechristo sounded too good to be true. We did too, we just didn't want to acknowledge as much to each other.

I doubt I would be telling you this if Mireille had paid the price, or if we had decided to come back. But we made up our minds to fight, to let him evict us from our home, and to let him completely starve the project of funds before we gave in. He did neither. As soon as he realised Mireille would prefer to let the theatre fail than give in to his demands – not in the end for emotional reasons, but because she didn't appreciate being toyed with – he stopped his bullying. He laughed it all off as a game.

So, what I'm trying to say is that we've grown up a bit, but we're no less determined. If anything, we're as excited by the whole thing as before we came. We love the language, the country, the city and the people (I'll tell you about some of them another time).

Love to Lizette and Jay.

PS: Didier and Helene are coming for two weeks. They say they'll be visiting twice a year until we return! And Mireille's sister, Veronique – did I tell you she works now for a Swiss media firm making documentaries – has persuaded the company to let her make a low-budget info-flick about the Teatro Sucre project. She's coming soon too, and then again in September. If the film ever transpires, I'll send you a copy. In the meantime, here's two camclips, one of Mireille dealing with the carpenters, and another of me on our terrace think-ing of less stressful days – evenings spent making cardboard cut outs for drama club, or Sundays aboard *Ginquin*.

August 2070

Back safely. Thanks for taking us to the airport yesterday. It was good to see you and Lizette and that scamp Jay, even if for such a short time. Didier's death was such a great shock to Mireille, I think the only way she can cope is to be extra busy again (shades of Helene), and we have so much to do here. Will write more in a few days. Take care.

May 2071

We've had to close the theatre. It was inevitable. There's no audience. Felix – bless him, apart from the odd flaw, we still love him – has run out of charity. And the government is passing emergency laws which would have shut us down anyway. I thought we might return to France or even England (from what you say), but Mireille wants to stay.

The money from Didier's will has finally come through. After his death last year, two women with no connection to each other – I find this shocking – made a legal claim against the estate. One had a 15 year old girl, and the other a nine year old girl who they claimed were Didier's natural daughters. They both said Didier had been funding the girls' education. Helene hired the most expensive lawyers, and a couple of private detectives. In the end, though, once the DNA tests were forced through, the claims were dismissed. Half the money has gone to Helene, and a quarter each to Mireille and Veronique. I think the idea is that Helene will make provisions for Veronique's children and ours if we have any (!?!).

Mireille wants to use the money (and the money from our flat in Paris which we've sold) to form a theatre group and go on the road, to travel round the country performing for free in villages and towns; and in Peru and Bolivia as well. If we live frugally and only employ a maximum of six players, we think we can do this for four or five years before the money runs out. Will the darkness last that long? We'll be dead by then, from exhaustion. Mireille believes it's our mission to take a 'rainbow of entertainment' wherever we can.

I hope all is well with you and Lizette and my little brother, take care.

September 2074

Mireille is pregnant. I am allowed to tell you now. Five months. Inti, a boy, should be born in January, all being well. I wonder how many others around the world celebrated their first sight of the sun as we did!

Thanks so much for your letter, and your news.

We have stopped travelling – at last – and, while we're waiting for Quito to want its grand Teatro Sucre up and running again, we've started a community theatre to work with the psychological victims and the schools and the unemployed. We're hoping that within a year we can find a way of covering our costs. Helene's given up arguing for us to come back, and will be visiting as soon as she can. She may stay for a while and help with the finances.

When will you and Lizette come, and my not-so-little brother? We would so love to see you. It has been a miserable time, and now it is possible to imagine the future again.

Take care.

April 2075

First we had Helene here for weeks and weeks and weeks, now we've got Mum worshipping at Inti's altar – and he's only three months old. I've attached several new camclips, more tomorrow.

Lots of love. Take care.

Doug Turnbull to Kip Fenn

January 2070

We are here in Sydney. After some months of renting, we bought this place (see pics). We can scoot to the beach in ten minutes (Miriam is there now doing group exercises), or be at the grand old opera house in 50. The skies are blue, and the sun shines as if there were no tomorrow (I won't mention the flies). The views across the harbour are breathtaking.

Lucy may come and live out here too. She's split up with her man (a cellist – a tosspot) after ten years, and the doctors have lost control of the rheumatism in her shoulder. She can play well enough, in short spurts, for teaching purposes, but not for performance any more. Susannah is expecting again, her third. She and her husband are staying in New York. He's climbing up some media empire hierarchy. I don't suppose Miriam would have wanted to emigrate if they had remained in blighty. We see them once a year. Funny isn't it how you get lots of grandkids from one daughter and none from the other? How's your crew, Lizette and Jay, and Guido, and that strange man Arturo?

As soon as this damn war is over, we shall expect you for dinner – as usual!

PS: I heard from Jude Singleton the other day. Would you believe it? She's still working – must be in her 80s – acting as an advisor to a think tank on war damage and environmental recovery. Rather her than me.

October 2071

Glad to hear you're back in the saddle. Rather you than me. Wasn't it the pet licensing authority that was in Pickle Herring House, or has it moved? Can't be many people taking on pets these days.

Miriam wants to go 'home', but we can't. It's all too complicated and expensive. Back home the cold and damp was normal most of the time, but here it's worse, it feels sharper for being so unnatural. The Aussies aren't coping very well. You'd think in such a big country with so few people we'd be able to avoid the food and energy rationing ... once they did battle with surfboards and cricket bats, now they fight in queues.

Nor are we coping well. Lucy's moved in, but she blames us for coming here in the first place. Miriam blames me for the same. Although it was her idea (seriously she thought the sun would make her young again).

I go out to the glasshouse to do battle with the aphids which multiply as fast as humans are dying across Asia.

Alfred Ajose to Kip Fenn

November 2072

The beaches on the east coast here in Zanzibar have seen turbulent times, but at low tide they are wide and white and flat. You can watch the old women collecting seaweed, but there are no tourists floating around in scuba gear any more, no kids building castles, no glamourpusses, no urchins selling fizzes and wiches at extortionate prices. It is a melancholy place, like your beach resorts in winter – like all beaches everywhere now.

I was walking along the sands today thinking about many things, but much about you my old friend. Is it acceptable to call you 'old friend'? I feel old. Do you? All that volleyball has prematurely aged my bones, my joints – and for this I blame you. It would be unfair, though, to blame you for the cold, heavy weather which seems to make all aches, including the ones in the head, worse. How can anyone not feel old in these days.

What do you think when you hear the news? I listen (for I cannot watch) for hours on end, and then I go to the beach to feel the sand between my toes, which is the only thing that takes me out of the present and back to a time before there was a weight on my shoulders. What do you feel?

What do I feel, you ask? I am too impatient to wait for you to ask. There is pity and sorrow and anguish. But these are feelings I've had for most of my life. I've suffered with my fellow Nigerians, whether they've been suffering from disease, from crime, from famine or civil war. I've never stopped crying. Can I feel more now that millions are dying?

But I do feel more. Something different. Something terrible. And there is no one to whom I can tell this but you.

I am filled with anger and resentment. I am bursting with it. Are you not?

You and I both have struggled our whole lives long, in different ways but with one aim, to combat inequality and make the world a fairer place. We have had two enemies, always two enemies, man himself and nature. But it felt like we were holding our own, if not making progress, and mitigating the worst of what man and nature could do to us.

And now this all. First man finds a way to wipe out every advance we ever made; and then nature spits in our face as if to remind us how petty our efforts have been, how pathetic they have always been.

But where is my anger to go? To whom shall I address my resentment? Should I turn towards Sango – he is the Yoruba god of thunder and lightning – before I die?

Meanwhile, I go to the beach and feel the cool sand beneath my toes ...

Fela is coming soon, for two weeks. He has business in Dar es Salaam and will travel here after. I was too harsh a father. I see it only now. And he repays me with a love and respect I do not deserve. He has become a good man, and kind. I wish him many sons, many sons and many daughters.

And to you old friend, I send my warmest greetings, wishing you and your family a peaceful and safe way through these dark years.

PART THREE

Arturo, Noteks and Old Photos

'On waking, the first thing I see is the wallscreen with the time, a message for my wife from her daughter, and a sunrise scene from Tahiti. As I move through my house, the temperature and lighting are just perfect. I go to the john, where the bowl 'knows' when and how long to flush. In the jacuzzi room, the water flow is controlled by a sophisticated central heating/plumbing sytem (and my razor has an automatic 'bristle thickness sensor'). In the kitchen/dining area, the stove, the fridge, the freezer, the dishwasher, the garbage processor, the breadmaker, the microwave, the mixer, the toaster and the coffee-maker (did I forget one gadget or ten) are all computer chip controlled to a lesser or greater degree. The lock on my front door is activated by a chip; as are the gate to the garage and the lights along the drive. My car has 137 computer chips controlling everything from battery state to traffic density information and seat angle. At work I use a keyboard, screen and phone, all completely reliant on computer hardware. In the office gym, even the traditional weights are in-chipped to provide display information. In the evenings, I don't lumber around the house being useful, mending our son's bicycle for example (the gears, suspension and lights are dependant on electronics) or seeing to a faulty window latch (it's hooked up to a sophisticated thief alarm). From morning to night, I've not used one appliance or piece of equipment that I could mend if it went wrong. On retiring, I find my wife in the bed. She's in-chipped too, for medical monitoring and hormone flow, but at least I can still fix her mood – some nights anyways.'

Out of Control by Chuck Harris (2049)

CHAPTER 25

IN WHICH LIFE GOES ON AFTER THE GREY YEARS

It is difficult not to believe that the Grey Years should be classified as the greatest catastrophe in human history. Certainly man himself, by means of war, never created as much devastation. One well-known historical demographer suggests the plague in the 14th century may have wrought a similar amount of damage proportionally; and a cohort of scientists give considerable credence to the idea that an eruption of Krakatoa and the subsequent climate disorder in the 7th century was so devastating that it affected human civilisation more profoundly than the Grey Years have done so far, or will be seen to have done a century hence.

Whether true or not, more people probably died prematurely as a result of the Grey Years than the sum total of all the world's population at any one time up until about 250 years ago. Looking at the figures, a simple calculation shows that two million or more people were dying each week during the Grey Years, or more accurately during the Grey Years and the subsequent year. Surely, every individual on the planet was affected; and yet they all – we all, *Homo sapiens* – carried on about our lives as best we could, concerned as ever with our own shelter, food, energy, mating, parenting, working and socialising.

During the Grey Years, Lizette and Jay and I had kept our heads down, so to speak, working hard, living quietly, making a daily commitment to watching the news, and trying – if not always succeeding – to acknowledge our relative good fortune. Thereafter, with the return to a more normal climate, not much about our personal lives changed in 2074 or 2075.

In the village, as everywhere, there was more obvious leisure activity outdoors. Local working parties formed to clean up the landscape (removing unsightly dead vegetation and planting new trees and shrubs), and we joined these whenever we had time. Lizette was an enthusiastic member of the Tilford Propagators whose main objective was to keep the working parties supplied with young plants, whether propagated at home – or should I say in the home – or bought with funds raised from charity events.

The Tilford Propagators had another source for their seedlings. In 2072, and at Lizette's instigation, they took over, from an absent-but-willing landowner, a derelict commercial greenhouse. They repaired the structure and installed s-glass units, and then, rather than using it to grow their own produce, set up a parish species databank, with the aim of being ready for the day when regeneration could start.

One of the group, a gardener by training, wrote about the project for a media outlet, and the concept took off more widely. It probably did more good keeping people busy, though, than in helping to restore the countryside. The earth contained plenty of dormant seeds and rootstock ready to sprout anew, and these tended to do so much better than the transplanted seedlings, which were easy prey to hungry, and fast-breeding insects. Damn it, nature will have her way, Lizette would say tetchily before explaining why some planting or other had failed.

Underlying these petty complaints at nature I detected in Lizette a deeper and ingrained antipathy towards biology and biologists (not gardeners) although she would never admit this overtly. I imagined it was a bias that came with the territory of her academic discipline, after many years of education, training and peer involvement in materials science. Theoretically, all biology had long since been reduced to chemistry; and biochemistry had been a major discipline for over a hundred years. Nevertheless, biologists worked at the level of living matter, trying to control nature but willing to live with it, while chemists were incessantly trying to break matter apart and recreate it from scratch.

Today, 25 years on, only a botanist or a dendrochronologist would be able to tell at first glance that something terrible had happened to the countryside around Tilford in the 70s. The last time I was there, in the mid-90s, the day the sale of Taunton House was completed, all was as lush and beautiful as it had been during my teens: the triangular green (still sloping, still a venue for cricket matches), the banks along the river Wey by the old bridge, the playground nearby, the pretty track to Elstead, once used by the monks of Waverley Abbey, a millennium earlier.

In the 10s and 20s, Julie and I, or sometimes Alan too, would take the car to Elstead on a Sunday and walk that track through to Tilford for lunch at the Barley Mow, or to Tilford and then walk in the reverse direction to Elstead for lunch at the Wool-pack. I loved the route, through the wooded edges of Hankley Common, with its surprisingly-high embankment above the Wey, views across the flood plain fields, and the oak tree with its hanging rope from where, with a leap, I could swing backwards and forwards above the river, or, in summer, jump for a swim.

***

Here on my screen is a nostalgic camclip of that rope swing, one taken by Horace, he who never dared to jump on the rope himself.

There are two boys whose names I don't recall, as well as Jeff Zimmerman and myself, all playing the fool. We must have been about 15. I am fully dressed (and shoed) and swing-ing on the rope dangling above the middle of the river. I can't get any momentum to swing back, despite my writhing efforts. I must have miscalculated how much movement I needed to return to the raised river bank, or, more likely, one of the others had blocked a safe landing. The whole gang is laughing. After a minute or so I let myself fall into the river. There is much applause. Here's another bit of the same camclip. Horace must have lent the cam to Jeff for the rest of us are racing around trying to pull each other's trunks off. Horace is making a particular effort with mine! And, a few metres away, an old couple are trying to have a quiet picnic.

Under cover of the screaming antics on the screen, Chintz has crept into the room, and is giggling too.

'He's a sweetie.' She thinks the boy trying, unsuccessfully, to hide his privates is me, but it isn't.

***

Not all of nature recovered as quickly as that on the lush banks of the Wey, especially in areas of the world which had been most acclimatised to strong sunlight and high temperatures. Genera, thousands of them, which had taken millions of years to evolve, were wiped out in a few short years. Their ecological niches were filled by aggressive, quick-growing, quick-breeding species. In much the same way as the efforts of the Tilford Propagators were less than successful so were most of the many and varied grander schemes, in the 70s and 80s, designed to re-strengthen species, or in some cases reinstall vanished species from scratch, through DNA databanks or re-creation schemes licensed by the Agency for Genetic and Cloning Techniques (AGCT).

The AGCT was one of the first UN agencies to become fully functional again in the mid-70s, after the Second Jihad War, and in the last of the Grey Years. It required relatively insignificant levels of funding, and the disputes tended to be more agri- or bio-technical than political. But, at the same time, most of the UN's other institutions, including the IFSD, were starved of funds and, effectively, in mothballs. Debate about a new world order had been under way at the highest level since the end of the war. Some statesmen went so far as to say there was no way back for the United Nations, and it was not uncommon for commentators to mention the EIPD World Union study that I had worked on.

While the international negotiations on the UN continued to be hampered by the Christian world's distrust of Al Zahir, Europe and North America were visibly considering other options. Soon after Al Zahir's assassination, though, in 2076, the Islamic countries made clear their determination to negotiate seriously and quickly for the resurrection of the United Nations. With the world so needy, and so many institutions all ready and waiting to be brought out of mothballs, it became clear there was no realistic possibility of starting again from scratch.

Once the international negotiations began in earnest, they were neither very speedy nor transparent, which resulted in the European Union prevaricating over an extension of the mandate for REACH. When, finally, we were given a three year extension, to 2079 (by when it was expected the EU would be ready to funnel its funds again through the UN agencies), we had lost six months' worth of operations.

I took the EU's decision-making delays in my stride, but Jean-Michele could not relax. He would come into my office, close the door carefully behind him so as not to be overheard by my secretary, and rant about the failings of politicians.

At project level, Jean-Michele had infinite patience, and would work through whatever problem, whatever hold-up until it was sorted; yet, oddly, he was hopeless at coping with the drawn out political processes of those above him, especially when the decisions they were making affected his work. The best way to deal with him in this mood was to let him rant and say little in return.

Several years later, when REACH was winding down, he did come once with Raisa to Taunton House, for a garden dinner party. While there, he moaned to me about having failed to secure a future position at a higher level. It was as if he'd come to visit with the sole purpose of quizzing me about this. I did not prevaricate. I advised him he would be better off sticking to a job not too far removed from the operational level where his best talents lay. He looked at me suspiciously, marched off to find Raisa, and left soon after.

As Jean-Michele suspected, I had replied to discreet enquiries about him from various selection boards without whole-hearted praise of his managerial abilities. Since I was convinced his skills would be wasted if he moved too high up the ladder, I did not feel guilty about this. When the REACH office in London was closed, Jean-Michele went back to Italy with Raisa, where they married – we were invited to the wedding but did not go. We lost contact with them after that. Much later, I heard on the grapevine they had two children, and Jean-Michele was doing an excellent job running Italy's national agency in charge of emergency humanitarian aid.

CHAPTER 26
IN WHICH HORACE FINALLY STANDS DOWN

During the Grey Years, and through to 2075, everyone moved around far less than hitherto, not only was energy so expensive but there were tight and complicated restrictions on private and business vehicle movements, not least through the rotor arrangements. We ourselves rarely went beyond the confines of our work and home areas, and others, even regulars like Horace, came to see us much less often.

By 2076, though, transport had become marginally easier, and Horace began to reappear on our doorstep every now and then. On one occasion, in early summer, he brought Tim, his podgy brother, who we hadn't seen for several years. Although the active part of their joint property business had stalled during the Grey Years, they still owned and rented a score of buildings. They argued a lot, and Horace usually tied Tim in knots. I bet, Lizette would say, they squabbled as children; they love it.

This particular visit, Tim appeared anxious and sullen. He sought, as soon as he could, a private conversation with me. I took him for a walk, through the village to the bowling green. In short, he was asking my help to persuade Horace against standing in the next election, due in the autumn when the National Coalition's five year mandate expired. According to Tim, Horace's health was deteriorating, and, by supporting increasingly bizarre causes, he was making a fool of himself in Parliament.

I was not convinced that Tim's appeal was motivated by real concerns, and suspected some deep-seated, perhaps unconscious, sibling ploy to get one over on his older brother. It was true that Horace wheezed a lot, but then who didn't at 75, and that his political comportment had declined. I had seen media reports of Horace being suspended from the House of Commons for several days as a result of bad language against a Green Party MP. Nevertheless, he continued to lobby tirelessly for policies that would benefit his constituents. Moreover, among his 'bizarre causes' was one I could not help but approve of: he campaigned persistently for Great Britain to lead the march towards a new international order, and regularly cited the EIPD study on World Union.

Later that day, while Lizette and Jay took Tim over to see the Tilford Propagators' glasshouse, I sat in the garden with Horace. We drank a light refreshing Wiltshire wine he'd brought with him.

'Made by one of my constituents in the late 60s. Larry. Amiable man. Went bankrupt in 71. Had no choice but to put his land in the hands of the Department of Agriculture. From vineyard owner and sophisticate to farmer and muck-raker. Damn good wine though. Looking for investors to start the vines again. When he gets the land back. I'm considering. What do you think? Not as warm as it used to be. Could stay cooler. What do you think? Half the experts says the Grey Years have done for global warming and we're on the brink of an ice age, and the other half pontificate about faster climate change. Giving money to Larry, be like playing the lottery.' I changed the subject.

'Tim says you're thinking of standing again.'

'If they'll have me. Selection committee's meeting next week. May invite me to continue, may not.' He said it with conviction as if he had no idea what might happen. 'What do you think, you've got your ear to the ground: warmer or cooler? vines or no vines?'

'I don't know Horace. Sounds risky to me. Hot or cold, people always need houses, but vines won't always grow. I thought you'd be ready to step down now, give some other likely lad a chance.'

'If the committee'll have me, and the voters want me, I'm still that likely lad.'

'You didn't even like Southampton when you were selected back in the 20s.'

'Long time ago.' His clipped delivery, which had become more exaggerated with age, softened and slowed down. 'Be 50 years in 77. Fifty years an MP. That would be an achievement.'

'Is it 50 years? I didn't realise. I remember the party the night of the election. I came with Gillian and Crystal ... Gillian had just told me she was pregnant again...' I sunk into my own memories. The names of Gillian's children only had to flit into my consciousness for a second, and it was as though someone had knocked all the air out of me, and then dipped me in a wash of sadness. Incidentally, writing these Reflections has helped me come to terms with the fates of Crystal and Bronze, although nothing can ease my regrets.

'A real achievement. I'd be only the third person in history to serve 50 years as an MP in the British Parliament – that would be something to put on the cover ...' I was not listening, instead I was wondering, for the thousandth time, if there might have been a course I could have taken that would have led to less anguish in the lives of Gillian, Crystal and Bronze. Horace stopped talking, and then restarted, insistently.

'What else does Tim say? Let me guess. Thinks I shouldn't. Bad for my health. Making an ass of myself. Thinks I should stop before I'm remembered for the wrong things. Let me tell you something about Tim ...' Horace's phone rang and he answered it. I probably went inside to urinate, it's what I usually did by this age when there was a break in conversation. When I returned, he repeated the question.

'So, what does Tim say?'

'He is worried about your health. I can see why.'

'No affordable lung transplants yet.'

'And, yes, he does think you're past your sell-by-date. I'm reserving judgement.'

'Big of you.'

'How many times has the Speaker expelled you from the House now?'

'Lost count. He's a fool.'

'Who?'

'The speaker.'

'Why don't you tell him,' I said facetiously.

'What do you want me to do? Tidy up my diaries. Won't be a pretty sight.' Diaries! Now he certainly had my attention. I had no idea he kept a diary.

'Diaries?'

'You didn't know?' He knew I didn't know because he had never told me. 'I've a publisher ready and waiting; he's legally bound to keep it a secret until I say so. Won't publish till I step down.'

'When did you start? Why have you never mentioned this?'

'About 50 years. Only political, not much personal – except where personal is political. Didn't need to write personal, Caxton did that for me.' Having spent but a few years in government, and only as a lesser minister, I could not imagine there would be much of political interest in Horace's diaries. 'Never told anyone. Not Tim. Not boyfriends. You're the first. People clam up if they know you as a diarist; they keep you out of the inner circles. Good advice from Tindle when I office-boyed for him. Told Spoon once I was thinking of writing a diary, he said, "Don't do it. Don't ever do it. Is that clear." I'd started long since. I took his advice to heart, and never did do it – tell anyone that it is.'

Having failed to win me over to his cause, Tim tried a playful attack on his brother over supper, appealing to Lizette's common sense, and expecting Jay's support simply because the boy preferred him to Horace. But what started as banter descended into a full-scale row. Lizette screamed at them to stop and sent them out of the room, in the same way she used to deal with Jay when he was six and misbehaved. Jay found it all most amusing.

But it was far from that. The brothers fell out for six months; and we never saw Tim again at Taunton House. Sadly, Horace did not achieve his 50 years in Parliament. He was reselected without difficulty, and, although right-wing parties were expected to lose seats in the forthcoming election, there was no real threat to Southampton, or so he said. But, about four weeks before the election, he suffered such a serious coronary thrombosis that he was obliged to stand down. Ironically, the Progressive Party chose a candidate nearly 50 years younger in his stead.

I went to visit Horace several times at a private hospital in Southampton, while he was recovering, and then later before and after his heart surgery. During one of these visits he explained that Tim had been anxious for him to retire from politics so that the two of them together could wind down their business, which, apparently, would take more effort and time than simply keeping it ticking over, and then retire fully, possibly abroad. If Tim thought Horace would leave Britain, he must have been senile.

CHAPTER 27

IN WHICH WE VISIT MERCURIO AND THE NOTEKS

A few weeks after the visit by Horace and Tim, and during the last ten days of Jay's summer holiday, we made our own journey, to Pembrokeshire, and then, on the way back, to Chew Magna in Somerset. It would have been very inconvenient to use public transport so we took our Toyota Ishfreel despite the cost of fuel and tolls – although the much-hated not-full-occupancy tax supplement had been scrapped by this time.

I loved driving the Ishfreel, a saloon I'd bought in the late 60s which served us well enough for nearly a decade. It was the quietest car I had ever owned, but more than that it reminded me of the petrol-fuelled vehicles I had driven as a young man, the ones which had razor-sharp acceleration. Since 2071, the hapless machine had only been used as a rotor bus for trips to the station or school or supermarket, and hardly ever been allowed out for a run on the motorway. This holiday was Lizette's idea, and focused entirely on her family, so driving the Ishfreel again was my private source of pleasure.

Although I was happy to visit Samuel, Lizette's older brother in Chew Magna, I was less sure about the trip to Stackpole Haven, the Notek community five miles south of Pembroke. Jay thought we were making a long overdue friendly visit to Mercurio, Lizette's younger brother, with no ulterior motives, but Lizette's aim was for Jay to witness the harsh uncomfortable reality of Notek life, though she was also very curious about Mercurio's children.

To my mind, Lizette had long since lost any control over Jay's behaviour, his plans or his hopes, but this did not stop her trying to affect them – nor, I could add, did her intelligence and a good basic understanding of psychology. I doubt she would have advised any other parent to behave in the way she did towards Jay. It was as though an emotional drive displaced her intellect.

Jay, though, had learned well how to bluff and how to pretend he was listening; and he had perfected the art of underplaying his own knowledge about anything and everything. Whereas once he had used this technique to avoid being faced with genuinely more complex tasks, he now used it to maintain a secret, smug power over Lizette. When she tried to push him to do better on his maths or science course work, he would feign ignorance in the face of her expectations. Then he would pretend confusion at her exasperation, and, within minutes, they would be arguing without knowing about what. Whereas I had had some influence over Lizette's behaviour towards Jay while he was young, I had none left by this time.

Jay had taken the 16 exams earlier in the year, and achieved modest results. Lizette was not satisfied with his progress, and regularly made disparaging remarks about his grades, as if, somehow, this might spur him on to do better next time. One of Lizette's greatest fears was that Jay would drop out of school, something he could legally do at 17, along with drinking, smoking and voting. Partly inspired by Mercurio's annual visits, Jay had developed a schoolboy interest in the Noteks, and often, at the pitch of his arguments with Lizette, would threaten to run away and join a Notek community. Lizette knew no more about what went on inside the Notek villages than I did, and what little we did know came from Mercurio and the media, which loved to expose Noteks as living way beyond social and cultural norms. Nevertheless, she felt informed enough to judge it bad – plagued with the deadly sins of sloth, lust, greed, pride, not to mention poverty, ill-health and inadequate hygiene – and that the sooner Jay saw the reality of Notek life, the sooner he would throw off his childish impressions.

We spent Saturday evening/night at Hereford with an old school-friend of Lizette's, arriving at Stackpole Haven around midday on Sunday. It was a surprisingly ordinary-looking village, similar to other rural hams planned and constructed in the 20s and 30s. A pond, a church-library, a grocery store and a pub called The Last Elm all clustered around a large oval green. Children were playing in one area of the green; groups of people seated at benches by the pub were eating and drinking; and bicycles were parked haphazardly all over the place. Lizette and Jay were both disappointed in their different ways, although I had no idea what they were expecting. A group of girls sitting cross-legged on the grass were busy knitting. When I asked for directions to the address we had for Mercurio, one of the girls, about 15, naturally pretty with long seaweed coloured hair, a spotted blue t-shirt, knee-length jeans, and bead bracelets on both arms, answered.

'Rio? You want my dad, he's over there, in the pub. We prefer it if you leave the car outside the village lines. Didn't you see the signs?' And she returned to concentrate on her knitting.

'Yes, sorry, but I didn't know where we would need to stop. We'll drive back and park now. In the pub you say? And your name is?' One of the other girls said something, and they all burst out laughing.

'Who wants to know?' she said. And they all sniggered. 'Friend of Rio's are you?'

'Yes. Sort of.' There was another whispered comment and more laughing.

'Yewla. My name's Yewla.' This time I heard the whisper, 'It's the tax men.' And they laughed again.

I returned to the car, pleased with my discovery, and pointed out the girl called Yewla, Lizette's niece, Jay's cousin.

A few people looked up as we entered the pub, but not Mercurio who was one of a group in the far corner playing chess. Jay noticed there were no screens or lottery machines. He said the place had the appearance of a heritage inn, and went to investigate the board games and books stacked on a dresser by one wall. Lizette and I observed Mercurio from behind until he became aware of our presence. I expected him to be horrified or perturbed at our sudden and unexpected arrival, but he wasn't phased at all. He expressed more delight than surprise, and calmly introduced us to the rest of his chess group.

We had made no arrangements about where to stay, thinking we would take advice on a nearby hotel from Mercurio, but the community had a guest house which was free that night, so Rio – as everyone called him – said he would take us there. On the way across the green, we stopped to say hello again to Yewla and her friends. This time she put her knitting down, stood up and came to give each one of us in turn, including Jay, a two-cheek kiss. Jay went bright red. (Jay to me a few days ago: 'You're making that up, I wouldn't have gone red.')

The cottage, a 19th century stone bungalow, was clean and tidy, and decorated with hand-woven fabrics, enamel artwork and ceramics. Mercurio helped us to carry the luggage in. Mercurio, Jay and I then left Lizette alone in the cottage for half an hour, to unpack and freshen up. We took the Ishfreel to a parking bay, and then accompanied Mercurio to a nearby farm where he needed to explain why he would be absent for a couple of hours. That afternoon he was due to service a harvester, he said, but it could wait until later. I had had no idea he was mechanic (why had I never asked?). He serviced and repaired all the community's farm vehicles.

Jay was intrigued because he had thought the Noteks lived without all technology. Mercurio explained how there were many different kinds of Notek community, some purists refusing to use tools or appliances that had been made with modern electronic or computer-aided technology, some only rejecting technology invented within the last 50 or 80 or 100 years. Most, though, as with Stackpole Haven, chose a boundary before the electronic age, rejecting all use of chips, but with specific well-defined exceptions where electronic technology helped to preserve the environment or natural resources (s-glass for example). Mercurio said most Noteks liked to talk about their communities as celebrating and preserving sustainable human cultures including many technologies, and not as communities which rejected human development.

From the farm we returned to the guest house to collect Lizette before moving on to a pottery, which filled a large extension at the back of one of the brick buildings. In 50 years, it hadn't weathered anywhere near as well as the stone guest cottage which was four times as old. Mercurio introduced us to Esos his six year old son, playing in a sandpit with some friends, and Esos's mother, Andrasta. She was no older than 30, but her very thin visage and huge sunken eyes gave her a haunted look. There were a hundred pots, glazed and unglazed, all over the workroom floor, and she was trying to reorganise them to make more space on the storage shelves. Jay asked if he could try his hand at one of the pottery wheels. Andrasta, far from pleased at the intrusion, glanced at Mercurio as if to ask whether the disturbance was truly necessary; he winked, smiled and gave her an encouraging nod. As I watched Jay make a mess of the slippery clay, I had a sudden flash memory of being taken once by my grandmother Eileen to a pottery on the south coast.

From Andrasta's workshop, Mercurio led us to another similar building but without an extension. It appeared to house several adults and children, all of them busy with play or work of some description. Here Mercurio found Yewla's mother, May, much older than Andrasta but more comely, if I can use that old-fashioned word. May was not only Yewla's mother, but a member of the Esos co-op, thus indicating more of a pattern in Mercurio's affairs than he had hitherto suggested. Indeed, to my mind this was a very different Mercurio from the one we saw at Taunton House, more thoughtful, more interested in our good opinion, more robust. It was as if, in the past, he had deliberately exaggerated all the aspects of his life that he knew Lizette would despise.

Mercurio continued to guide us round, to farms and workshops mostly, and a Notek shop on the main road some distance from the village centre, and to explain about his life. I found the place remarkably ordinary, if somewhat quaint. I did notice the Notek community land looked cared for, and less damaged by the Grey Years, than other rural areas we had passed through, but then it was well known that Noteks nurtured their land well. This was one reason why, over the decades, they had been able to argue for and win special legal status. Jay was unusually enthusiastic with his questions, especially about Yewla, schooling and leisure activities; Lizette remained oddly quiet, confused or annoyed by Jay's enthusiasm.

When Mercurio left us to return to work, Yewla and a half-brother, Almond, offered to show us Stackpole Quay and the beach at Barafundle Bay. I declined because my ankle had swollen up, but Lizette and Jay went, and gave me a full report later. That evening we congregated at Mercurio's house which, we discovered, he shared with Andrasta's sister. There were a dozen others, including Andrasta, May and her current partner, Mercurio's children and Almond. A large trestle table had been set up in the garden. Andrasta and her sister had prepared a splendid meal: a gazpacho-type soup, cold duck and many salads, and a 'delicious strawberry-filled ice-cream'. I am using Jay's memory here. We talked about this a few days ago, on his birthday, before he left on holiday. He enthused particularly over the ice-cream: 'A few years later, when I dropped out of Reading to join that Notek community in Cumbria, I expected to be eating that delicious strawberry-filled ice cream every day.'

Over supper and with the help of a potent elderflower wine (this I remember), Lizette's quiet manner gave way. Perhaps she had herself been bewitched by the peacefulness and harmony of the community and wanted to remind herself why life in the real world was real, or perhaps she was determined to try – for Jay's sake – to show up some faults in the Notek way of being. She began by asking a variety of seemingly innocent questions, but soon took on a more goading tone, grilling Jay and his friends about the community's economy. Before long, she was in full flurry claiming that if everyone were to become a Notek there'd be no science, no research, no development, no progress, no future.

But she had misconstrued the indulgent mood around the table, believing our hosts were not taking offence, and went so far as to accuse the Noteks of being no better than parasites, who were only able to survive because they fed off a developed and responsible society. Andrasta was the first to crack. She got up in a fury, collected Esos, who had ice-cream round his lips, and stormed off. At that moment, I too thought Lizette had gone over the top, especially given the gracious way Mercurio had received us.

Yet it was Lizette who suffered. Mercurio himself looked thoughtful and said little. He let his friends enjoy a deserved and sustained offensive against Lizette, using their well-rehearsed, almost religious, arguments. What is the point of science? of research? Why do we need development and progress? What do we have to hope for in the future? In what actual specific definable ways have electronics made life better? Why do we need camphones and computers and chips? What does your life have that ours doesn't? Why should man live to 95 rather than 80? Why has the world fought two abominable wars which utterly wrecked its ability to cope with a natural disaster – an inevitable natural disaster? How is life different now – really different in its essence – from 100 years ago, or 200 years ago?

The basic Notek philosophy counts on the following ideas: there is a natural limit to economic progress and to man's ability to enjoy wealth; capitalism has done well to get Western societies to this natural limit, but thereafter expectations of lives improving endlessly are counter-productive and damaging; wealthy nations should not seek 'sustainable progress' but 'sustainable balance'; and excess wealth should be fairly shared with those less well-off.

Lizette did her best to argue about how science should and could improve medicine, agriculture, energy efficiency and environmental protection, but the Noteks knew how to respond. They were not opposed to science and research itself, but to nine-tenths of it which was wasteful and unnecessary.

In a fully-committed Notek society there would be sufficient funds for useful science, research and development.

Lizette became increasingly irritated at not being able to score any useful points – not that Jay was listening, he'd long since been taken inside by Almond, ostensibly to look at paintings – and would have gone on for much longer, had Mercurio not intervened. He offered an olive branch by stating that Lizette's area of research, as far as he understood it, was the kind supported by the Noteks. But Lizette would not stop, her tongue loosened by alcohol, and so, eventually, Mercurio's patience evaporated. Why, he wanted to know, had Lizette never visited before now. Lizette's stock answer was that she had never been invited. I had always supposed this was true. Mercurio revealed that he had begged Lizette many times when they were younger, in their 20s and 30s to visit, and she had regularly scorned him and his invitations. Lizette looked extremely uncomfortable, and suddenly very tired. She glanced down into her empty glass, and then back up at her brother.

'Well I'm here now aren't I.' This was said with attempted defiance. 'Well I'm here now aren't I.' The second time the words carried a mixture of apology and sorrow. I was dumb-struck by the new information – Lizette had clearly deceived me about the relationship with her brother – and the change in her demeanour.

'Yes you are,' Mercurio said. 'Yes you are.' Then someone filled all the glasses again, and Almond suddenly appeared and said he was taking Jay to see the children's tree house in a wood nearby. I leaned close into Lizette, put my arm through hers, awkwardly, and whispered so no one else could hear.

'You were very brave to come here, and to speak out. It's as though you were prepared to be shot down in enemy territory. I didn't realise before but you've come here for a reconcilia-tion, and in a moment, this moment it has been achieved. It wasn't that painful was it?' She nodded, meaning I know not what, and clutched my arm tighter. When I asked if she wanted to go, she said no.

I decided to divert the focus of conversation by asking about the prayer that had been said before supper: 'For what we are about to receive may our children, and our children's children, and our children's children's children be privileged to receive, amen.' This is how and when I first heard of the Church of Moral Atheism.

It was a church, I understood, in the broadest sense of the word (any body professing a common creed) based on an understanding, a hope and a belief. The understanding was that god never was or never would be and that therefore we, human beings living in a complex society and world, must be responsible for ourselves, our fellow man, our fellow creatures, and the environment in which we live. The hope was that our children would have good lives, free of hunger, danger and disease. And the belief was to be in a fixed moral code acceptable to all humankind, only this had yet to be elaborated. The Church was a new fad, we discovered, which had been spreading through the Notek communities and elsewhere for several years. A few social academics and philosophers had written papers about the movement, Mercurio explained, and the International Notek Confederation – much larger and more important than when it was originally formed in the 50s – had launched a major study to define a moral code for the church that would be acceptable to a two-thirds majority of Confederation members.

CHAPTER 28

IN WHICH I TALK ABOUT WISDOM FORCE

We remained at Stackpole Haven for a further two days. Lizette and Jay did more exploring while I sat for hours in the pub talking with members of the community or reading in the library. Surprisingly, Lizette fell in love with her brother again. This was the first time, she confessed, since he was 11 when, in consequence of some huge grievance, she had relinquished her role as his guardian angel.

On the Wednesday, we drove to Chew Magna, to Samuel's three storey mansionette 'at the opposite end of the Sanderson family spectrum' as Lizette put it. The property came with a long drive, large well-manicured gardens, and several outhouses – a conservatory, a play room, an office. Samuel and Lynn had three children: the oldest Saul who worked with his father in their tidal engineering consultancy firm; Irene, who had travelled a lot before the Grey Years and had visited us in Taunton House, worked as a journalist on women's magazines in London; and Mahonia, who continued to study architecture at Warwick University. All three lived away from home, although Irene was visiting at the same time as we were, and Saul lived nearby with his wife and baby son. Despite the rich trappings, Samuel and Lynn were hospitable and down-to-earth, and not at all pretentious. Again, I had been slightly misled by Lizette, who, I realised, could only see the members of her family through a magnifying glass.

Samuel was semi-retired, so both he and his wife had time to lead us on various trips. Lizette wanted to go to Weston-super-Mare, to lay flowers by her parents' memorial stone, and Jay went for a swim on the beach. Another time, Irene took Jay and Lizette out in the family skiff on a nearby lake, while I lunched with Samuel and Saul near their offices. Sanderson Engineering Consultancy Services, they told me proudly, had helped on tidal barrage projects in 47 different countries. The business had been healthy before the Toba eruption, but now, with post-Grey Years investment, they were overwhelmed with opportunities. This meant the firm would be able to expand rapidly if Saul wished.

They did not have to sell the technology to me. For 30 years or more – since the advances in systems durability and safe materials with long-term resistance to marine growth – we at the IFSD had promoted the exploitation of tidal turbines as a reliable and regular source of electricity for coastal areas. And yet, surveys said, we had not come close to fulfilling 10% of the potential demand for this kind of technology, even in those regions where power use was way below the UN average.

I knew full well that Samuel had grown tired of the travelling and extended stays away from his family required by many of the company's contracts in the past, nonetheless, I decided to sing the praises of the UN's Wisdom Force.

During its early heyday, in the 50s, there were nearly a million retired citizens from wealthy countries working in and for developing countries. The basic idea was that retired professionals of whatever ilk – engineers, surveyors, geologists, architects, teachers, doctors, software programmers, company managers – volunteered for terms of duty, of one to three years, with no other purpose than to transfer their knowledge to those less well off. The programme had run aground during the Jihad Wars, in common with many other UN functions, but was rebuilding itself in earnest. Although only minimum pay was provided, the programme's popularity stemmed from the way it made the voluntary contracts sound as pleasurable as a holiday: five star accommodation, excellent health and safety care, domestic help, a social network, and part-time hours to suit.

That same evening, at my suggestion, Liam Nash joined Samuel, Lynn, Lizette and me for a gourmet meal at The Wild Salmon in the centre of Bristol – Jay having opted for a film at the nearby superscreen. Liam, Diana's cousin, had stayed in contact with me since our first encounter at Diana's bio-fest. Apart from intermittent emails, we had met half a dozen times over the years, usually at his instigation, and usually for a lunch in London. Because he lived in this same area and worked in a similar industrial sector, I thought he and Samuel might get on. But I had an ulterior motive. Liam, having retired some years earlier (and buried his wife), had signed up for a term of duty with the Wisdom Force, and was heading out to Namibia to help plan and build a new water filter manufacturing unit.

The five of us got on well. Lizette gave a more detailed report on our trip to Stackpole Haven, and we spent much of the time debating the pros and cons of Notek values. Liam and I ganged up against the Sanderson trio, all of whom were prejudiced against Mercurio. Lizette may have undergone a reconciliation with her brother, but her long-held views about the fundamentals of his way of life had not changed. Like me, though, Liam appreciated what the Noteks had achieved and what they were aiming to accomplish. Also, unlike the others, we were both willing to acknowledge that the Noteks had had a beneficial influence on our society, our culture. It was not until the waiter was serving coffee, though, that I managed to bring the conversation round to Liam's forthcoming venture to Namibia.

The following day we set off to return to Surrey. All in all, the tour had been a success, working out much better than I'd expected. Lizette had got tetchy with Jay now and then, but this was nothing unusual. She and I, though, did have one row on the way home. I was driving, Lizette was expounding on the great benefits of materials science, and Jay was listening to music through his earphones – the Rainbow Sharks, he informed me the other day, his favourite band for many years.

'You and Liam, last night ... defending the Noteks. I agree they could survive, but not at that comfort level. It's the energy provision that makes the difference and they wouldn't have so much if it wasn't for the s-glass, the polymers that make wind and water turbines so efficient, and h-fuel storage technology. And to subscribe to the notion that you can cherry-pick your science and research investment ... It's fatuous. Scientific development and invention doesn't follow prescribed patterns. If it wasn't for pure research into materials and matter, Liam's filters would be a hundred times more expensive, Samuel's turbines would still be stuck – literally by marine growth – in the pilot project development stage, and your great IFSD would be the International Fund for not-quite-so-Sustainable Development.'

I changed the subject.

'What do you think ... will Samuel consider the Wisdom Force?' There was silence for a few moments, and then Lizette erupted.

'You did it on purpose. You invited Liam, so as to encourage Samuel. I don't believe it. You sod.' I said nothing. 'I don't want my brother going off to some god-forsaken place halfway round the world, dragging Lynn with him. I can't believe you did that.' Lizette stormed on. She was particularly cross at the fact that I hadn't discussed my 'devious plan' with her beforehand, which was 'very uncharacteristic' of me. I did not mind being called devious, but I hated the idea that Lizette liked me being predictable, so I argued back – definitely not the right thing to do. Our raised voices, apparently, made no impact on the Rainbow Sharks, for Jay never removed his headphones once.

Three years later, in 2079, Samuel and Lynn went to Lima, Peru, so that Samuel could help train Peruvian engineers to build their own highly efficient and low-maintenance tidal turbine units, instead of importing them from Japan, Italy or Britain. He took a one year contract initially, and then extended it by a further two years, which is how they came to be there when Lizette and I undertook our tour of South America in 2081.

CHAPTER 29

IN WHICH I GET A NEW ANKLE

On our return from the west country, I went immediately to an orthopaedic specialist at Guildford Hospital. For years he had been treating the severe rheumatoid arthritis in my left ankle, and for years the pain and discomfort had grown progressively worse. I had survived so far through a combination of painkillers, a surprisingly comfortable ankle bandage-brace, thanks again to Lizette's beloved materials science, and a micro-surgical reconstruction which miraculously helped enhance the joint for nearly two years. I also employed a walking stick and special shoes.

This time the specialist proposed a second, more complicated and costly bio-engineered joint reconstruction. He promised it would give me a minimum of five years pain free hiking. I agreed. But, within 18 months, I was once again in agony. Late one afternoon – it must have been September 2078 (Jay had not yet left for Reading University) – I was hobbling back from the bowls green, when I bumped into Sami. He wanted me to inspect the quality of his cucumbers (purple) and the size of his marrows (enormous).

Now that rationing had come to an end, and Iona was no longer concerned that growing food might indicate hardship, Sami was keen to start exhibiting again. I hadn't been in his garden for years, and the ostentatious fortifications took me by surprise. He confided that he used the security lamps to extend natural daylight, but that this was not illegal – energy use restrictions had not been fully lifted by this time – because they were only powered by energy collected from the s-glass on his own property. Most of this energy, he said, came from a huge new L-shaped s-glasshouse. Inside, he showed me an exotic array of tropical vegetables, but, oddly, no fruits. I thought Sami's efforts at excess gardening were eccentric if not absurd, certainly compared to Lizette's hobby gardening and the purpose-driven organic horticulture in Mercurio's community, but, nevertheless, I praised his efforts.

Which goes to show how a little hypocrisy can take you a long way – literally. After applauding his okra, cocoyams and dazzlingly-coloured chillis, he was ready to let me leave. As he unlocked the side gate, I held on to the fence to ease the pain in my ankle. He insisted on taking me inside for an examination. I gave him a brief medical history of my ankle and the name of my consultant, to which he replied, 'Oh my god'.

Stupidly, I had allowed myself to accept treatment until then without doubting the advice of my surgeon. According to Sami, the reconstruction surgery on my ankle had been a waste of time, money and pain. There was constant pressure for doctors, he explained, to choose the least-cost option, regardless of whether this led to higher costs in the longer run, whether these costs were paid by the state or by the individual. It was ever thus, with the state trying to minimise short-term costs, and the medical establishment insidiously (or subconsciously if the word can be applied to an establishment) trying to maximise its income. What I needed was a new ankle, Sami said. It would be five times as expensive as one micro-surgical reconstruction but would last ten times as long. More importantly, he added, it would give me much greater mobility with far less discomfort.

'Go to the surgeon, ask for a second opinion or referral, to me at St George's. I'm so sorry that I haven't paid more attention to your discomfort before now. I never thought to ask. It's so very rude of me. We can do it half on the health service, or more, so it won't worry your insurance too much.' Iona had come into the room with a tray of drinks and edibles. I thanked him and her profusely.

Although I did get myself referred to Sami within a few weeks, it was some months before I could undergo the necessary surgery. In the meantime, Sami's prescriptions and an improved ankle bracelet helped control the discomfort. The new ankle, when it came, transformed my life: gone was the constant threat of pain day and night, gone was the routine of pills and cold-presses, gone was the ankle brace, gone was the stick, and gone was my chronic reluctance to leave the house or office to do anything at all. It was a magnificent ankle with, I guess, 85% of the movement of the previous one before it went bad. The monetary cost was high, even discounting the health service share, but there was an additional price to pay: not only was I obliged to inspect and applaud Sami's vegetables several times a season, which I didn't mind, but Iona took advantage of her husband's good neighbourliness and added us to her dinner party guest list, which Lizette did mind.

I should admit that I had no qualms about taking advantage of the most recent advances in bio-engineering despite my personal belief that Western societies had spent and were spending far too much money on medical research, and many other things besides. Politicians often find themselves in deep water when their private lives are put under the microscope; but I am no politician, and I have no psychological objection to classifying myself a hypocrite.

I spent the spring of 2079 becoming accustomed to the way my new foot felt, and revisiting various walks around Tilford, especially my favoured hike across to Elstead – though it took a while before I could manage the whole distance one way, with a bus ride home.

It was in this period that Lizette again became occupationally depressed. The year before, the year Jay left home, she had applied to take over as Sidney Jensen's departmental deputy, which would have given her more managerial responsibility, and allowed her to hope for a professorship in the future. Sidney, however, opted to bring in a younger woman, Olive Norrington, with an exceptional research track record. Lizette felt slighted. She made an effort through 2079 to look for a new position, knowing we would be free to move anywhere as soon as my contract with REACH expired, but most of her applications were half-hearted. She went to two interviews, and was offered one position, in Norwich, but turned it down. By the end of that year, she had come to terms with spending the rest of her working life at Guildford University, a decision partly eased by a growing respect for Olive, who had, Lizette grudgingly admitted, enlivened the department.

Chapter 30
In which Josephine Lock employs me

I, on the other hand, could not come to terms with my situation. REACH's mandate, and my job, terminated in December 2079 when administration of the ongoing projects was transferred to the European Union executive in Brussels. Surely my life was not over. I was 80, and relatively fit, all the way down from the mind to the ankles. It would have been churlish to complain about the mild symptoms of rheumatoid arthritis elsewhere in my body which, with my ankle clear of pain, had become more noticeable.

Lizette was not insensible to my octogenarian angst and fears about retirement. She stepped up our social arrangements with trips to the theatre in London, more visitors at the weekends, and, inevitably, more tasks in the garden and bridge practice. It was around this time that Horace's book, *Reflections of a Political Lightweight*, was published, and that Lizette first proposed, half seriously, I write my autobiography and call it *Reflections of a UN Heavyweight*.

Incidentally, Horace's book was a racy read. Not only did he reproduce as much printable Parliamentary scandal as could be squeezed into the story of his own career, but he had one truly newsworthy tit-bit which catapulted the book into the bestseller lists. He revealed – to much astonishment – that he had had a brief affair with Terrance Spoon. The same Terrance Spoon, now deceased, who had been married with four children, and had been prime minister for several years in the 40s. Unfortunately, the book and the revelation turned Horace into something of a media darling; he was able to make more of a fool of himself in broadcasting studios than he would have done had he still been an MP in the House of Commons. A newly-constructed heart certainly ensured his zest for attention continued unabated. At Taunton House, Lizette rarely bothered any longer to help me entertain him which meant I alone had to cope with his garrulous turns.

When I looked back on my life then, I realised that apart from a tedious period at the Department of Industry and Technology in the 20s, I had been very fortunate in the progress of my career. I had never had to struggle to find jobs, they had found me. I decided, therefore, it was finally time to be more proactive, to tout around for any modest employment. I drew up a list of people I could contact, and I tried to draft what I might say to them. This proved far from easy. I had never been good at keeping in touch with colleagues, and so there was no way to disguise a communication as having any purpose other than canvassing. 'Hi, how are you? By the way, I'm not doing anything at the moment. If you hear of any opportunities coming up ...' Ridiculous. I couldn't do it. The most I could do was mention, in the normal course of social contacts, my distaste for retirement.

In the summer of 2080, I received a surprise call from Jude Singleton. Lizette and I had just returned from a week in the Midlands staying with Pete and Clarity, to find Jay camped out at Taunton House. Two years earlier, he had scraped into a course at Reading University on 'The Information Interface' only to drop out after nine months to join a Notek community in Cumbria, and this was his first visit home. Lizette lost no time in losing her rag. She was shouting when my phone rang. Jude Singleton, who was around ten years older than me, must have been in her 90s. We had met occasionally while I was working for REACH in London Bridge; and we sent each other New Year cards.

'Have you heard of Josephine Lock?'

'No.'

'Let me ask you another question then. How's your interest in old photos?'

'You know I sold my collection before leaving The Hague. But I follow the auctions onscreen, and I've been known to trek into London for an exhibition. It's one of my only pleasures these days.'

'Self-pity, that's not you Kip.'

'No, I've put it on, like a hat.' She laughed. 'So who is Josephine Lock?'

'Josephine Lock, née Shuttleworth. The only child of Ronald and Deborah Shuttleworth, later known as William and Deborah Caxton. Caxton left Deborah a very rich woman. She squandered some of it, but soon learned – with the help of a second husband who died in the 60s – to handle the power and guide the Caxton assets. She passed away last year, and left over a billion euros to her daughter. Josephine, who's about 60 now, was married to a Captain John Lock, but he too died years ago. There are several children on the scene who take up some of Josephine's time, and for whom a chunk of the inheritance will be earmarked. Much of the rest of her time and money is dedicated to various charities. But she has one abiding personal obsession – old photos. She already has a large collection, which is curated on a freelance basis by one of the specialists at Bradford. But now she has this money, she wants to do something big, something very big indeed. Are you there, Kip?' The shouting between Lizette and Jay had escalated, and I moved out to the garden to avoid any of it getting through to Jude.

'I'm here, Jude, all ears. How do you know this Josephine?'

'Green Aid. We both sit on an advisory panel. She's a special person, exceptionally humane and giving. She's spent most of her life working for charities of one sort or another. She's very attentive, with a tendency to become involved. Overly so. It's only with the help of tactful assistants she manages to get through a hectic schedule. I think it's a reaction to her father. It's as though she believes the very worst things written about him, and is trying to make up for his moral corruption with her own life. The photo thing, that's different, it's a private passion. A weakness, she calls it.'

'And she wants to do something big with this weakness?'

'She wants to starts a new museum on the origins of photography, here in London. In collaboration with Bradford if possible, but competing with it if necessary. She's proposing a generous budget: for a property, for acquisitions, for staff and for investing to provide a secure future for a minimum of ten years. But that's not all. She plans for the new museum to launch and lead an international project to create a single portal providing simple and efficient access to the world's most important early photographs regardless of their owners. She dreams of being able to switch on her screen and within seconds being able to use one portal to find any photograph over 200 years old by date, by artist, by subject, or by location along with a relevant encyclopaedic-type commentary. And ...' She paused.

'And?'

'And, she's thinking of involving you.'

'Me? Why?'

'If it was the museum alone, she could pick any number of experts from here or abroad who would jump at the chance of such an opportunity, but the portal will be a different matter entirely, involving sensitive negotiations with historic photograph libraries around the world, and Josephine sees the two projects as integrally linked. She wants someone with your administrative and diplomatic experience to oversee the whole scheme and there aren't many like you, with time on their hands, and with such a detailed knowledge of old photographs.'

'She knows a lot about me?'

'From me, I'm afraid. Although not, of course, about your personal dealings with her father. You'd be paid, but not much. Not because she can't afford it. This is my interpretation, of course. She imagines you having ... wants you to have, the same passion for the project as she does. Do you want to meet her?'

The front door crashed as Jay left. After putting the phone down on Jude, I felt dazed and elated.

Four weeks later, I travelled by train to Tunbridge Wells from where a skinny youth with ear-rings and a dappled jacket drove me (in a Duo which took ages – I've always hated the Duos, with their minimal leg room) to Caxtonbury, a beautiful 15th century manor house, complete with moat, near Cranbrook. This is where Josephine lived when not in London. I was nervous throughout the journey, scared that I might not like her and that, if there was no chemistry between us, or that my earlier dealings with her father somehow interfered in our business, she would look elsewhere for someone to realise her dream. But Josephine created her own chemistry with people. We had already spoken several times on the phone, and she had researched me thoroughly.

She wasn't at all how I had imagined her, a media celebrity elaborately made-up, with chic clothes and shaped hair. She wore a long hanging tan shirt over dark red slacks and appeared surprisingly small. There was no disguising of age in the flesh on her face, but nevertheless she had girlish cheerful features, and radiantly piercing eyes, which seemed ready to hypnotise. At a distance you would never tell how much energy she packed into that fragile body; close-up she was a controlled fire-cracker, not one that scares but one that enchants.

I spent the afternoon at Caxtonbury, a name which had been imposed on the property by Caxton. While being shown the gardens, Josephine talked about her father, who had died while she was still a teenager. She had come to the conclusion, many years ago, that he had been an astonishing man, astonishingly clever and astonishingly awful, but he had never deserved to die so young, to be murdered by an assassin. I referred to my earliest meeting with him, when he was a Shuttleworth and I was a schoolboy, but not my later encounters. Thereafter, neither of us mentioned her megalomaniac father again.

We ate lunch with a quiet middle-aged man named Leo Vaughn, who helped Josephine store and catalogue her prints and negatives; then the two of them showed me a sample of the collection. Stunning. Josephine had upwards of a hundred rare early photographs and glass plate negatives, from the 1840s, and a thousand more from slightly later. Most of the rarest and important photographs had been bought, at very reasonable cost, from a French institution which, in desperation, had sold off some of its treasures during the Grey Years.

Josephine was bubbling over with excitement as she tried to talk me through her different holdings, explaining the provenance of each print, or amusing me with an anecdote about its purchase. Leo was run off his feet, doing all the work, removing fragile prints, metal daguerreotypes and glass plate positives from their storage, giving them to me to examine and then returning each one to its proper place.

I do not remember exactly what she showed me that day, but there was one of William Henry Fox Talbot's prints called *Pencil of Nature* (not in good condition), a remarkable daguerreotype of Siberian workmen taken by J P Alibert, some beautiful Le Gray photos, and a Hippolyte Bayard albumen print of barricades in Paris (which reminded me of a Le Gray photo of Palermo after Garibaldi's conquest). I also recall several particularly appealing French stereoscopic daguerreotypes of reclining nudes, which were similar, but earlier, than the stereoscope prints I had owned. Josephine would have kept us both there until midnight, but Leo, who was heading all the way back to Bradford where he worked, had to leave after a couple of hours. He said he wanted to tidy up first, and suggested Josephine and I retire to a more comfortable room to discuss what they had nicknamed the Project.

Josephine and I talked non-stop, in the garden over tea, then in the drawing room, where all walls were covered in a patchwork of framed reproductions of old photos, and through a delicious supper served by the cook who appeared happy to double as a waiter. While drinking coffee, the dapple-jacketed youth interrupted us to ensure I was taken back to the station in good time to catch the last train to Gatwick with a connection to Guildford.

Over the next few weeks, by email and phone, we prepared a simple plan of action, which I then wrote up as a proposal and she discussed with her legal and financial advisers. I was to manage the whole project in two overlapping programmes. In one, it would be my task to prepare a detailed operational plan (with a budget breakdown, objectives, staffing levels etc.) for the museum, which, when ready, would be brought to a project development board set up and chaired by Josephine. Subsequently, and with the board's approval, we would purchase a property and appoint a curator who would handle the museum's furbishing, launch and operations. Josephine and I, and other advisers we chose, would buy the stock for the museum. She saw no reason why we shouldn't start this immediately, since it would be a long and stealthy task finding potential collections to purchase.

The second programme would also involve me preparing a detailed proposal on how to approach the complex task of realising Josephine's dream of a single portal for the world's most important 19th century photos, getting it approved by the project development board, and then implementing it myself.

My retirement landscape no longer looked flat and barren.

CHAPTER 31
IN WHICH I GO TO THE THEATRE IN QUITO

For several days in a row now, I've had the pleasure of Guido and Mireille visiting in the afternoons. Today they have gone to Paris for a week, and then they'll be back in London for a few more days. They look middle-aged now, but they were still young people when Lizette and I visited them in 2081. I couldn't say when the change took place. Although I communicate with Guido in Dutch by email and on the phone, when together with Mireille – the two of them are usually inseparable – we speak in English since Mireille's Dutch is no better than my French or Spanish. Where Guido hesitates over a word, Mireille completes his sentences for him. They are a sweet couple, but I do not feel close to them.

They enquired politely about my progress on this book, though they both share a disinterest in the past or their families' heritages. Guido has never asked to see any of the chapters, and, when I've emailed him queries about our life together in Oldwijkgaarten, he's replied pleading a faulty memory. Their son, Inti, is a waiter and a would-be movie actor. He studied drama in San Francisco. Mireille and Guido thought he would return to Ecuador, and are disappointed that he's decided to settle in the United States.

Mireille and Guido themselves are on the road half the year, touring all over South America with their famous Grupo de Teatro Quito. Whenever they have a new show start-up, Guido gives me net access rights so I can watch the broadcasts if I choose. Over the years, I have made attempts to tune in. I can see the theatres are full, and the audiences enthusiastic, but I don't watch for long. Theatre is meant for the stage not the screen, and in any case the flow-translation, which works well for business and basic communication, never gets close to interpreting theatre language adequately. I stuck with one of their shows, an adaptation of Amado's *Gabriella*, through from beginning to end, and it was fantastic, although, to my mind, it owed more to the 21st century film than the 20th century book.

***

I did see one of their plays for real, before they started Grupo de Teatro Quito, and while they were still in charge of Teatro Sucre. This was on the grand tour Lizette and I undertook in April 2081. We were away six weeks in all, an exhausting six weeks, but one I could never have done without Lizette's companionship (and Sami's wonderful ankle).

Bel, as in Belinda, who the Project had employed as a general purpose dogsbody and who worked out of Josephine's office in Soho, London (part of her extensive apartment), organised the itinerary for us. Although I did have Project business in both Lima and Rio, and thus her help with travel arrangements would have been partially legitimate, I paid her overtime out of my own pocket. Bel was as bright as a button and as sharp as a pin, and managed to buy us some government-controlled permits for the Galapagos Islands. Most people booked up two years or more in advance to visit the famous islands, but she discovered a broker who dealt with permit returns and cancellations and was authorised to re-sell them. We went to Quito, then to the Galapagos Islands, Lima, Cuzco, São Paulo and Rio. I could fill this chapter with details of the journey, but will restrict myself to a few highlights.

Six year old Inti was one such highlight. This was our first physical encounter. Content to have his own audience, he never stopped performing for us. Already at the airport he gave us a one minute show, a dance and a poem in Spanish, on the moving walkway. At the colonial-style house in the San Marcos quarter, owned by Guido and Mireille, Inti showed us the tiny amphitheatre, with seating for four, constructed in the corner of the elaborately tiled patio. There was a weather-proof screen there, and a cam connection. I recognised the place, for Inti and Guido had used it to talk to me by cam-phone.

Inti looked not unlike Guido did at that age, but there was none of Guido's diffidence. I never once noticed the boy slope off to his room to do something on his own. He wanted to be with the adults and involved in their activities. And there was plenty of activity in the house. It seemed as though the phones were always ringing; and there were people coming and going all day, not only those connected with the show, but neighbours, or those who had worked for the community theatre during the Grey Years.

Guido and Mireille had long planned to take a week off during our visit, but, because of the late switch in our schedule to accommodate the Galapagos Islands, we ended up arriving when they were much tied up with a production. Nevertheless, they made us feel very welcome. Our bedroom, although cramped, had been brightly decorated with a floor vase containing a large bunch of bird-of-paradise flowers. They reminded me of Diana.

Guido and Mireille were immensely proud of Teatro Sucre, not only of having restored the building and theatre in 2069-70 (with Felix Montechristo's money) but in re-resurrecting the theatre as a going concern during the previous three years. Many of their shows were the talk of Quito, and consequently a sell-out. They knew how to choose the best touring groups, from as far afield as Europe, and they had a talent for putting on their own spectacular shows.

The one we saw, *De Aqui Hacia el Sol*, a musical about the Grey Years, had been written by two local writers. It was designed and directed by Guido, although Mireille, as the co-producer, had also taken a hand in the direction. I thought it an exciting show, even without fully understanding the text, while Lizette judged it simplistic and over-cinematic. The story revolved around two families, rich Catholic and poor Quechua, with organ music employed effectively for the former and panpipes for the latter. What I remember most, though, was the dazzling way each aspect of the show moved progressively from dark to light and from grey to colour – I'd never seen Electralon material used so effectively.

I had been to Quito twice during my time at the IFSD. The old centre was a joy to wander around, with its craft shops, Indian markets and trendy eating places; and it was certainly no trial to revisit the Baroque churches with their gold-rich interiors, although Lizette was more impressed than I by the religious relics. But I had not been to the Galapagos Islands. My expectations were so high that I couldn't fail to be disappointed, not by the islands, and definitely not by the tortoises, the iguanas, the boobies, but by the way we were led around like sheep, our every step ordained and monitored, and by the way the whole place felt like a wildlife zoo. I did, though, understand intellectually that these very restrictions were necessary to enable I, and many other tourists, to experience the islands' treasures.

The park for giant tortoises, along with a UN-licensed cloning centre similar to one I'd seen in China for pandas, was interesting, as was the Galapagos Island Survival Foundation Exhibition which explained how the islands had coped with climate change excesses – updated to include the Grey Years – and sea level rises. The Foundation had been set up and supported for many years with IFSD money. The best part of the week was three days sailing around the smaller islands on a modern Brazilian-made ketch. We searched out sea lions, penguins, tropic birds and the waved albatross, and ate lobsters, crab, small tuna and goat all caught by our skipper and his son.

In Lima, we stayed with Samuel and Lynn, both of whom had fallen for Peru in a big way. Lynn rambled on incessantly about the Inca civilisation, while Samuel appeared genuinely happy with the work and the opportunity to pass on his learning. He hadn't realised, he said, that he would end up becoming involved in investment decisions, by dint of growing to like his pupils and wanting to help them. Moreover, he found it galling that some Peruvians might be getting rich on the back of his charity. Notwithstanding this and several other criticisms, he was very positive about the Wisdom Programme.

While Samuel and Lynn took Lizette sightseeing, I filled up the week on business. Firstly, I negotiated with the government's ministry of art and heritage for an agreement in principle to incorporate an important state-owned collection of photos in our universal portal. Secondly, I finalised a deal to purchase a private collection of 19th and early 20th century Andean photographs, including several by the Courret brothers and Martin Chambi. The seller and I had agreed on a price and conditions, but, months later, the government intervened to prevent the collection leaving the country. It was my mistake. There had been no formal legal requirement to do so, but I should have sought permission for the private purchase directly with the ministry of art and heritage. At the very least, I could have informed them about my negotiations.

I was on a learning curve: the buying of historically-important art, or access to same, required different negotiating skills from those I'd employed for decades in the giving of welfare-important development aid.

From Lima, we flew to Cuzco, for various trips, not least to Machu Picchu where I secretly relived, for a moment or two, the excitement of my early holidays with Diana.

In São Paulo, where we stayed in an unmemorable hotel, Lizette insisted on a city tour. It included lunch at the highest restaurant in the Southern Hemisphere, truly high enough to fully appreciate ant-man's achievements. I had dined there 20-30 years earlier, with a Brazilian minister, but then it had had some class, now it was no more than an over-priced tourist guzzleshop. On another day, we sought out the Museum of Modern Art, where I rediscovered the beautiful wood/metal panels by Hector Julio Paride Bernabo I'd once seen in Salvador. We also went to the world famous science museum, Museo Biomass, which used scintillating displays and 3D-integration exhibits to demonstrate man's use of wood and other vegetation to provide heat and fuel, and, of course, to show off Brazil's pioneering role in the modern history of biofuels, such as Vivido. Mostly, though, we were in São Paulo so Lizette could meet up with a Brazilian friend who had done a PhD and some lecturing at Keele University, and so I could spend time with Arturo, Fatima and his children – my grandchildren.

CHAPTER 32

IN WHICH I EXPERIENCE ARTURO'S FAMILY

Arturo had retired from O Futuro and sold his ranch in Goiânia. He now divided his time between a huge mid-block apartment and sky-garden in São Paulo and a villa in the hills overlooking Florianopolis on Ihla de Santa Catarina. I never went to the villa, but from the camclips Arturo sent me, it looked glamorous, like a billionaire's home.

The apartment in São Paulo was richly appointed also, with dark marble corridors and columns and gilt wall cornicing, both of which gave the place an ostentatious feel. Arturo himself had the appearance of a man who had lived too long. He had grown fat. Cosmetic surgery on his face had long since decomposed the features. He wasn't yet grotesque, but a cartoonist would have required little imagination to sketch him. If I exaggerate, it is only because there was nothing left of my son or his life that I could engage with. When I enquired about his cloned daughter Alicia – as I had done by email without any answer – he said she had behaved very badly and disappeared years earlier. Disappeared!

Arturo had two main interests: golf and tropical fish. The palatial apartment was full of fish tanks, some of them built into the walls. When the screens weren't in use they showed soothers, live broadcasts of fish swarms swimming in coral reefs.

Not long after arriving, Arturo showed me his proudest possession: a tank with a dozen unremarkable slender fish, each one about ten centimetres long with blue and yellow partial stripes. He told me they were called Brachydanio AM, and asked if I had any idea where the name came from. I did not. Nor was I happy to know when he told me. The species had been named after him, Arturo Magalhães, because the pattern of the partial stripes, looked at sideways, showed quite clearly an AM marking. I assumed this was an accident, until Arturo told me otherwise. He was the director of a specialised lab which genetically manipulated such fish to order. When I reminded him that independent genetic experimentation on animals for commercial gain was banned at the UN level, Arturo shrugged his shoulders and explained that the Brazilian authorities had deliberately shown no interest in enforcing the international law.

I learned, during my two visits to the family, that Fatima, who I had not met before except by camphone, was about to have her jaw and forehead skin re-stretched and her earlobes extended. She proudly trumpeted, using a mixture of Portuguese and passable English, the various enhancements she'd already subscribed to over the years, such as the sockets – they looked like moles – for cheek miniscreens which she only wore on special occasions. Without a trace of modesty, she also mentioned her vaginal muscle implants. I responded, without thinking and enough subsequent embarrassment for the two of us, that Arturo must be a lucky man. Fatima's quizzical expression suggested she hadn't understood my remark, or that I had missed the point.

I met Ignacio, the oldest child, only the once, at a family meal, to which I went alone without Lizette because I saw no reason to inflict Arturo's kin on her. He arrived late, dressed in skin-tight clothes like a cycle racer, and had the confidence of someone much older than his 16 years. After giving a mock bow to Arturo who was watching an American golf tournament on the wallscreen, he planted a sloppy kiss on his mother's mole-marked cheek. Fatima was grateful for his presence, not angry at his tardiness. He sat down and delivered a quip that caused his younger brother and sister to laugh. He turned to me and said something in Portuguese which he asked Tina to translate.

'Welcome to Brazil, to the land of dreams.' He was barely with us an hour, before he rushed away.

Juliano, 13 years old, spoke rarely either time I was at the apartment, preferring the company of his games console and the largest screen he was permitted to use at any given time. The closest affinity I managed with him was for about half an hour when I feigned interest in one of the football games he was playing, and used my earphones to get a bitty sense of his commentary.

As for Tina, only ten at the time, she was strangely aloof from all that happened around her, and would often fail to reply when spoken to. She had no time for the tropical fish or for Juliano's games, but she did enjoy dressing up. On one visit, she took me into her bedroom to show me a cat, Salvatore (named after a current singer). He was sky blue, which I found very disturbing. I had grown used to jet black tulips, purple cucumbers, lavender-flavoured berries, and had seen, onscreen, illegal genetically-modified hamsters and rabbits, plus I was trying to get my head around the idea of fish species created to order. But sky-blue cats ... I would not have thought it possible. The sight of it made me feel physically sick.

I was not using the translator earphones at this point, partly because they functioned inadequately with children who could not or would not make the effort to talk more deliberately than usual, and partly because Tina had sufficient English to complement my inadequate Portuguese. Thus, I was in a state of moral consternation for a full two minutes before I comprehended Tina's explanation: she preferred Salvatore orange, the colour he was dyed last week. Then she gave me a comb and asked me to groom him, which I did with relief.

The day we arrived in Rio de Janeiro, 8 May 81, was the day two chemists from Pittsburgh in the United States announced they had created life in the laboratory, and could do it again. The media went berserk with the news, and so did Lizette. As far as she was concerned this was the holy grail of scientific research. She stayed in the Leblon beachfront hotel all day glued to the screen watching interviews with the two scientists themselves, and the debates with politicians, religious leaders and others. One of the traits I loved in Lizette was her endless enthusiasm for science and scientific developments. Barely a week would go by without her returning home from work bursting with news of some discovery or invention reported by the science media during the day. Despite my limited knowledge I would usually encourage her to explain more, to colour in the scientific picture for me.

On this occasion, though, I had to leave Lizette to her own devices since, as in Lima, I had pre-arranged appointments on behalf of the Project. The oldest Argentinian photographs (mostly taken by itinerant US photographers such as Charles DeForest Fredericks), and the only ones we wanted for the portal, were held in a private collection, and the owner Max Voll, a billionaire, had agreed to see me in Rio. We met at the Club Militar, a glitzy restaurant in Urca at the back of a beach, directly beneath the Sugar Loaf.

As with most of our eventual collaborators, Max was keen on the plan but wanted to be reassured that the benefits would meet the costs, and that public screen access to his collection through our portal would not compromise the ownership security attached to the photographs (i.e. that they would not be directly printable, downloadable or grabbable). In terms of costs, all we asked is that the owners put copies of each of the photographs they had agreed to share into a database format that we would supply. On the benefits, I explained that we fully expected the portal to increase, not diminish, interest in the original collections, and that we would pass on 85% of the page view income. The Project development board had already decided against free access and that our content pages would be billed on Solar's lowest mainstream charging level – close to 0.01 euros at that time. I was not as technically knowledgeable as Max, but, having been sufficiently briefed by our technical advisers, I was able to provide confident assurances on portal copyright security.

CHAPTER 33

IN WHICH I NEGOTIATE FOR BRAZILIAN PHOTOS

Also that week, in-between day trips with Lizette to Petrópolis and Búzios, I negotiated portal access to the most important photographs owned by the Brazilian state, including several daguerreotypes from as early as 1840 by Louis Compte. And, miraculously, I was also able to buy, from Senora Maria Pedrosa, an archive of late 19th century Brazilian photographs for our collection which included 37 Ferrez prints! It is a negligible story but I cannot resist telling it.

I located Maria Pedrosa at the end of a trail which started with old auction catalogues. I had noticed a series of lots at one particular auction firm, spanning several years, which appeared to come from the same anonymous collection. I guessed there might be more. I contacted the auction house staff who gave me, somewhat unwillingly, the details of an agent they dealt with. Then, I engaged in a drawn-out email dialogue with the agent, who, eventually, set me up with a meeting.

Maria Pedrosa, who was a similar age to me, had been a star of Brazilian soap operas in the 20s, 30s and 40s. She was very wealthy and lived in a mansion behind fortress-style walls in the Santa Teresa suburb of Rio. Four husbands had come and gone over the years. The last one, from whom she had inherited the photograph collection, died in the late 60s. She no longer ever left her home, but she did have a small army of live-in staff, and there was a constant stream of visitors. Not only were there both advisers and cadgers wanting something from her, but there were the rich and/or famous who had once loved her on the screen and who petitioned to come to her weekly dinner parties. All this I had learned from the agent or my own research.

But she was one of the most memorable people I have ever met, both in body and in character. When I entered her opulent receiving room, she was standing seven or eight metres away with an elbow on a grand mantelpiece. She looked every inch a movie star, and could have been mistaken for half her age. Admittedly, my eyes were no longer very sharp.

When we sat down in antique armchairs, she remained a good four metres away. At this lesser distance, her light-golden curly-haired wig looked real enough, but I could detect heavy layers of make-up designed to hide the age of her skin, and the clever way a slinky gold gown appeared to make her look youthfully slim and not agedly slouched. Whether she didn't care, or had no means to change it, her voice sounded croaky and old; and she farted constantly. The agent, a handsome dark man, around 40, impeccably dressed in a pressed white suit, sat in a third lounge chair. When Maria's English gave out, he translated; and then, later, when Maria and I had finished talking, he was the one with whom I finalised the details.

For nearly an hour, Maria quizzed me incessantly, wanting to know why I was in Brazil, what I'd done in my life, how old I was when I'd first had sex, how many wives I'd married and children I'd sired. She wasn't the least impressed by my career at the IFSD, although I could see she perked up when I mentioned my collaboration with Pam, the film director. She was very interested in the fact that I had a Brazilian son, and, when she enquired further about him, I told her, reluctantly, about his work. I thought she might kick me out – few other topics could elicit such violent reactions in people as cloning – but the reverse was true. She herself had a cloned son, she said, thanks to the O Futuro group; moreover, she thought she remembered meeting a techno-clinician called Arturo. When I enquired about her own son, she waved an arm, flashing inch-long purple nails, to dismiss my enquiry, as she had done with all my other questions.

At the end of her inquisition she spent another half an hour giving me a well-rehearsed monologue résumé of her life story. Thus I learned that her mother had acted in a 1980s film, *Edu*, about the origins of cinematography in Brazil. On my request she asked her assistant to ensure I was sent a copy. It is a beautiful movie. I have it on Neil. Perhaps I can persuade Chintz to watch it with me this evening. I am missing Jay's near daily visits. I wonder if he would judge me as being too long-winded in this chapter. It is certainly taking me a very long time to write. I think my concentration is fading.

I realise that by naming certain early South American photographers, and Max Voll and Maria Pedrosa, I am giving them too much relative importance. Most of my negotiations for the Project were conducted by camphone or email, and I would certainly not have made trips, involving time and expense, to Lima or Rio without other reasons. The most important photographs and photographic collections we had earmarked for the portal were in Europe and the US, and therefore the only special journeys I made, during earlier years, were to negotiate portal access with the important curators and owners in East and West Coast United States, Moscow, St Petersburg (far too late for Alan or Anna), Warsaw, Berlin, Prague, Paris, Marseilles and Milan. That said, I did make trips to Shanghai and Tokyo as well.

By early 2082, we had appointed a director, Giselle Dufkova, to take charge of the photograph museum side of the Project – to be called The Josephine Collection – and we had poached Leo from Bradford to look after the photographs themselves. This meant that, much to my regret, it was sensible to hand over most of my photo-purchasing role to Giselle. By early 2083, we had also appointed a technical director, Lorraine Lomax, who was to manage all the museum's computer-based operations, including the portal, which was to be known as Portia for no other reason than that its official name, the Universal Portal to the World's Earliest Photographs was too clumsy for common use.

The success of The Josephine Collection and Portia was largely down to the dedication and skills of Giselle and Lorraine. But it was Josephine herself, with her special talent for enthusing others and making the impossible sound possible, who was responsible for finding and attracting both women in the first place. I feel sure that if I had been the one to approach either of them they would never have considered leaving their highly-respected, well-paid positions. Yet, there was also a point where Josephine's ability gave out, she lost patience with detail, and got angry if she hadn't found anyone to whom a task could be delegated. Thus, the courtship of Giselle and then Lorraine followed a similar pattern: Josephine wooed them to the Project, and I married them to it; she fired their imaginations and made them believe in the dream, and I showed them why we should, and how we could, make it a reality.

Both Giselle and Lorraine were exceptionally gifted individuals. The former, a quiet studious lady, had spent 25 working years at the Société Française de Photographie and was looking for a new challenge. She loved the idea, as sold to her by Josephine, of abandoning Paris and working in London. Unfortunately, the Société Française de Photographie resented her leaving and it wasn't until the 90s, long after I'd gone, that it finally agreed to allow its photographs to be accessed through Portia. An American by birth, and with a much livelier personality, Lorraine had lived in London most of her life. Recently, she had spent five years helping the Royal Horticultural Society and its international affiliates re-launch a series of themed portals for universal read-only access to all existing and relevant pre-19th century publications. The results had been much applauded in the media.

CHAPTER 34
IN WHICH DIANA AND ARTURO PASS AWAY

I am racing too far ahead, and need to backtrack to the months following our South America tour.

In June that year (2081), Diana died, from kidney failure. I went to the funeral in Amsterdam. Guido arrived just in time on a delayed flight via Miami, having left Mireille to cope with looking after Inti and their theatre's busy schedule alone.

We sat in a row with our friends Peter and Rudy. Peter's wife Livia was bedridden and in a nursing home by this time, having been crippled by a stroke. I don't know where Rudy's sister Ulla was. Nearby were Mireille's mother, Helene (exquisitely dressed but undeniably old), who had travelled from Paris with an escort, and Mireille's sister Veronique who had come from Geneva. It was not surprising to see them there since all the Rocard family had been very fond of Diana, as a consequence of her friendship with Didier, who had died a decade earlier. Diana's younger sister Dominique, her partner Waltar and their two sons, Jurian and Lukas, with their wives and several children sat in front of us, as did Dimi, Diana's oldest sister, who was in very good shape for 90 odd.

A haggard-looking Karl gave a moving speech, but one which neglected the middle portion of Diana's life, the part during which she had lived happily with me, and during which she and I had raised Guido. After the service, there was a wake at Karl's house, but neither Guido nor I wished to go. Instead, we took the train to Leiden for a nostalgic stroll around the town and through Oldwijkgaarten.

Nothing had changed. Centuries of architectural history had not been affected either by the wars or the Grey Years. Our old house and the surrounding gardens appeared the same, well-cared for, with children playing on the lawns, and colourful roses blooming in the borders. I would have been content to walk in silence, but Guido had a need for confession. He felt guilty about having emigrated to South America and deserting Diana, especially as he was her only son. He never meant to stay away a lifetime. She had resented his distance, he confided (for he had never mentioned this before), and wanted to know if I had too. I said I had missed him greatly, but I'd never resented his choices, especially since I understood that he was devoted to Mireille, and that they had found a fulfilling life for themselves. Your mother should have appreciated that, I told him, so don't think about her resentment as anything other than an expression of her love. It may not have been apparent at times, I said, but you were the most important thing in her life, more important than Karl, me or even the theatre itself. At which point he burst out laughing, and said 'now I know you're re-inventing the past'.

We met up with Peter and Rudy later and took the tram to Rudy's house in the Amsterdam suburbs. There we spent a melancholy and, for me uncomfortable, evening talking about Diana. Peter's memory had begun to fail, and he was unable to censor out of the conversation his memories of and anecdotes about Diana and Karl; either that or, when talking about Diana, he became confused between Karl and me. Peter had known Diana together with Karl long before I came to the Netherlands, and then, when they reformed as a couple in Amsterdam, he and Livia both remained friendly with the two of them. This had not affected my friendship with Peter and Livia since, by then, I was seeing them infrequently – they only came once to Taunton House – and, until recently, they had always been careful to avoid discussing Diana in any context that involved Karl.

As far as I could tell, Rudy's life had not been as rewarding as Guido's and, as a consequence, they had grown apart over the years – it wasn't only the geographical distance between them. Rudy had separated from his wife, who had taken custody of their child, Arnout. And, although Rudy had tasted success as a professional musician, his standard of living had fluctuated with the popularity of jazz.

Four months later, in October, Karl and Dominique organised a memorial service at a small theatre in Amsterdam, and I heard Rudy play for the first time in 20 years. He had such a sweet touch. There were other faces, familiar friendly ones who sang Diana's praises, or who acted out sketches, sad and funny, from her favourite plays. I was sorry Guido and Mireille had decided not to come, but they followed the event onscreen, and the three of us talked about it at length afterwards.

I couldn't resist taking a personal swipe at Karl, for it must have been he who decided that the memorial service/show should include a two-hander sketch from Angelika Stockmann's *The Children's Land*. I asked Guido if he remembered, when he was about eight, being woken by his parents shouting at each other, and coming out of his bedroom to try and stop their argument. He did, along with a vivid recollection of being afraid that we might be about to break up, and that he might lose one of us. I explained that it was during the production of the Stockmann play in Antwerp that Diana had got back together with Karl, and that the secret relationship had been the root cause of the argument – although I didn't realise as much at the time. I was convinced Karl's staging of an excerpt from that play was no coincidence.

Diana's passing led me into sadnesses and regrets which went on, in one form or another, for weeks, and were then resurrected in the run-up to the memorial and in the weeks after that. The memories of her colourful, magical warm companionship could easily send me into a maudlin mood if I let them. And, obviously, I had regrets about the final years of our relationship, not only for myself, but also because of the possibility that our behaviour may have contributed, albeit slightly, to the decision by Guido and Mireille to leave Europe. I felt truly privileged to have known her, to have spent part of my life in her orbit, and to have fathered her son, yet I could not regret our eventual separation, for then I would never have met Lizette with whom I experienced the most complete and rounded relationship of my life.

By contrast, I felt very little emotion at the news of Arturo's death. It was as though he had never managed to pierce his way through to my heart. He had arrived too late, when my emotions were already spread too thin. I tried to act as a father, and, I guess, he tried to behave as a son. A cynic might argue that for several years we played out our respective roles, one giving mock respect, the other providing financial support. Again, I am probably being too clinical in my assessment. While Arturo was here, studying, dependant on me, I'm sure I did care for him, as I do now – in a distant kind of way – for his daughter Tina, and his grandchild Maria.

Arturo died in 2082, of skin cancer. I was too busy and tired to make the trip for his funeral, and so expressed condolences and made excuses to Fatima by camphone. She told me that Arturo was already suffering from the cancer when I was there, in São Paulo, but that he had not wanted to burden me with the knowledge. She also told me, nervously, that I had not been mentioned in Arturo's will. Before dying, however, he had proposed I might want a pair of his tropical fish, the Brachydanio AM. Fatima said she would arrange and pay for safe transport. I declined politely, as I did her offer for any other memento. She informed me the family would be leaving São Paulo and moving to live permanently at the property near Florianopolis, a place where her children's grandfather would always be welcome. I returned the offer, suggesting, as sincerely as I could manage, that she and her family should come to England one day and stay with us at Taunton House.

I cannot resist adding a short postscript to Arturo's story. When Tina was here a few weeks ago, she told me her father had left instructions for his ashes to be mixed with fish food and fed to the Brachydanio AM. Fatima had done as instructed, with a tear in her eye, but the fish died in transport to the villa near Florianopolis.

I could mention that, within three months of Arturo's cremation, the United Nations concluded, as part of the ongoing post war negotiations, a comprehensive, permanent and mandatory agreement on human and animal cloning. Concessions were made to the pro-cloning scientific and political communities permitting a greater variety of cloning activities and techniques than had been allowed hitherto under the previous UN code and by the AGCT. However, whereas the old rules were wholly inadequate – being neither mandatory or widely accepted – the new international law imposed such strict licensing and operational conditions, with punitive sanctions for non-compliance, that the commercial cloning operations in Brazil and China, for example, were finally obliged to close down.

CHAPTER 35
IN WHICH GISELLE AND LORRAINE WORK MIRACLES

Chintz has abandoned me. She declined to watch the old Brazilian movie, *Edu*, claiming that she hated all foreign language films; and she no longer pops in to see me when she's off duty. How can she be so fickle? Guido and Mireille have been and gone today, and Jay returns tomorrow. He will find me much weakened, and struggling to conclude this chapter. However, he should be content to discover that I am skimming over his two year drop-out period, and the angst this caused Lizette who thought he would end up spending his life with the Noteks as Mercurio had done.

***

On returning to Reading University, a move much applauded by Lizette, Jay continued with the same course, on 'The Information Interface', although he switched the focus of his modules away from scientific information towards social and environmental knowledge. Subsequently, he went to Birmingham to do a year's teacher training. Lizette was unable to suppress her disappointment at his career choice. Jay and I both had to cope, in different ways, with her infrequent, but nevertheless stinging, attacks over his lack of ambition and achievement.

On the whole, by this time, Jay felt comfortable enough to spend some weekends at Taunton House, occasionally bringing boyfriends with him. But, if ever Lizette began to make snide remarks about his profession, he would engage her in argument for half an hour or so, then storm out and not return for several months. I tended to defend him, especially before any argument had escalated, and then after he had gone, but my interventions never served any purpose. Instead, they usually led Lizette into a semi-emotional attack on me, there being a surfeit of teachers in my background.

Personally, I believe teaching is one of the most important and noblest of professions, and that Lizette was wrong to give her research undertakings far more value than her education work. Within a few days of such arguments, Lizette would find a way to apologise. In my case, where the apology was genuine, it was unnecessary. In Jay's case, the apology took the form of an unwelcome excuse without any trace of repentance for – what Jay rightly viewed as – her illegitimate judgement on him and his life.

My five years working on the Project passed all too quickly. In the preparatory stages, when Josephine chaired the development board, and we worked together as a small team, the meetings were often long and unstructured. And yet, such was the pleasure of Josephine's intensity and enthusiasm, and the nature of our endeavour, that I usually felt a touch of disappointment when she finally shuffled her papers together and said: 'Ladies and gentleman, enough. You have been so patient with me, and so generous with your time, I really must let you all go now. But we have made progress, haven't we, such progress.'

During 2082, we acquired an interesting property near King's Cross, in Chalton Street, a stone's throw from the British Library, and, by 2083, with Giselle and Lorraine both in place and formal committee structures operating, the implementation stage was well under way. Nevertheless, Josephine continued to be very demanding and involved, and this led to a spate of awkward arguments over minor decisions. Thus, wisely, Josephine agreed to step back leaving me to preside over most meetings. She continued, however, to chair the main development board which met to decide on key budget issues and the more important artistic questions, such as those concerning photograph purchases and the evolving parameters for Portia.

King's Cross was inconvenient for me, so, when the office refurbishment works were completed on the second floor (i.e. before the gallery areas on the ground and first floors), I planned to spend only two days a week there, with Bel organising my meetings accordingly, and to sleep over at a local hotel. When Josephine learned of this, she insisted I make use of the self-contained guest suite within her own apartment and join her for supper on a regular basis. Only when she advised me in advance that the suite would be occupied did I make alternative arrangements. Thus, we settled into a useful pattern, with the weekly supper together serving as our main point of contact.

Even with Josephine in the background, rarely a month went by without her causing one mini-crisis or another. Josephine, for example, continued to want everything done yesterday, while Giselle would not be rushed. She worked earnestly, kept long hours but became surly and uncommunicative if asked to speed up some action or other. The only effective way I found of dealing with this was to sit down with Giselle and look at the detail of the work required for a specific action. If I could demonstrate where a time saving was possible, she would accept it, and the surliness would evaporate. If I could not demonstrate where such a saving was possible, then at least I was sufficiently briefed to argue Giselle's case with Josephine.

Another problem arose because of Giselle's dissatisfaction with Leo Vaughn. Having convinced the Collection's executive board of the need for a second curator to manage special exhibitions, she employed a compatriot, Henri Pouile, who was more than ten years younger than Leo. Thereafter, she began a very deliberate process of obliging Henri to encroach on Leo's responsibilities. Her idea was that either Leo would resign in protest, or Henri would end up taking charge of the main collections anyway. But Leo was no fool. As soon as he had sufficient evidence of Giselle's manipulations, he went straight to Josephine. She then came to me, insisting on fair play for Leo. I won't suggest it was easy, but, after three months, I did mange to persuade Leo to take the lesser position – i.e. curating special exhibitions. Moreover, I convinced Josephine that Giselle was right to have wanted to replace Leo, and that Henri was perfect for the job; and I gave Giselle a stern warning not to be so devious again. Much unpleasantness might have been avoided, I advised her, if she had only approached me early on with her doubts about Leo.

Although the Société Française de Photographie used the lame excuse of Giselle's defection to justify its obstructive attitude to Portia, I am certain its director, whom I personally went to see twice, resented our initiative. Britain's National Media Museum, in Bradford – which was only a few years away from its centenary – did not need the pretext of Leo's departure to precipitate stolid opposition, not to The Josephine Collection, which it fully supported, but to Portia.

Arnold Cowerbridge, the museum's chief executive, argued publicly that the portal we were trying to build should be directed through, and launched from, his museum, a national museum with international credibility. Our venture, he told *The Guardian* media, was doomed to failure. Even if we managed to launch Portia, he suggested, it should be called 'Partial Portia', for it would not be able to provide access to a very significant number of the most important early photographs, such as those in the Bradford museum.

When, in response, *The Guardian* came to me for an in-depth interview, I stalled, and went to Bradford to talk to Cowerbridge. He was an unpleasant looking man, half my age but equally tall, with a trimmed moustache, flared ears and a sneering mouth (not entirely disguised by the moustache). He smiled a lot, though, which improved his appearance and helped in conversation. His glass desk was devoid of clutter, and spotlessly clean.

I explained to Cowerbridge that Josephine Lock, who had pledged more money to the preservation and promotion of early photography than any other private donor in history, had been deeply offended by his remarks in the media, especially as they came out of the blue without any previous discussion. I reminded him that he had deflected all our approaches up until now. He smiled. Then I gave him a very brief résumé of how much we had achieved so far, leaving him in no doubt that we had made zero compromises on the scale of our venture and that we were on schedule. The smile drooped. Next I told him I had five important media interviews pending, but first I wished to clarify what potential if any there was for collaboration between his organisation and mine.

Without giving him time to reflect on what I had said or to respond, I moved swiftly on to the second part of my pitch – a direct appeal to his vanity. I told him how much we admired and respected him and the museum, and that although Portia would survive and flourish without his support, this would be a pity, a great pity for those who used Portia and for Bradford itself.

Which led me on, smoothly, to the substantial list of advantages for the museum of taking part in Portia. This was the same list as I had used on countless occasions with other archives, collections and museums: an additional revenue stream; a new and important service for the world (pompous I know, but sometimes pomp works) making the earliest photographs more available than they had ever been before; and improved exposure – as it were! – for each collection accessible through the portal. Only minor collections, I intimated, should be insecure about Portia, since their contributions would be outclassed by the larger institutions (such as Bradford) which held the most important early photographic items (such as Bradford's first negative). Nevertheless, I advised, without Bradford, Portia would not be 'Partial Portia', but 'Portia providing access to all the world's most important early photographs except those held by the Bradford Museum'. Naturally, I did not mention our difficulties with the Société Française de Photographie.

And, finally, I closed the pitch with three offers, especially for Bradford, which had been agreed with Josephine and Giselle – we'd not yet employed Lorraine: a partnership on exhibition exchanges, allowing Bradford special rights, giving it temporary but regular gallery space in the capital city; a general effort in our signage, publications and websites to promote the importance of the Bradford archive and holdings;

and, with respect to Portia, a specific acknowledgement of support from the Bradford museum.

Cowerbridge listened carefully to all I had to say, so carefully in fact that I suspected his refusal to negotiate earlier and his media outbursts were all part of a planned campaign to get as much out of us as he could. By the time I finished speaking, he was smiling again. He promised to think over my proposals.

For *The Guardian* interview and others that followed, I trusted my instinct, making no counter-attack against him, and playing up the hopes of Josephine, 'our benefactor', that collaboration would lead to 'a fantastic new resource for the world of early photography'. A few weeks later, when Cowerbridge was in London, Josephine took him to one of the most exclusive and expensive restaurants in London, and, then, over the next three months Cowerbridge and I negotiated a substantial framework agreement – which is not to say that, subsequently, Giselle and Lorraine didn't have their own problems working with Cowerbridge's staff on the details.

On the whole, Lorraine caused me fewer headaches than Giselle. This was because, on the technical side, she was a wizard, and on the artistic side, where Josephine was more sensitive, she advanced no firm opinions. She did have a gratingly loud voice, and an abrupt manner on the phone. This was a considerable disadvantage because one of her principle responsibilities was to help make it as simple as possible for our collaborators to prepare their own collections for use through the portal. Where the collaborators were prepared to take advice and instructions by email, Lorraine was as patient as necessary; when they rang, though, wanting to sort out a problem directly, Lorraine's manner and apparent impatience led to a few complaints.

I decided the best way to resolve this problem, which might get worse in the run-up to the launch, was to allow Lorraine an assistant, which she needed, and to ensure she not only took on a person with the right skills but gave him or her the technical liaison responsibilities.

A more persistent migraine of a problem for me, though, was caused by Josephine's whimsical approach to Portia's development, and Lorraine's spiky reluctance to make apparently insignificant alterations to already agreed parameters. Mostly, I sided with Lorraine, much of whose work was more complex than Josephine or I could understand, and so I learned to try and divert Josephine from responding to my weekly briefings on Portia with impractical new ideas.

CHAPTER 36

IN WHICH THE JOSEPHINE COLLECTION IS LAUNCHED

Steadily and unsteadily, smoothly and with hiccups, we moved towards the launch of The Josephine Collection in March 2085. Using Josephine's millions we amassed a remarkable collection of 19th and 20th century photographs, books and other paraphernalia – although not equipment, this was a decision made early on – while Giselle and Lorraine, along with Henri, Leo and our other staff supervised the development of the facilities to house them.

On the ground floor of the Chalton Street property we had three large galleries, and, on the first floor, two further galleries, a library/reading room and a meeting salon. The extensive basement was dedicated to storage, but, in addition, we had storage areas on each floor. With so many different photograph materials – papers coated with myriad kinds of chemicals, glass, metal, cellulose, ceramics, even wood and cloth – storage was a complex and technically-demanding business. After much heated discussion, and on Giselle's insistence (she nearly resigned over the matter) we had opted for an expensive storage concept which combined maximum light and atmospheric protection with compactness, flexibility and accessibility. From what I could tell, it paid for itself several times over within a few years.

Giselle and Josephine had two major run-ins prior to the launch, both caused by Josephine. Giselle was devoted to the concept of a launch exhibition entitled *War and Peace*. In a collection of Russian photographs I had purchased at auction, there was a stunning portrait of Leo Tolstoy. Giselle worked out, from the date, that Tolstoy must have been writing his great book at the time; and, from there, she developed the idea of using The Josephine Collection photographs to show contrasting images of the world at war and at peace in the 1850-70 period.

In an uncharacteristic display of egotism, Josephine objected and said it would be more appropriate to launch with a special exhibition based on her own favourites from the

Collection. I suspected – Josephine forgive me for this – she may have been involved with a new man at the time, and wanted to impress him, but any such suggestion would have been way beyond the brief of my relationship with her. In the end, we put on both shows, in separate galleries, thus temporarily reducing the permanent display area by one room. This was not so complicated since we had, in any case, planned to rotate the permanent displays every six months.

The second dispute came when we were beginning to make preparations for the launch party and the opening of the museum. Josephine turned up one day unexpectedly with a young black woman, Leona Sumani, so pretty she could have been an actress or model. She was to be the Museum's new public relations manager, Josephine commanded, and her appointment would be confirmed by the next meeting of the executive board. Giselle in a moment of stress, threatened to resign (again), whether because of Leona's looks or the way she was foisted on her, I'm not sure. She calmed down when I reminded her that she herself had been 'chosen' in much the same way, and that much of the museum's public relations would necessarily come through Josephine's personal connections.

My own fury at Josephine's capricious behaviour dissipated quickly. The next time we were together in private (subsequent to Leona's sudden introduction) Josephine confessed to thoughtless actions and apologised sweetly. I doubted there had been anything thoughtless in her behaviour at all. Instead, I recognised an artful touch of dissembling combined with mock naivety. Nevertheless, I accepted the apology. The incident and my own sudden anger helped remind me how remarkable a person our benefactor was, that every cent we had spent had been hers, and yet, overall and relatively, she had been so uncontrolling, so undemanding, so uncapricious.

The opening of The Josephine Collection went better than we hoped. We held two launch parties. The first was for friends of the Project, who came from far and wide, such as

Max Voll from Buenos Aires. The second was for the media and political and artistic celebrities. We – I should say Leona – streamed the invitations for both events over the course of a day each, so as to avoid crowding problems. Josephine, who never sought publicity for her own sake but who was fully aware of its usefulness, gave a handful of interviews to the most potent media, particularly those with strong outlets in the US. In addition, Leona farmed Giselle and me out to the lesser media, taking care to guide Giselle, who had a sloppy screen presence, to radio and print journalists (I knew this because Leona told Josephine and Josephine told me).

We learned from the extensive, and largely positive, media coverage that The Josephine Collection was the first new major artistic institution in London since before the Second Jihad War. One commentator went so far as to say the opening of the museum presaged 'a reawakening of the city's cultural spirit', another called Josephine 'the Daguerreotype Angel'.

Several months later, a young and eager BBC-connected producer, Cos Williams, approached me (via Leona) wanting to make a quality documentary on the building of The Josephine Collection. I consulted with Josephine and the staff. We agreed on giving our full support, but on the condition that the programme only be broadcast or sold after Portia was up and running – we thought the opportunity of publicity such a programme would generate would be wasted if Portia was not yet operational. Cos agreed, and, thereafter, I spent one day a fortnight discussing progress and plans with Cos or being interviewed by his researchers in preparation for their further work with our staff. By taking such a focal position between Cos and the museum, I was able to direct, as it were, the director and help him to appreciate certain key aspects: above all the unique contribution of early photographs to our history, culture and society; but, also, Josephine Lock's unrivalled benefaction to early photography; the dedication of our staff; and the generosity of our collaborators without whom the development of Portia would not have been possible.

With her staff assistant and a dedicated team of knowl-edgeable, mostly retired, part-time volunteers, Lorraine managed to complete on schedule the detailed cataloguing and comprehensive search criteria for the tens of thousands of photographs in the Portia database. Whether originally positive or negative, whether albumen plates, salted paper or collodion prints, calotypes or daguerreotypes, Portia could display every photograph in a variety of forms, in real size and tone or enlarged to fill the screen, or, in the case of negatives or negative images, as a reversed image. A standard set of six buttons also allowed for limited tonal and textual adjust-ments. Accompanying catalogue information (date, size, subject, photographer, process, country etc.) was available onscreen with or without the photographs and could guide the viewer easily through the database to similar items. All the photographs and the information about them appeared with a prominent link to their original collections.

Launching Portia, in February 2086, was largely a virtual affair, superbly arranged and executed by Lorraine. We employed an external consultant to find us the net/email coordinates of relevant media contacts around the world, but Lorraine's team did almost everything else. Before seven days had passed, we registered a million hits, from nearly 50 different countries, three-quarters of them entering more than five content pages. Within three months, Portia achieved a weekly average of two million hits and an average income of around 60,000 euros, 50,000 euros of which was transferred automatically to our collaborators. More significantly, our collaborators all reported a doubling or trebling of interest in their own collections.

In addition, we held a non-virtual party at Chalton Street, with attention focused, not on the exhibits, but on the wall and freestanding screens throughout the galleries. We all watched a display, programmed by Lorraine, showing off Portia's attributes and workings, and Josephine gave a short speech – I have a recording of it on screen now. She has a generous word to say about everyone involved with Portia and the museum, including me.

'And finally what can I say about Kip Fenn? He has been our guide, our leader, our commander, directing our travails with such foresight, patience and fairness that I doubt my dreams for this museum and for Portia would ever have been realised without him.' She stopped and looked around until she caught my eyes. I was standing with Lizette to the side and at the back, but I was taller than those around me. It was as though there were only two of us in the room. 'Thank you, Kip, thank you from the bottom of my heart.' And she blows me a kiss across the top of the crowd.

EXTRACTS FROM CORRESPONDENCE

Jay Sanderson to Kip Fenn and Lizette Sanderson
October 2079

I'm in Cumbria. In Caldbeck. I'm taking a year off uni. I should have talked to you about it, but I didn't decide till back to Reading last week. It hit me, all of sudden, that I needed time to myself, some real time. I should have done it last year, before uni, but I can go back next October – I checked.

I know Mother will go potty when she reads this. I'm at a Notek community, it's bigger than Mercurio's, and makes money from Lake District tourists, but we're still rigorous, pre-electronic, like Stackpole Haven. I'm doing odd jobs, labouring mostly, but I'm learning fast, especially how the mill works. We buy in the grain (organic and certified Traditional, of course) from all over the place, and grind and mix different kinds of flour. There was a bobbin mill here on Cold Beck River once which had a wheel nearly 13 metres in diameter. It was said to be the second biggest in the world.

Brin is here too, he was the friend who came last Christmas and who Mother said must have been dragged through a hedge backwards – but then you said that about me too. Brin's graduated now, as an information officer at St Mungo's, the Caldbeck Notek Community Library. It used to be St Kentigern's Church. Kentigern, also called Mungo, was an early Christian missionary. I'm told, Kentigern means 'high lord' and Mungo 'my dear friend'. We live in an 18th century cottage, similar to the guest house at Stackpole Haven, made of stone. It's very basic, but homely.

Hope all's well with you. (How's the ankle Pa?)

November 2079

If you want to chastise or moan or argue, Mother, then direct your letters elsewhere – I won't be reading them.

December 2079

So sorry Pa not to be with you for your birthday, especially as you've reached the grand old age of 80. We're very busy, and, as always I'm very short of money for travel (no, that's not a beg – on your birthday that would definitely be out of order – you know I don't want any help). But I hope you like the tie, it's silk, and handmade by a friend. It'll look smart on you.

Love to Mother.

PS: We've a covering of snow, which should brighten up the trek to High Pike for midnight on New Year's Eve.

August 2080

Thanks for the prodigal son welcome. Not! I'll try again next year. As it goes, I've decided to spend a second year at Caldbeck.

August 2080

Pa, thanks for your letter, but sorry, I can't make it back again now. And I don't care if Mother 'doesn't really mean it'. But good luck with the photo project, sounds exciting.

November 2080

The wet summer was bad for our market gardens, and now the cold has come early. Much as I love this landscape, it can get very dreary at times. But I don't mind. Brin's taken over running the library. I'm his assistant, although I don't do much with books. I manage the Learning Exchange – did I tell you about this before? It's not much more than a card index which is used to put people wanting to learn a skill in touch with those who can teach it. And vice versa. It would be far easier with a computer (don't ever tell anyone I admitted that). It's the same principle as the barter markets, only with people's skills instead of their goods, and it takes a bit more managing. Yesterday, I had an enquiry from an accountant in Carlisle who wanted to learn calligraphy. We've two girls here into calligraphy, and one of them needed some bookkeeping assistance. It doesn't often work out so easily. If there's a lot of demand for one type of skill, then we try and set up a class. It could be here, or in Carlisle, or in Penrith, we're not as isolated socially as Mercurio's happy family. I also run the children's book groups (which I love doing), and organise the CMA (Church of Moral Atheism) meetings, which take place in the library. I hesitated for ages over joining the CMA (Brin hasn't joined), but most others here are members. Membership doesn't entail much more than a commitment to a decent way of living and sharing.

And did I tell you I do the school groups now. Once every couple of months, we get a school group coming to look round the community. I do a vote thing at the beginning giving them a choice of five out of ten possible places to visit (the mill, a farm, a market garden, the fish ponds, the library, a potter, a weaver, a beehive keeper, a herbalist ... did you know sticky willy is good for psoriasis?), and then, because they think they're being hard done by, they want to see more than they think they've been allowed. They press me for one more visit, and then another. I love the kids' enthusiasm, and the way they ask so many questions.

October 2081

Hi Ma, Hi Pa – surprise – I'm here at Reading, in a student pad with a couple of other lads, one who was brought up a Notek, and the other who's done a year with a community in Derbyshire. It was good to see you again. I feel bad about having stayed away so long. And I know it must have been dispiriting for you to watch me drop out and live with the Noteks (Ma, especially – sorry). But, honestly, I feel the two years have done me a lot of good.

PS: I left the CMA. Brin never joined. He thought there was something faintly anti-gay about the emphasis on hope for future generations. I agree with that now. (He's left Caldbeck – did I say? – gone to Tierra del Fuego. But, as it goes, we'd split up by then. He'd become very introverted and antisocial.)

PART FOUR

Alicia, Dying and Centennial Thoughts

'If I am asked to look into the future, which happens all too often (why do people imagine I have a crystal ball in my pocket), I close my eyes and shake my head. It is a comfort to find the darkness, for the future of mankind is far blacker. The 20th century was the blackest in human history, until, that is, the 21st century. I've no doubt that 100 years hence, man will be scratching his head and wondering why, despite being richer, cleverer and nobler than ever before, the 22nd century was the most terror-full and destructive in all history.'

Please don't ask me about the future in *The Tap Dancing Essays* by Crispin Gregory (2086)

'One way of interpreting history is to see *Homo sapiens* in a constant struggle against his primitive, animal in-stincts. For the best part of 10,000 years, it has persis-tently sought to improve itself, through cooperation and civilisation, but until the 19th century this effort was largely haphazard, guided largely by imagination and guesswork. While some philosophers, preachers and leaders pressed humankind forwards, in what we would now judge as a progressive way, others – many others – did not. Only with the understanding allowed us by the sciences of evolution, psychology and genetics, for ex-ample, can we begin to try and chart a deliberate route towards peace and prosperity for the whole human race.'

Survival of the Fittest in International Politics – Towards a View of Progress by Zoe Bergmann (2082)

CHAPTER 37

HAVING DOUBTS ABOUT MY DEATHDAY

It is Thursday 3 December 2099. A memorable day, if such a term has any meaning to a man whose life and memory have but two months to go. This morning, my doctor, the gentle but direct Rupert Lipman, apprised me of the results from a sequence of tests carried out in the last few days.

'Fine, Mr Fenn, everything is fine.' He agreed to increase the dosage of some of my pills, in particular those which completely numb the pain in my joints, and those which ensure my neural alertness: I've hardly written a thing, I told him, during the last two weeks. The tests, he said, showed that the increases were fully consistent with my planned death date, and that, with one more increase in four weeks time, I should be able to maintain my current well-being status through to the end of January – which is good news. Having completed so much of this manuscript ahead of schedule, and then having slowed down in the last month, I'm anxious to finish soon.

But now, for the first time since signing up for my death-day, I am having doubts about dying.

No sooner had the doctor, his assistant and Chintz all left together (a cheery, friendly word from Chintz would have been welcome), than another nurse came in to ask if I felt strong enough to see an unexpected visitor, one who preferred not to give a name. I expected a journalist or a researcher interested in my old friend Oakley or in the history of the IFSD or possibly in my 100th birthday vis-à-vis the forthcoming centennial. Any such person phoning me here at Willow Calm Lodge is given a number for Jay. Usually, he says I am very ill and cannot see visitors. Occasionally, therefore, those with chutzpah turn up at the Lodge and try their luck. Most of the time, I refuse to see strangers without an appointment, but this morning I felt more carefree than usual so let curiosity get the better of me.

The woman who entered was tallish, with a dark-skinned face, light make-up, and long hair pinned back tightly into a pony tail. A chocolate-coloured roll-neck sweater beneath a beige fleece and light brown jeans lent her a stylish but modest appearance. She smiled in a warm, giving way, like a colleague, not a journalist trying to create an instant friendship.

'Visitors usually make an appointment. I only have ten minutes.'

'I would have made an appointment with Jay if you'd not been able to see me now, straightaway.' She spoke English with an amateur fluency and a strong accent, part American part Brazilian. And, then, as she sat down in the chair by the bed in front of me, I noticed how familiar her features appeared.

'Are you from Brazil? Have we met? Are you related to Arturo Magalhães, or his mother Conceição?' She laughed kindly, but sadly, for I could see hesitancy in her eyes and too many frown lines reflecting a life of troubles.

'Yes, yes and yes. For an old man – I hope it's not rude to call you old, when I'm old myself – you're sharp. I am Alicia. Alicia Magalhães, now Gonçalves. You held my hand once, and I showed you my bedroom. For years I had a camclip, but then I lost it.'

'Alicia. You're Alicia. I have that camclip.' All of a sudden, I was no longer carefree, but taken over by emotion. 'I was looking at it only a few weeks ago. I've been writing my Reflections, an autobiography of sorts ... Do you know that half a century ago, your father ...', I saw the lines on her face involuntarily tighten, and her eyelids flutter, '... Arturo surprised me ...'

'I know, he told me. Which is why I came like this.' She got up and leaned over to kiss me on the cheek. 'Hello Grandfather.'

'Alicia. Alicia. Alicia. I thought you were dead. Everyone – even Tina, your sister, who came here in September – thought you were dead. You disappeared 20 years ago.'

'I know. It's not true, though. What Arturo told you is not true. But I'll tell you my story. Not now, soon. I'm here for a while. I'll come every second or third day, and we'll talk. Will it be good for you? Now I must tell you one more thing. I have a daughter, Angela, who was 20 last month. She is married to Quasim and they have a son, Renato, six months old and as healthy a baby as you could ever imagine. We're all in Portugal, in Porto, where I live with João Gonçalves – not Angela's father. So, Grandfather, you are a great grandfather, and a great great grandfather. Now you see why I call you old.'

Alicia did not stay very long, but promised to return on Saturday when she would tell me more about herself. For the rest of the morning, I felt joy again – the first time, I think, since before Lizette fell seriously ill. Although writing these Reflections has taken me on an emotional roller-coaster ride, it has been by proxy only. I was tempted to call for an extra bath, or drift off into a dreamy sleep, one in which Alicia and I might stroll through the gardens, along by a river, hand-in-hand, chatting about old times, family parties, our shared history, as if we had known each other forever. Yet, after my chat with Dr Lipman, I realised I must press on with this writing.

There is little left to tell.

CHAPTER 38

COMPARING THE 21ST WITH THE 20TH CENTURY

It is not only Alicia's arrival that is interfering with my ability to concentrate. The world is going mad with centennial fever. The nurses and doctors talk continually about their own and other people's plans for New Year's Eve; the media is full of programmes reviewing the century just gone, or previewing the century to come, or advertising centennial programmes; and I'm receiving more email than usual, invites from people I haven't seen or heard of for ten years or from organisations I've long since left behind. I have standard replies so it doesn't take long to deal with them. But the general buzz of excitement is distracting, and it will only get worse as the days tick by to the end of the year, and, 31 days hence, to the end of me.

The coming centennial has led me, as well as everyone else, to reflect on how life has changed during the century. I do not claim my thoughts are original since I've culled most of them from the media. I have no doubt, for example, like many commentators, that for an individual in the rich developed nations life has not changed anywhere as much this century as it did during the last one. The very reverse might be true – i.e. more advances in this century than ever before – if one considers scientific understanding, industrial processes, medical techniques etc., but these are beyond my knowledge, and I am only reflecting on daily life for an ordinary person.

During the 20th century, there were so many major advances. To list but a few: transport (the car and the aeroplane); health (sewage and fresh water systems, electricity, antibiotics, vaccines, organ and joint replacements); communications (the telephone, the internet); the home (central heating, carpets, labour saving kitchen appliances, personal computers); more time and money for leisure pursuits (volleyball, television, holidays, eating out); and the individual's relationship with government (human rights, the vote for all, media freedom). If I take this same sample collection of categories (transport, health, communications, the home, leisure and citizenship) which affect the daily life of an individual such as me in Western Europe, it's not easy to identify any in which there have been changes as fundamental as those experienced by my forefathers.

In transport, the fuels and engines might have changed and the outward appearances may have gone through fashion trends. In the 40s Diana had a Fiat Klimt!; and, currently, Jay has an Archangel Flitter which, frankly, is a triumph of design over function. We still, though, use cars, buses, trams, trains, metros and aeroplanes. Yes, we learned to plug our cars into cables or to fill up with hydrogen, and we became accustomed to planning trips according to toll costs and to monthly toll bills, and to using dashboard congestion busters, yet traffic jams continue to blight our society. Despite commonplace fictional predictions, evident in my childhood, of traffic moving to the skies, there is no real prospect, even today, of a mass aerocar/aerohover transport system – for obvious reasons of safety, cost, fuel consumption, traffic management complexity etc. But, at least vehicle traffic creates negligible atmospheric pollution; and far less noise than in ages past, since engines naturally became quieter, and because – though it took decades – European Union laws now encourage improved road surfaces.

In terms of our health and well-being, I'm living proof of many advances. One hundred years ago, I would probably have died in my 80s or 90s; but who knows exactly how many years have been added to my life by better information on diet or by improved medical advice and treatment. Life expectancy certainly crept up during the first four decades of the century, but nowhere near as sharply as it did in the 20th century; then, during the wars and the Grey Years, it slipped back again. I am certain, however, that the quality, as opposed to the quantity, of life for older people, certainly in Western Europe, has improved significantly. If, a century ago, I had lived to 100 I would not have done so in comfort, free of pain, and neurally alert.

Certainly, there have been far-reaching developments in communications during this century, but few would argue they are more significant than the actual inventions of the telephone, radio/television and the internet. Large wall-screens were not ubiquitous when I was a child in Surrey and a student in London. Moreover, then, there were important limitations on computer memory and speed, and on digital information flow through the net, and these, in particular, restricted the way people accessed sound and moving images. And, although cams, for personal use and surveillance, were becoming more popular, these too were unsophisticated (limited by memory, quality and battery technology) and consequently the cam infrastructure, and the associated public debate on personal freedom issues, was in its infancy.

Our relationship to computers and screens was thus immature at the start of the 21st century, and it took a while for the way we store and access information, of all kinds, and how we relate to screens to become more fluid and natural, more freewheeling. It was not until the 30s-40s that most of us were at ease communicating directly with screens to find information, access a film or documentary, or talk to a friend as smoothly as if we were talking to a librarian, a store atten-dant or a neighbour on the front porch. By then, of course, we could transmit and receive across the world – as easily as our forefathers made telephone calls – high quality private broad-casts, camclips or films of any event: a journey, a conference, a family reunion. For the running cost of a highly efficient light bulb, we could Livepicture our lounges or bedrooms with streamed views of Mars, Himalayan pandas, an Australian termite colony, a Red Sea coral reef, a Bangkok brothel, the latest volcanic eruption, Fifth Avenue or Tiananmen Square pedestrians, views from a friend's lounge or bedroom, Tokyo stock market transactions, abstract art images, and so on.

In our homes, no change has been more evident than the use of wallscreens, but there have been many other not so spectacular (!) developments. Houses are far more energy efficient than they ever used to be, and I'm sure – no, I'm more than sure, I'm certain, because Lizette told me often enough – the materials for house construction, furbishing and decorating have changed a lot (s-glass is an obvious change, and now z-glass), but not so that you would necessarily notice. Lots of gadgets have come and gone and come again. My personal favourite was the bath/shower thermostat that guaranteed a regular water temperature every time without fuss or fiddling. I first experienced them in hotels, but, unless you remained several days, there was no benefit since it took effort to calibrate the controls. I didn't have one in my own home until we moved into the Oldwijkgaarten house. I could also mention the major changes in food packaging (one of Lizette's favourite topics), but I'm already spending too long on this deviation. What we do not have today, despite 20th century fiction implying we would, is domestic robots. Most regular tasks around the house or garden are too complicated by far, and can be done much more efficiently by humans. Besides, we enjoy many of them; and they can provide welcome relief from sedentary occupations.

After several decades of increasing wealth during the latter part of the 20th century, the developed countries went on getting richer in the first half of the 21st century, and so we had more money and time for leisure. Nevertheless, I don't believe this century has given us anything truly new or important in terms of leisure. In the 1990s, the internet had already created international gaming communities, and it was only an extension of this that led to the gaming pubs which I used to frequent (unwillingly) in the 10s and 20s with my buds. Already by the end of the last century there was no corner of the globe left unexplored by intrepid tourists, and there was no action sport or adventure not available to those with the right amount of foolishness and money. As for virtual reality 'trips' into the so-called Matrix world, it soon became clear that very few of us wanted to sit around with goggles on all day, especially when the real world is so exciting as it is.

It is true that movie holidays did not take off until the 20s but they were no more than a repackaging of the kinds of experiences you could buy at adventure complexes, such as Disneyworld, and later Dracula Park, Bride's Galaxy, The Wild

West, or on adventure tours (white water rafting, skyscraper climbing and game park trekking come to mind). I remember discussing this fad with my father Tom once. We had gone to a guzzleshop after seeing Pacciotti's glorious bio-flick *Garibaldi*. This must have been in the early 30s, for it was not long after our trip to Malta. Tom was so taken with the film and Vincent Mallow's performance as the Italian hero that he mused on whether he would be able to buy a Garibaldi holiday. Then he wondered if he would prefer to re-enact being the first real (as opposed to fictional) astronaut on the moon (Neil Armstrong), or the first (fictional) spaceman to encounter extraterrestrial life as in the film *Planet Sister*.

For my part, I confessed that if I were forced to take a movie holiday I would want to be Manuel from the film *Trumpet Boy*. I said I would choose the scene where, having defeated the evil Reefland dictator, Manuel walks proudly into the main government building to address the country's parliament. Although all the establishment cronies are sniggering and joking, for they expect Manuel to act and talk without maturity, he wins them over with a powerful speech full of traditional ideals and practical suggestions for how to achieve them.

A year after this conversation, Tom sent me a camclip of himself as Garibaldi, kitted out in red shirt, scabbard and beard – which was a shock because I had never seen him with more than two day's stubble. With him was a band of compatriots apparently engaged in a gun fight along the length of a Palermo back street. An attached note said: 'Didn't fancy having to wear a spacesuit, and, in any case, Fragrance hates all that space stuff.'

Finally, to finish off this digression, the only major innovation in terms of citizenship that springs to mind is the electronic identicard. The European Union introduced a standard format in the 20s and this lead to a huge civil rights campaign in Britain and elsewhere. It was not until the late 20s, when faced with chronic and acute immigration problems, rising crime trends and the spasmodic chaos caused by First Tuesday Movement activities, that the Union began to enforce their use. By this time, identicards also had the ability to hold a vast amount of additional private information, such as medical records, emergency telephones numbers, photos, written/voice signatures, Galileo position coordinates, all of which were usefully accessible to the card-holder through his/her individual access codes.

Over time, it has been shown, by research and public acceptance, that carefully-planned and regulated identicards provide, for society as a whole and individuals, far more advantages than disadvantages. Civil liberties may have been breached in many well-publicised cases, but the debate is no longer over whether we should have identicards, but whether one day the United Nations should agree on a basic harmo-nised – and, obviously, voluntary for the time being – format which could replace passports. Such discussions are part of the ongoing New Century Mandate, agreed at the 2095 sum-mit in Geneva (celebrating the UN's 150 year anniversary), which, by further strengthening the UN system, aims to maintain the momentum created during the last quarter century of peace

I stress that this brief and flawed analysis is only valid from my perspective as a citizen in Holland and England. I understand only too well from a lifetime of business errands to every corner of the world that many of the major innova-tions and advances in the 20th century, so significant and life-enhancing in the developed countries, did not touch many in the developing world until the 21st century, with many more impoverished, ill and hungry yet to benefit. Thus a Brazilian or Nigerian or Chinese individual the same age as me might believe his world had changed far more during this century than it would have done had he had lived in the previous one.

When I think forward towards the next century, I am full of hope, but it is not a hope that paradise can be found tomor-row if only the right beliefs or policies are pursued. I believe history has shown clearly enough how idealism, whether religious or political, can be so very dangerous if not tempered with realistic expectations and a firm commitment to peaceful, humanitarian and sustainable principles. Nor do I dare hope that war or plague or famine will vanish, for they will not; nor do I hope that all men and women will suddenly take on a Zen-like calm and be more happy, for they will not. No, my simple (and wobbly) hope is based on only two cornerstones: one political and one religious.

The starting point for my hopes is the United Nations. Despite, or because of, the Jihad Wars the UN is far stronger today than it was 100 years ago. It has its own army with the authority to intervene in sovereign states in a few well-defined circumstances; a plethora of powerful and improving institutions which effectively redistribute five or six times as much wealth as they did in the late 20th century; a rudimentary justice system that may well be able, in the near future, to regulate aid, competition, trade and environmental issues fairly and effectively; and well-equipped and funded emergency response teams to deal with sudden disasters. Moreover, the New Century Mandate appears to demonstrate that all the fine words from the world's major regional groupings about further strengthening the UN will be translated into action – eventually.

The other foundation for my hopes is the Church of Moral Atheism. I would not have said this in the mid-80s when I retired, and when the Church was largely confined to the Notek and other alternative communities. But since then it has swept through Europe and the Far East, attracting millions of adherents, many of them writers, artists and intellectuals. Catholic and Muslim religious fervour is as strong today in parts of the world as it was prior to the First Jihad War, but now that non-religious social and political intellectual leaders have an alternative to offer those needing religious-type passion or wanting religious-type guidance, it is possible to believe that the Church of Moral Atheism might forge a new way for man to mould his future.

I must stop, I am in danger of preaching, which is certainly not in my nature.

CHAPTER 39

IN WHICH I LIVE HAPPILY AND PEACEFULLY

Jay is in excellent spirits. All is well in his relationship with Vince. There were reasons, personal to Vince which I shall not go into, which led him astray. It is possible, Jay says, they may 'reaffirm' their marriage vows next year, on the tenth anniversary of their wedding. Normally, Jay is careful not to talk about the future, and especially not 'next year'. I wouldn't mind, but he thinks it would be tactless. On this occasion, though, his enthusiasm got the better of him, so I was tactful and did not say 'I'm sorry, I won't be able to come'. If I had, he would not have taken it as an offhand quip, a joke, a way of dissipating the ever-present tension about my death date. Instead he would have apologised – three times.

During his visit this morning, he cleared up the Chintz mystery. One of the other nurses, whom he chats to now and then, told him Chintz has a strict policy with patients who have signed up for a deathday: exactly three months before the day, she closes up, shuts herself off emotionally. It's the only way she can cope, or so her colleague told Jay.

***

As I've already commented, there is not much left to say about my own life. Lizette went through a tough period in the mid-80s. It began with a work row, in 2083, over plans for one specific area of future research efforts. The department head, Sidney Jensen, had taken a neutral stance, leaving Lizette in dispute with Olive Norrington.

One Sunday, Olive and her partner Marcella – a senior lecturer in psychology, and named, I presume, after the movie heroine – had come for lunch at Taunton House. It was already late in the afternoon, and we had all been drinking. I was showing Marcella some 19th century photographs through Portia, when an explosive argument between Lizette and Olive erupted in the other room. It stopped abruptly. Olive shouted through the house to Marcella that she was leaving, and we heard the front door slam. Marcella collected her things, apologised, and raced off after her friend. This argument, or whatever had caused it, left Lizette moody for weeks, but she would not talk about it.

By the end of the year, Lizette had begun to consider leaving Surrey University. In the spring she told me there was a job vacancy at her old college, the Farnborough Science University which, having closed during the Grey Years, was up and running again. It would mean, she said, the end of her research career but a comfortable few years stoking her retirement funds. She also, finally, explained a few details about the departmental row, admitting that Olive had been in the right all along. In May 2084, Lizette informed me she would be starting at Farnborough in October. This was not a moment too soon, since Sydney was about to retire as head of the department at Surrey University, and Olive would be taking over.

I semi-retired from my duties at The Josephine Collection immediately after the launch of Portia, in February 2086, and then fully retired in December the same year. The staff organised a party at Farmer King's, a newly opened zini bar in the next street, to which both Jay and Lizette came. I was fêted with presents and mini-speeches. The night before, at a private supper in her apartment, Josephine had given me the most astonishing gift: an original Marc Ferrez photograph of Copacabana beach, wild and undeveloped. It was housed in a Perfect Frame, meaning I could hang it on a wall without having to worry about damage from light, humidity or heat conditions. It must have cost her well over ten thousand euros. When I tried to express my thanks, Josephine dismissed them saying the gift was only 'a very small token' of her gratitude for my contribution to the Project. I put it in a prominent position on a wall in the office at Taunton House (replacing an over-sized reproduction of Le Gray's *Garibaldi* which moved into storage).

The following year, 2087, was the year the world held its breath, as it were, while the caldera in Yellowstone Park,

United States, growled more loudly than it had ever done before. It was also the year Great Britain won the football World Cup for the first time in more than 100 years (alas I'm still waiting for GB to win any volleyball cup), and our neighbour, Sami, smashed the international record for a marrow size. According to Guinness World Records, the heaviest marrow was 55.1 kilograms, and Sami's was over 56 kilograms.

I had been invited to inspect his specimens in early September, while the vegetables were still growing. He rattled off a list of weights and sizes, which I thought were village records. When he tucked a special set of scales under the largest of his marrows, and confided a dream that he might beat the world record, I thought he'd gone loopy. A few weeks later, the very same specimen hit the headlines. Journalists began arriving in their hoards, parking their strange vehicles in our lane, and coming to us and other near neighbours for additional comments and colour. Iona pranced around the village as if she were a queen, and, no doubt, dreamed Sami's marrow would give her more than 15 minutes of fame. Lizette, who had never liked the woman but tolerated her because I was Sami's patient (he was treating rheumatoid arthritis in other parts of my body by this time), began to loathe her. Fortunately, their brief celebrity status left Sami and Iona with such a long list of potential dinner party acquaintances that we were no longer in demand. By 2089, they had moved, to a bigger house in socially-upmarket Hambledon.

My life during the later years of the decade – it seems like yesterday – was not only happy (apart from the deaths of friends) but peaceful. The happiness came from being with Lizette. Our partnership, nearly 20 years old by this time, was a rich one, full of enjoyment in each other's company and many shared pleasures – not least 'affection, tenderness and other pleasant things'. Lizette did have a sporadic tendency towards depression, and could be demanding at times, yet I never sensed or believed these difficulties were caused by me. Indeed, the reverse was true. She made it seem as though I helped her through the bad times, that I was a rock onto which she clung temporarily during the storms. In consequence, I always felt wanted, needed, loved.

And the peacefulness came from the fact, I suppose, that I did adjust to a routine without deadlines or meetings or responsibilities, my tenure with Josephine having served well to ease me into full retirement. Not that my involvement with The Josephine Collection terminated the day of my retirement. As an unpaid non-executive director, I sat on one of the advisory boards, which convened every quarter. Moreover, at Josephine's initiative, she and I met once a month for lunch. Less often, I saw others from the museum, usually Giselle or Belinda, who had become a highly competent administrator. In addition, there were certain photo-world individuals – Arnold Cowerbridge for one, and Max Voll for another – who considered me a friend and, when in London, would invite me for a meal or to join them at a gallery or auction.

I visited Jude Singleton, who had reluctantly entered a sunset hospice – not dissimilar to this one – and had opted for a medical regime leading to a deathday 18 months hence. But I think she made a mistake in telling everyone, for it made contact with her near the end awkward. I found saying goodbye on my last visit a very unnerving experience: I could not find the words, emotions, or actions to equal the occasion. One day, perhaps, when our society has become more comfortable with the notion of death, those of us with planned death dates will be able to have our parties before lights out, not after.

At Taunton House, we continued to receive guests regularly. Jay, who had taken a job teaching in London, visited fortnightly, sometimes with a friend; and during school holidays would stay for several days at a time. I enjoyed having him around, he was helpful and companionable. Already by this stage he had begun to take on a paternal role with me, worrying about my health and prompting me to do more exercise or to try a newly marketed Chinese remedy for arthritis. He was less comfortable with his mother who, on occasions, would still let loose flurries of criticism. They originated not so much out of disappointment with him, I came to understand, but out of a deep-seated inability to let herself accept the situation, because it would be wrong to do so. From what I learned about Mervyn Sanderson, her Pa, I suspect this tendency came from him through a combination of genes and the domestic environment which he dominated.

And now from preaching it appears I've moved on to psychoanalysis, which suits my writing disposition no better.

Horace continued to stop over on his way back to Southampton. Tim had died in 2084, leaving Horace devastated, uncared for and lonely. He appeared to lose all of his ebullience over night, as if he had been waiting for an excuse not to go on performing; and, at the same time, he developed a form of senile dementia. A doctor took nine months to find adequate medication. He became maudlin too, and would hark back to his youth and our days at Witley Academic.

Then, in 2086, urged on by his publisher, he completed a second book. It was published under the title *Uncommon Times* and promoted as 'a companion volume' to *Reflections of a Political Lightweight*; but it revealed nothing different or new. Consequently, the media ignored it, and this vexed Horace more than the meagre sales that followed. He hired a driver/assistant at his own expense and went on a gruelling book signing tour.

Less than halfway through, at a literary-arcade in Exeter, he was seated at a table with his books piled high, waiting for customers, when a stroke saved him from any further embarrassment. He died the same day. His body was brought back to Southampton. One of Tim's children who lived not too far away and suffered his uncle better than others, organised the funeral. Horace would have been disappointed at the turnout. Too many of his friends had already died, and, others, especially those in the Progressive Party and other Conservative Alliance parties, had been alienated by his scandal-rich autobiography. I couldn't help wishing he had made it to 50 years as an MP, for the achievement might have given the media more to focus on in their obituaries than the secret affair with Terrance Spoon.

Our other guests at Taunton House were mostly Lizette's family and friends. Mercurio kept up his annual ritual, although age forced him to relinquish the bicycle for a car – 'the scourge of post-Victorian man' – adapted to Notek standards. Samuel and Lynn visited too. Gratifyingly, they often talked about how much they had enjoyed the experience in Peru. If they had been any younger, they both said, they might have taken another contract. We also saw Irene Sanderson, Lizette's niece, for she lived in south London, and would drop in to visit before or after an ice skating excursion to the sports complex in Guildford. She was curious about our interests, following Lizette into the garden to ask questions about the fuchsia varieties, or browsing with me through old photographs on Neil. When Lizette and I began taking mini-tours, she was full of advice: beforehand, on what to look out for; and, afterwards, on what we had missed. We never saw Saul and his family, or Mahonia, who had married an architect, given birth to twins and moved to the Shetland Islands.

Nor did we have any contact with Esos, although Mercurio kept us informed of his news. He moved for a while to a Notek community in Denmark, but, after three years, returned to Pembrokeshire. He is still there, at Stackpole Haven, with his father. Yewla showed up a couple of times at Taunton House, once when Mercurio was there; they argued the whole time. He hated that she had left the community and that she was happy working in the real world, for a company which made children's broadcast programmes. However, they must have patched up their relationship for, when the two of them came here to Willow Calm Lodge some months ago, they demonstrated a good rapport.

Having brought me a beautiful bunch of lemon yellow roses and sunset gladioli, however, they did have one argument – I couldn't tell whether it was testy or tongue-in-cheek – about the glittery vase on the windowsill: Yewla loved it, Mercurio hated it. I didn't dare tell them why it was there.

Although much in tune with the bright and tacky end-of-the-century fashion, I think it's a ghastly thing in itself, forever trying to upstage the flowers that it holds, sometimes succeeding, sometimes not, yet how can I help but love it.

Mercurio looked very weathered, but retained an impish look around the eyes. Yewla was pregnant, visibly so, and, therefore, must have been with child already when she visited with Irene a couple of months earlier.

As for Lizette's friends, I would say we saw Rhoda too often. She had retired, but rather than taking retirement as an opportunity to slow down, she speeded up. She was one of these middle-aged women who dress up and make up as though they were 40 not 60, and who not only delay the onset of the menopause with pills but deny it forever with self-psychology. She was always on the move, searching for a new man. I've no idea why she thought she would find one at Taunton House. Jay said she was a typical Maysie – middle-aged young, single, independent and exciting. By contrast we did not see Pete and Clarity often enough. By the mid-80s, Pete's health was poor. Since he refused to travel, and Clarity would not leave him on his own, Lizette and I made the trip north once a year, usually in the summer.

In the late 80s I lost Peter de Roo and his wife Livia. Livia went first, in 2089. I travelled to near Leiden for the funeral, sad at Livia's death, but looking forward to seeing Peter. But he was a shadow of his former self, with grey skin, and a rake-thin and stooped body. Rudy played a beautiful tune on his sax – apparently Livia's favourite – at the funeral, and Ulla spoke some words I could not hear for her sobbing. Four months later, I returned for Peter's funeral, which was less depressing, probably because Guido was there.

After the funeral, we spent a nostalgic evening with Rudy and Ulla and a few others at Rudy's house in Amsterdam. The next day, Guido and I together went to the old Oostlander family house in Utrecht to visit Dominique and Waltar, who were relatively fit and active (still are, I hope), to catch up on their news and the progress of their children. I hoped Guido would return with me to England for a few days, but he was obliged to fly straight back to Quito.

The peace of my retirement years was regularly punctuated by bad news. Barely a month went by without my finding an obituary of someone I knew. I became so accustomed to the idea of past friends and acquaintances dying that I regularly checked two obituary netsites, one dedicated to United Nations staff and the other focused on international politicians. The names and biographies triggered memories, and led me into reflecting back over my working life in a way I had not done before. Otherwise, I continued to play bowls in Tilford, once a week usually, but never very well. I became friendly with a handful of other players, and would stroll home with one or another of them for a drink and a chat.

I also continued trying to work my way through a teach-yourself bridge course. I would sit in front of the screen and play demonstration hands with three very attractive photo-constructed young ladies (I could choose from hundreds of composites), and the games would proceed as slowly or as fast as I wished. At any time I could stop the game, ask for hints or explanations; or I could instruct the screen to intervene whenever I played below a certain standard. I could even set one of a dozen styles of cross-table banter – which had a higher humour content than I ever encountered playing bridge for real. But learning was a pain: I could never recall what cards had been played and, however odd it might sound to others (and to Lizette), whenever I made a mistake, I could hear my father Tom calling me a 'stupid idiot' as clearly as if he were one of the players onscreen.

While Lizette continued to work, my life was relatively quiet. Somewhat whimsically, I called this period my yoga and yeast years. Jay teased me, saying if I lived any longer I'd turn into a Notek. The idea irritated Lizette, which may have been Jay's objective, but I found it intriguing, flattering almost, as though there were more to my personality than I had realised.

I had Sami to thank for the yoga. He suggested I take up the discipline soon after installing my new ankle, but I ignored his advice. Then, as the arthritis progressed, he urged me further to consider yoga as a natural way of keeping my joints as supple as possible for as long as possible. With the right commitment (ten minutes every day permanently), he said, I might need less pills to control the pain and keep me mobile. He directed me to a tailor-made course of exercises – onscreen, and demonstrated by an elderly man, not unlike me, with movements restricted in the same way as my own. Daily practice was laborious initially but, after about three months, the exercises had become as much part of my daily routine as breakfast, watching the news, or preparing a pot of Ceylon tea for Lizette on her return from work.

And I had Jay to thank for teaching me how to make bread, a skill he picked up in Cumbria, and for finding a shop nearby which sold fresh yeast, without which the process would not have been so satisfying. I liked that I could conjure up breakfast baps or olive bread with very little cost in terms of time or money; and, besides, kneading dough was good exercise for my fingers.

Apart from the trips to London, the visitors, the bowls, the yoga and the yeast, and the onscreen auctions, there was plenty to read – I was partial to biographies at this time – and I spent a fair amount of time listening to and extending my classical music collection. I also became attached to Alan's clinic in Bangladesh. As a significant donor, I was sent regular reports on its activities and budgets; and the administrative staff were friendly and forthcoming whenever I called by camphone.

CHAPTER 40
ALICIA TELLS HER STORY

Alicia has now met up with both Jay and Guido; and, Mireille and Guido have spent time with Jay and Vince. They all get on, or so they say, and intend to stay in touch. Mireille and Guido are coming tomorrow for the last time.

Alicia visited a couple of days ago and told me more of her story. She grew up at Arturo's ranch in Goiânia, accepting that her natural mother, Edna, had died during childbirth, and loving first Luz and then Fatima as her own mother. But as brothers and sisters came along, Ignacio, Juliano and then Tina, her own position in the family became more tense: Arturo seemed to be permanently angry with her, and Fatima was too weak not to be prejudiced towards her own children. Alicia, like 'Cinderella' (her own description), was given far less spending money than her siblings, she was taken fewer places, and was given endless chores.

At 14 she ran away, to Rio, and became a night club prostitute. She avoided the drugs trap and was lucky with friends, and was especially thankful to a man called Rodrigo whom she called São Rodrigo – 'without him I would have been washed away in the Rio sewers'. In time, she gravitated towards the safer and more lucrative call girl scene. At the age of 17, she decided to make a journey home. It took a while to find her family because they had moved to São Paulo – this was about three years before Lizette and I went to South America. On day one she was welcomed as 'a prodigal daughter'. On day two, though, she had a violent argument with her father. A fish tank got broken, and she stamped on one of the fish floundering in a puddle on the marble floor. Arturo lost his temper and told Alicia the truth: she was a clone, and Edna was nobody, just a girl he had married for fun, who died from a drug overdose.

The news devastated Alicia. Immediately, she ran away again, back to Rio where not even São Rodrigo could comfort her. She felt 'worthless', like a 'freak', like 'nothing at all'. She told me she had known a few clones in Rio and they had all been 'messed up, more messed up than everyone else', and some had died very young. As a child she had seen documentaries about the terrible things that had happened to children cloned in Brazil – especially female clones from a male parent – and, although she saw other films and read books that showed how most clones were healthy, she gave more credence to the bad stories than the good.

She decided to run further away, to Los Angeles. There she hitched up with a charity group ostensibly aimed at helping cloned individuals integrate themselves into society. This particular organisation attracted her and other foreigners because it offered not only clone counselling but help with work and residency permits. Alicia got sucked in for a while, until she realised it was a clearing house for slaves. All the instruction and help came with a persistent message: you are nothing, therefore expect nothing but be grateful for any mercies. After six weeks, she was offered a poorly-paid job as a domestic servant in the household of a rich Mexican family in Baja California, 300 kilometres from Los Angeles. She was pressed to sign a contract which committed her to the job for five years. She refused. The organisation threw her onto the street. She went back into prostitution, this time with as many chemicals in her blood system as she could get her hands on. More and more she came to believe all the clonist media hype, and expected to die at any time, from a defective organ, a failure to resist a virus, or from an overdose, because she was not psychologically strong enough to be alive.

***

While Alicia sat by the bed telling me this story, she appeared to grow more calm and self-confident. It was as though she was not telling me about herself, but about someone who had been in her care, someone she had cared for and guided to safety. Some of the time, when she was talking or responding to my questions, she took hold of my hand, as if it were me she were trying to lead to untroubled waters. She has promised to come again in two days time.

Tomorrow is the day I must say goodbye to Mireille and Guido. They do not know about my deathday. Outside of this hospice, only Jay knows I have scheduled my death. It was distressing enough to decide on a definite limit to my own lifetime, but then I had to make a decision about who to tell and who not to tell. My overriding aim was, and is, to give friends and family the minimum amount of sorrow, both before and after my death.

To begin with, I considered whether I should tell Jay. After Lizette's departure he became my closest friend, and then my carer. I honestly did not believe his behaviour towards me would alter in any significant way if I told him. Indeed, having made up my own mind and before finally signing the papers, I discussed the idea with him in some detail. He objected vehemently – as any loving son would – using practical and emotional arguments, not least that such a course would be unfair to those who loved me. But anyone who loved me, I responded (trying to match Jay's tone) would respect my decision. It boils down to quantity versus quality, I concluded. I'd prefer to enjoy the days and weeks left to me than have extra time just to be a spectator at my own mental decay show. In time, he accepted my decision, albeit grudgingly and under pressure – as any loving son would. I am sure this was the right approach with Jay. He may have become slightly more over-attentive and condescending, especially as time is now running out, but, if I hadn't told him, he would have been very deeply hurt afterwards.

With Guido, my closest relative apart from Jay and my only living natural son, it is not the same. He may be pained when he discovers my deception, and then feel guilt at not having found more time to spend with me in recent years. But I am planning to speak to him by camphone on 30 or 31 January, and then, within an hour of my death, he will receive a letter. I have already written this letter, and Jay will organise its delivery. If I should die prematurely, then Jay will act accordingly. In any case, Guido will know from these Reflections that I believed it for the best to act in this way. It would have been an excruciating experience to have him, with or without Mireille, here for days or weeks prior to the end – excruciating for him and for me. We have been apart too long, and there is no easy rapport between us, as there was a long time ago when we worked together on *Ginquin*, which would see us through the anti-drama of hours and minutes ticking away towards the final moment, the moment when I let the paradise poison-soaked disc of rice-paper melt slowly on my tongue.

Having sorted out my own mind with regard to Guido, it was clear that I would not tell anyone else either. But that was before Alicia. Such is my sudden and deep affection for her, and her apparent affection for me, we are as father and daughter, once estranged and now together.

This last chapter, these last few pages, seem to be transforming themselves into a kind of diary which is definitely not my intention. Perhaps I am losing my ability to concentrate, or perhaps I simply do not have much to say about these final years of my life.

***

Guido and Mireille, who departed yesterday, gave me all the news from Paris, mostly about the Rocard family (several distant relations of Mireille have become famous or infamous), but also about Guido's relations on Diana's side and his friend Rudy. They described their own plans for a centennial eve theatrical extravaganza in Plaza Chica, Quito, which they are to host, and which is to be given a major live broadcast. Guido promised to email me the relevant net details and times, and I promised to tune in; and when he went out to the loo, Mireille whispered (to imply she was telling me a confidence) that Guido was secretly planning to deliver, live on air, a special message for me close to midnight Ecuador time. There are not many presents you can give a 100 year old man who has no possessions other than those stored (in a room at Jay's house) and waiting to be distributed to his heirs, and who rarely leaves his bed – but that might be one.

When Guido and Mireille walked out of the room, both of them smiled. They were confident of seeing me again – which is for the best. I felt sad, very sad for a few minutes, and then, astonishingly, I caught myself thinking of Alicia, and feeling happy again. This fickleness of human nature, in others and in me, never ceases to amaze.

***

Alicia, who came this morning, continued her story as follows. In 2077, she fell pregnant and aborted the foetus without a second thought. But, thereafter, she could not stop wondering about being fertile. It gave her a fresh perspective on herself, one which included, for the first time in years, a sliver of pride. She began to believe that if she could give birth to a normal child, she could be normal herself. She weaned herself off the drugs, and chose her clients more carefully. And then, when the time was right, deliberately avoided contraception with one handsome regular client. When a pregnancy was confirmed, she packed her bags and flew to Lisbon to start a new life. Since she had managed to stay in the United States for over two years on the back of a month's visa, she hoped Portugal would pose no problem. And it didn't. Within weeks she had found a man, João, a carpenter, who wanted to marry, despite her condition.

When I nodded slightly, Alicia stopped and asked me why. I began to explain about how Lizette was already pregnant with Jay when we fell in love. But, having talked at length with Jay, Alicia already knew this.

'I'd like it to be the same, but it's not is it? I was desperate and I cheated my way into João's heart before telling him the truth. I had too many tricks. With you and Lizette it was different, no? An accident of fate? I was not an accident of fate, and nor was Angela.'

'But João didn't mind. You are together still, so the marriage must have worked.'

'I owed him too much. It had to work. I could never want anything different. Yes, I love him and he loves me. It was not easy. I thought Angela would be the end of my problems, and I would feel good again, as I did when I was a girl. I planned to go back to Brazil for a holiday with João and Angela, but I couldn't. I hated Arturo too much. I told myself, over and over, I'm normal, I'm normal. And then I discovered I was afraid again. This time not for me, but Angela. She wasn't a healthy baby and I kept thinking it was my fault. One day I was worried about her heart, the next about her liver, and then about her brain. I was – what do you say – a hypochondriac about her. João wanted a child of his own. I wanted one too – at first. But then this fear came, and I couldn't do it, I couldn't have another one. My unhappy João. He took me to doctors, and persuaded me to join another organisation to help clones, a proper one this time, but I couldn't change what was in my head.'

She paused here. During our previous encounters she had looked at me hesitantly, but now she gazed at me intently as if trying to discover who was behind my eyes. It was such a strange moment, I don't think any girl – Popsicle comes to mind – had done this to me since my student days.

Feeling abashed, I broke the silence: 'You'd been through such a lot, it's not hard to understand.'

'It wasn't only that I was a clone, but how I'd lived, what I'd done.'

I could think of nothing to say, so we sat there silently for a few moments. Then, all of a sudden, she flicked to life, with a warm happy smile filling her face. She told me about her life with João and Angela, about how she trained to become a tour guide for American tourists, travelling up and down the Douro river twice a week, and spending more time in port wine lodges than with her husband. And she told me how João became an artisan earning good money from making tables and desks to order. Angela filled out as a teenager, became healthier, grew taller than both Alicia herself and João, went to university, fell in love and gave birth to Renato.

'I never wanted her to get serious with a guy so quickly. I never pressed her to marry or have children. I didn't push my troubles onto her; she understood about my background, but not about the fears in my head. She went that way. She's an apple pie girl – not complicated. She cooks and shops and goes to the beach. She finished university with a degree in business, and was working in a big store. Now she'll go back in six months, when Renato's one year old.'

At this point, Alicia used my screen to access her private memory store so as to show me a collection of camclips and camstills of her family. When she pointed out Angela's husband, Quasim, I asked what he did for a living.

'Quasim. He's lovely. His parents are Moroccan. They run a large fruit and vegetable import company. Quasim works there part-time, but he's studying to be a town traffic planner. In one year, he'll be qualified. It is a good profession, it pays well, but if he gets a job, it might be a long way from Porto. We'll see.'

'Won't you mind?'

'Yes, of course, but things are changing for me too. My fear has gone. It's why I am here. After Renato was born, I went back to Brazil. With João. We tracked down my brothers and sisters, and this is how I found you. Tina had only just returned from London. This is not all. I have one more thing to tell you.' She leaned over and kissed me on the cheek, then took hold of my hand and said: 'I'm pregnant myself – nearly three months – with a boy.'

'Oh, how wonderful.' I am not very good at communicating on an emotional level, but I felt elated. 'João must be a very happy man.'

'He is. We are. And you know what's so strange? It happened in Brazil.'

A nurse interrupted us to make a routine check on my monitoring equipment, to remind me to take my pills (which I

had forgotten), and to forewarn me that my lunch tray –
salmon trifle and spinach wafers – was waiting.

'I should go,' Alicia said, 'I will check times with Jay and be
back tomorrow or the day after.'

'I'll look forward to it.'

'It's good news, my Grandad, is it not? By July, you'll have
another great grandchild. A boy. I'll bring him to see you, in
September or October, I promise.'

CHAPTER 41

IN WHICH I PLAY BRIDGE WITH LIZETTE

Lizette retired from her academic career in July 2090. The Farnborough University gave a splendid party, to which several of her past Surrey University colleagues were also invited. Sydney Jensen was there with a strange-looking woman who Lizette said was his sister. He had recently published a book on the history of the use of plastic materials in the transport industry – we had a copy in the house. Olive and Marcella were there too. Despite not having seen them for several years, we fell easily into a friendly banter, which, on this occasion focused on the writer Gregory. He had died a few months earlier, and the publicity had led me to seek out some of his books. Marcella hated him and his ideas. She called them pop psycho-history, and claimed they were nothing more than a concoction of bubbles and sugar.

There were plenty of young people there too, and it felt good to hear from them that Lizette had been a fine teacher and popular. One of her colleagues, an overweight middle-age woman called Jane, who had been at the university ever since Lizette first worked there (having been laid off when it closed and then re-employed), was half-glossy and outspoken. She said this to me: 'I don't know why she ever went back to research, she is such a talented teacher.'

On the way home, when I enquired about her, I discovered Jane was none other than Lizette's bête noire, the most troublesome person in her department, the one she referred to as 'Findzinski' or 'that Findzinski woman'. So then I quoted what she'd said, about Lizette being a 'talented teacher'. It was part of a pattern in our behaviour: she over-impressed by science and scientific discovery and undervaluing the job of teaching, and me arguing that education was as useful to society as science, if not more so. I thought I had partly won this battle when she went back to Farnborough, yet she could never rid herself of the idea that teaching was a job of secondary importance. I wish she had known my mother, Julie or, better yet, my grandmother Eileen.

Lizette planned to pursue several interests in her retirement, all of which involved me. I did suggest she might want to try wearing whites and playing bowls, but I never had as much success in persuading Lizette to share my interests as she did in coaxing me to share hers. There was the garden. We did a lot of digging, planting, potting, mulching, weeding; we browsed books, many of them from the 20th century – Lizette had a special fondness for the David Hessayon classsics – and netsites; and we made regular expeditions to the Royal Horticultural Society gardens at Wisley.

There was also the bridge. Lizette had always been an aficionado. It was a family pastime, and we played when together with Samuel and his wife; Mercurio too enjoyed a game. In Brussels, Lizette had indulged twice a week. When we moved to Taunton House, she played only occasionally with friends, until, that is, she switched to Surrey University where she found a thriving bridge club. Once every few months, I was taken along for a 'social'. Then, with a playing partner, she joined the larger and more serious Guildford Bridge Club and rarely missed a Thursday evening session, when competitions were played. I was rarely required. In retirement, though, she decided that she wanted to spend more time at the club, and so every Tuesday afternoon she and I played together informally against other mixed ability couples. It was fun, at times. We met some interesting and some not so interesting people.

This is when Lizette began to employ me as a social crutch – I don't know how else to put it. She had always been proud of my achievements, particularly my career at the IFSD. To my knowledge, though, she had never boasted about me to friends or acquaintances, as she began to do at the bridge club during those Tuesday afternoon sessions.

Lizette's other burning interest was to visit parts of Europe she had never seen. Thus, for about three years, we embarked on a series of expensive, comfortable and well-organised mini-tours, lasting no more than three or four days each. Among other places, we visited Bergen, Corfu, Helsinki, Kiev, Linz,

Porto, Rome and Zagreb, most of which I'd been to on business but not as a tourist. Some of our trips were arranged to coincide with bridge conventions. Lizette's playing partner, a woman called Carla Rawlins, would travel separately. While Lizette played with her in the formal tournaments, I would either watch or take in a few historical or cultural sights alone. On these trips, whether purely for tourism or for bridge, we met many people, and Lizette's incessant need to brag about me became a constant pain.

It was an incremental process. In the beginning, Lizette would use the chit-chat sessions at the bridge club to explain that I had been not only 'a UN official', which was how I described my past career to strangers, but a 'very important UN official'. I guessed she was trying to make up for my inadequate card play, about which I felt, if not guilty, then censurable. Within a few months, though, she had progressed to introducing me as if I was the most important UN official on the planet – never mind that I had retired 20 years earlier and that I had failed at director-general level. If this did not impress, she would move on to elaborate other achievements of mine, by mentioning REACH or The Josephine Collection.

I began to worry there might be more to her behaviour than a crude attempt to compensate for my bridge skills. I wondered, for example, if she was embarrassed by my age. I thought to broach the subject with her but cowardice prevailed: I was painfully aware that, over the years, she and I both had often derided our ex-neighbour Iona, Sami's wife, for precisely the same kind of self-aggrandisement talk.

About 18 months after Lizette's retirement, Jay saved me, us, from this ridiculous predicament. I confided in him about my growing discomfort in going places with Lizette. Speculatively, he suggested that the behaviour trait might be connected with her depression. I had not detected any unusual symptoms of depression, nor had she mentioned any. A different person might have quizzed his son for more details, but I was reluctant to admit my ignorance, a habit acquired from too many years in meetings and negotiations. I did ask

Jay if he might be able to persuade Lizette to see a doctor or psycho-counsellor. She didn't trust his opinions on anything, he commented, but he promised to try.

One weekend, and without any apparent immediate cause, Lizette announced she had been feeling depressed and had booked an appointment with her local doctor, for whom she had much respect. When I probed gently, she refused to discuss the subject any further.

A week later, in the afternoon, Lizette came into the lounge where I was snoozing on the long sofa. She woke me gently, sat down by my side, snuggled up to my shoulder, all soft and giving, and curled her arm through mine.

'Have I been a pain?' I shrugged my shoulders. 'It's like I've been charging around through a fog trying to find something, or get somewhere. It's hard to explain. But I can think clearer now. The doctor gave me Chalaminth, only a mild dose for three months. It's working. She said my odd bouts of depression might have been caused by retirement. I had no idea. Did you notice?'

'I didn't know you were depressed, you never said.'

'No, I didn't really know.'

'You mentioned it to Jay.'

'Did I? How have I been difficult?' I could sense her thought processes working. 'How have I been difficult? Why didn't you tell me? You sod.' She mock punched me and I evaded the questions.

Chalaminth was the latest wonder drug, first released in the 80s. I do not pretend to understand how these medicines work, but, because of this one, Lizette developed the self-confidence to reflect on her own behaviour and feelings, and to talk them over with me. At the root of the problem – she worked out – was the fact that she had staked too much of her sense of self and worth as an individual on her work and career. Thus, on retiring suddenly from a near full-time post to nothing, she had become insecure and vulnerable and sought to cover over such feelings with activity.

Having acknowledged the problem, and faced up to it, Lizette slid off the Chalaminth more quickly than her doctor advised. She said she felt much better, more alive, more conscious than she had for months. And, because she became less determinedly busy and less manic, our journeys abroad were more widely spaced, I was hauled off to play bridge less often, and our social intercourse with friends and strangers alike returned to a more measured rhythm.

CHAPTER 42

IN WHICH THERE IS NOT MUCH LEFT OF ME

For about two years, we continued our pleasurable jaunts to Europe. Then, in 2094 Lizette had a horrible fall. We were walking through the botanical garden in Monte Carlo when she fell and broke her left hip. The emergency services were excellent, given the awkwardness of our location, but then we faced tedious administrative delays and other difficulties in organising the flight home. By the time Lizette had recovered from her operation and undertaken months of new joint physiotherapy, she had lost all enthusiasm for further travel.

As I hope I've indicated, Jay remained an important part of my life, a regular visitor to Taunton House. The tension between him and Lizette invariably present to one degree or another until this time, had ebbed and flowed in response to Lizette's moods or Jay's life choices. There was a tense period after he chose to study teaching, and another when he opted for a secondary school post in Ealing, London, teaching pure geography – Lizette wanted him to teach one of the sciences – and yet another when he announced, in October 2090, that he was going to marry Vince Wells, the advertising designer friend we had met several times.

Lizette had accepted Jay's homosexuality better than she had done his teaching career, but she did not condone the idea of gay weddings in general, let alone her son going through with one. Jay claimed then, and still does today, that he married Vince for love, and scorns the idea that he wanted to spite his mother. He knows, however, that I suspect there was an element of filial revolt. Fortunately, Jay and Vince chose to indulge in one of those expensive wedding holidays, to the island of Bermuda, over Christmas that year, thus allowing Lizette to ignore the whole episode. In Jay's defence, I would say he has taken the marriage seriously, and it has lasted longer than many orthodox heterosexual marriages.

Things between Jay and Lizette remained tense and complicated after her retirement more or less until she went on the Chalaminth. Thereafter, we all got on surprisingly well.

And then, after Lizette's accident, Jay began to recognise that Lizette had become old and fragile, and that, like me, she required more help and support. In 2095, Jay won a much sought-after head-of-department position at a well-respected school in Highgate, in north London. It was only a small department, teaching sustainable balance, with three other staff, but Jay was so enthusiastic about the job even Lizette was full of congratulations.

Today, Jay has five staff, and expects to be considered for deputy headmaster within a couple of years. He'll make it. Vince, too, changed jobs in the mid-90s, from advertising (the excitement of which had worn off) to product design; and the two of them bought a pretty Victorian terraced house in Muswell Hill. It had three bedrooms, a backyard and a permanent parking permit. As a house-warming present, Lizette took them six fuchsia plants, ones she had nurtured from cuttings and planted up in attractive glazed Spanish pots. She arranged them on the concrete steps at the back of the yard along a high wall, and she organised the installation of a reliable and automatic watering system. From then on, whenever we went to the Muswell Hill house during spring or early summer, Lizette took a bottle of plant food with which to feed the fuchsias. The last time I went to the house in summer, in 2097, just months before Lizette's death, they were still dripping crimsons, purples, and violets.

I do not wish to dwell on Lizette's illness, which proved the most tortuous time for Lizette and those around her. It began with intestinal ulcers, and progressed towards increasingly serious attacks of peritonitis one of which ultimately killed her. In retrospect, I am far from convinced she had the best treatment. I suspect the first surgical intervention which should have relieved her condition, exacerbated it instead. When we moved, in August 2096, she did switch to a different consultant but, by then, the damage – if my suspicions are correct – had been done. How can we ever know the truth of these things. There are so many cases reported of clear-cut medical malpractice and mistakes, what about those which are not so clear-cut? However sophisticated our equipment has become, doctors are only human.

But how unfair that modern medicine should have kept me in such good relative health to 100 years of age, well past my sell-by date, yet been unable to cope with Lizette's physical and mental deterioration. Lizette, herself, was a saint, there is no other word to describe her. She was stalwart and unselfish; she rarely complained – a characteristic which does not always serve an individual's best interests with the national health service – and she regularly tried to minimise the emotional and practical demands on myself and Jay.

On the practical side, I was no longer able to drive or walk very far so I rarely accompanied her to the surgery or hospital for tests. During the periods when she was hospitalised, I went twice a day by taxi and used a hospital Swifty to negotiate the long corridors to her room. On the emotional side, I loved her too dearly to want to do anything other than talk through every nuance of her illnesses and treatments, and share as much suffering as she allowed.

To my surprise – I confess this freely – Jay demonstrated how much he cared for his mother by visiting often, and making himself as available as possible to act as her chauffeur. Without his help, I don't know how we would have managed our move from Taunton House to a rented bungalow in Finchley, on a street called Meadowland View (but only in the imagination), not far, in fact, from here. The trauma of the move did nothing to ease Lizette's illness, but with my own mobility declining fast, we had no alternative. I guess Jay's readiness to help us out caused strains in his relationship with Vince, and may have led to Vince's first affair. But this is really none of my business, and I am only glad things are working out between them now.

Lizette died a week short of her 79th birthday in October 2097. The funeral service was held at Golders Green Crematorium. Jay made all the arrangements. It was a busy funeral, with a reception held in private rooms at a nearby tavern. I was too distraught to take much part in the proceedings.

Lizette's brothers, Samuel and Mercurio, and Jay all coped well with the social responsibilities. As it happens, it was the last time I saw several members of Lizette's family: Samuel's oldest son Saul, with wife and near grown-up children; Samuel's youngest daughter Mahonia, with husband, also an architect, and twins, not yet architects!; and Mercurio's son Esos, so similar to Mercurio when younger.

I did not expect to remain much in contact with Samuel or Lynn either but, surprisingly, they made an effort to visit me in Meadowland View whenever they were in London. They were among my first visitors here at Willow Calm Lodge; and, since they are planning to come in January (Jay says) they may be among my last. (Which reminds me, I must ask them if they've heard any news of Liam.) After the funeral, I lost touch with Lizette's friends: Clarity and her daughter Joan went on extended sojourns to Kurdistan; and I don't know what happened to Rhoda, but surely she must have grown out of being a Maysie by now.

There was not much left of me after Lizette's death. We had shed an array of things in the move out of Taunton House, but we still had a bungalow full of possessions, many of which were Lizette's. Jay helped me go through them, and make decisions on their distribution or disposal. It was an unpleasant task. Within six months, I had a stroke that left me unable to walk, partially paralysed in my arms, and incontinent. Fortunately – or, as I thought at the time unfortunately – there was no damage to my brain, and I was as conscious of my disabilities as I was of Lizette's absence.

Thus, in the spring of 2098, I went into hospital where three months of treatment stabilised my condition. Then I moved into this hospice which Jay found. After extensive discussions with Dr Lipman, and a talk with Jay, I decided in October, 12 months after Lizette's death, to sign up to a deathday, and to spend my last year writing these Reflections. The journey – inspired by a letter from Lizette and made possible by Jay's unflagging support and Lipman's pill menu –

has been exhausting but rewarding; painful and pleasant by turn, sad and joyful.

In these closing paragraphs, I will resist the temptation to pass any further judgements on myself or my times, with one exception. I have regrets, many of them to do with Crystal and Bronze, but there are other, lesser ones, such as not having gone to St Petersburg to spend time with Alan, losing Guido to South America, and having had minimal contact with my grandson Inti.

More generally, though, I can see now how I have lived most of my life on autopilot, not stopping to appreciate the taste, the colours, the feelings of life. I don't mean that I did not enjoy a good meal, film or political discussion, but rather that I did not enjoy the enjoyment – I'm not sure how else to put it. It is possible that there were good reasons for this during my 20s, when I was with Gillian, and when I was caught up with Caxton, but there were 20 years with Diana, mostly content, which drifted by in a haze of domestic routines, work deadlines and theatre society.

I wish that I had been more conscious of my good fortune in being alive, and in being alive in a rich peaceful country, and through such a golden age of human history. It was only in the 60s that I began to reflect more on the pleasures and essence of being alive. I link this change in me to the First Jihad War and to meeting Lizette. The war was long predicted. I remember Alfred saying to me in 2043: 'The IFSD is swimming against the tide. It's only a matter of time before there's a real war – five years or 20 – it's inevitable now.' But when it came, it still shocked the Western world out of its political malaise. And as for Lizette, her enthusiasm for the real – as opposed to Diana's imaginary – world, and in particular its scientific foundations, opened my eyes.

Unfortunately, my conversion came too late – the best had passed. Yes, I was lucky enough to have found Lizette, and, yes, we had a good second half, as it were, together; but the world had fallen into decline, the golden era of oil and chips was long gone. I – we all in Europe and the US – had been living through a great age, surrounded by a fairyland of riches, in a culture prosperous, free, full of art and science and invention and imagination, and we hadn't noticed how special it was, not until war tore us apart, and the sun's shine was taken away.

I am aware of a dichotomy here, a set of incompatible regrets. How can I reproach myself for not having luxuriated (enjoyed the enjoyment – I am at a loss for words) in the golden era when I believe it should never have been so golden, not with so much of the world poor, hungry or diseased? Having spent much of my life in the service of the United Nations trying to ensure a more balanced distribution of wealth, how can I not regret that we achieved so little, and that our failures led to such terrible wars, to terror, destruction and death, and, because the wars had left the world so deficient in resources, all of that terror, destruction and death multiplied tenfold during the Grey Years.

But I recall Pravit Krishnamurty saying, of the development aid we were trying to negotiate in the 30s, 'You know and I know it is not enough' and, 'It will never be enough'. And I try to understand what common sense tells me: it could not have been any other way. As I have said, I tend towards Zoe Bergmann's view on this – although I certainly would not have done so as a young man. And, as I've also already said, I do have hopes for the new century, modest ones. Recalling (or paraphrasing) something Flip once said: if you look carefully enough at history you can detect a progression, not of nature which always has its own balance – and you'll have to go to a biologist for that – but in the civilisation of men and women, mankind and womankind.

Since I've never had any difficulty in separating out the professional and quasi-political aims I espouse from the ordinary human actions I take, I do not really perceive any need to resolve the dichotomy.

CHAPTER 43

ALICIA VISITS ONE MORE TIME

This morning, before Alicia's visit, I spoke to Dr Lipman. I did not inquire directly about the consequences of delaying my own death, instead I asked him if he had had much experience of patients reneging on death date contracts, and deciding to hang on 'for dear life'. We had discussed this early on, but then I'd had no doubts about my decision or about my will to carry it through, and hadn't needed to pay any attention. This time I did. He told me that about a third of his patients change their minds in the last four weeks. Of these, half deteriorate very rapidly; a quarter take longer, a few months, to die and do so without comfort or dignity; and a quarter do get a tad more life, of acceptable conscious quality. But there are other factors, he explained. Most of those few patients whose pain and discomfort can be controlled longer than expected do not appear to benefit from the extra time because of the 'emotional confusion' experienced by the individuals themselves and/or their close friends and relatives.

I had thought to close my conversation with Dr Lipman at this point, but I succumbed to asking him, without any further artifice, whether I might be one of the few that could hold on for a few extra months. I have a new great grandson on the way, I said, in June. He'll be the first born of my kin in the 22nd century. Dr Lipman's head nodded very slightly, he pursed his lips, as if about to impart bad news, and informed me that I was on such potent medical doses that, in his professional opinion, I'd be 'ga-ga or dead' long before the summer.

Since the day she arrived, I have scarcely been able to stop thinking about Alicia. I am a schoolboy again, daydreaming, but not of Melissa or even Gabriella. I have come to terms with saying goodbye to Jay. I assume this is because our relationship is mature, tidy. But I did not foresee Alicia's arrival, and if I had, I would never have guessed that I would adore her, or that she would tell me she was pregnant and wanted to return. So, when she came this afternoon, and after we'd spent 20 minutes or more looking at family camclips –

hers and mine – I told her that I would be dying on 31 January, and why. She wept, which made me feel terrible. And then she stopped suddenly, as an actress might when a director says 'cut'.

'I'm so sorry, that was terrible of me to do that, to cry. That's so selfish. It must have been painful for you to tell me. What use is crying. I'm going home tomorrow. And in January, when all the centennial business has finished, I'm coming back. I'm coming with João, and Angela and Renato – they'll come, I'll make it work – and we're going to have a late fiesta for your 100 years. Is it good? Will it be good?' She was holding my hand.

'Yes, Alicia, it will be good. But please arrange it with Jay. He can help with the fares; please, please don't be shy about that. And, before you go I have something for you. I'm not giving it to you now because I'm worried I might die before you come again, because I won't I promise, but because I want you to have it now. It's under the bed. Don't open it. Take it home with you, and share it with João, and then, if you can, pass it on to your son.' In anticipation of Alicia's last visit, I had asked Jay to unbox the Ferrez photograph and frame and parcel it up in gift paper. Months ago, I had thought about giving it to Tina, but changed my mind.

'Then I too shall give you a present. I was thinking this already on that first day with you, and I've already talked to João. The name of our boy shall be Kip. Will it be good for you?'

'Yes, Alicia, it will be good for me.'

EXTRACTS FROM CORRESPONDENCE

<u>Kip Fenn to Guido Oostlander-Fenn</u>

31 January 2100

Once before you received important family news by letter, and now this time it is me choosing not to tell you something face-to-face. By the time you read this, I will have gone, and my hope is that I will be cremated quickly without any fuss, and my ashes will be buried near my mother's in a garden at Parsonville. If all goes according to plan, we will have talked on the camphone earlier today. You will have asked me how I am, and I will have said I am fine. But I have only been of sound mind, and relatively free of discomfort for this past year because I chose to fix a death date and take increasingly strong medication until then.

If you and Mireille had not planned to come in the autumn, I would have asked you to do so. I wanted to see you both very much, thus your visit was beautifully timed. But I did not want our last hours together weighed down by you knowing about my deathday. This was my selfishness, and I am apologising now as sincerely as I can. I did not want you returning to Europe just to see me die, not for you and not for me; nor did I want you to be conscious of me moving weekly, daily, hourly nearer the fixed date. I saw this happen to a friend of mine. You could say this should have been your decision not mine. But I took it anyway. Perhaps I was wrong. It is of no matter now. Jay was the only person who knew my death date for certain, and since I see him nearly every day, it was not possible to hide my decision from him. He has been a stalwart friend and confidant, helping me to organise my thoughts and write my Reflections. You will be sent a copy (in which I plan to append both this letter, some of those written by Diana, and some by you) and I hope you find my story interesting and accurate. As I write this I am thinking about those days we spent together on *Ginquin*, and I am wondering whatever happened to our boat. Perhaps if you ever come back to live in Holland, you will seek her out. Beneath her decking, she holds some of my very happiest memories.

Guido, I want you to know that you have been a star in my life, from your birth until my writing of this letter, more than 60 years, whether near or far, you have been a source of comfort and joy in my heart. It has been a privilege to be your father, to know and to love you.

Remember me to Inti, and to Mireille, and, above all, to yourself – take me with you into the 22nd century.

All my love.

Lizette Sanderson to Kip Fenn

October 2097

My darling Kip, if you are reading this then the worst has happened. I am so sorry for leaving you. It seems wrong and unfair that you should have had to look after me, and watch me slide away. It is 3 September as I write, you have fallen asleep on the sofa in the next room listening to one of your favourites, the Berlin Philharmonia playing Zanichelli. To-morrow, I go to hospital again. I fear I might not have another chance to write this letter.

It's a silly letter really, a selfish one with three requests.

I'd like you to do that thing with my ashes, put them in a pot, a flower vase. It was Rhoda's idea, she read it in a magazine. Do you remember us laughing about it. Best of all, I'd like it if my ashes could be turned into glitter – it's possible, some potters (but please not the Noteks) have the equipment – and used for the glaze. I'm confident you'll appreciate why I'd prefer a flower vase to a plant pot.

Secondly, tell Jay how much I loved him; look after him, as I know he will look after you.

Finally, I want to say this: do not mourn my passing, rather hold on to life, on to what we had together, on to what you are – and set it down. I mean I want you to write your Reflections, Kip. You have lived so long, seen so much good and bad, joy and suffering, you have done so much for the people around you, for me, for Jay and for the world, even though I know you do not feel this. Write it all down. You've thought about it before, and I should have encouraged you, but I didn't – as usual, I was thinking of myself not of you. Do it, write your Reflections, don't let yourself be forgotten.

We had a good time, though, didn't we. It wasn't all plain sailing, but you kept your hand so firmly on the tiller of our sailboat that when the inclement weather came along I couldn't help but feel safe and loved and in love.

List of characters

This is a full list of characters appearing in one or more of the trilogy volumes (excluding those referred to only once) by surname (where mentioned in the text) or, otherwise, by first name. For national leaders, dates for their period or periods of office have been noted (as listed in *Encyclopaedia Universal*, 2098 edition).

A

Abd al-Jabbaar, David (son of Sami and Iona) – VOL 3
Abd al-Jabbaar, Iona (wife of Sami Abd al-Jabbaar's) – VOL 3
Abd al-Jabbaar, Sami (Kip's neighbour) – VOL 3
Acklow, Rosemary (therapist) – VOL 1
Ajose, Alfred (Kip's friend) – VOL 1, 2, 3
Ajose, Fayola (Alfred's wife) – VOL 2, 3
Ajose, Fela (son of Alfred and Fayola) – VOL 2, 3
Akilina (Anna Mastepanov's cousin) – VOL 3
Almond (half-brother of Yewla) – VOL 3
Al Zahir (Muslim leader) – VOL 2, 3
Amado, Jorge (Brazilian author) – VOL 1, 2, 3
Anders (stillborn child of Diana and Kip) – VOL 2
Andrasta (Mercurio Sanderson's friend) – VOL 3
Angela (daughter of Alicia Gonçalves) – VOL 3
Antonia de Malancas, Pedro (aka Pam, Mexican director) – VOL 1, 2, 3
Arklington, Betty (US president: 2047-51) – VOL 2, 3
Armstrong, Neil (US astronaut) – VOL 1, 2, 3
Asquith, Jill (Alan Hapgood's friend) – VOL 1
Asser, Eduard Isaad (Dutch photographer) – VOL 1, 2

B

Bayard, Hippolyte (French photographer) – VOL 2, 3
Beale, Martin (teacher) – VOL 1
Beato, Felice (British photographer) – VOL 2
Belinda (administrator) – VOL 2, 3
Bergmann, Zoe (German historian and author) – VOL 3
Brin (Jay Sanderson's friend) – VOL 3
Bronwen (Lionel Wilcox's secretary) – VOL 1

Buffer, John (volleyball coach) – VOL 1, 2
Bunting, Tamson (British artist) – VOL 1, 2

C
Carter (Caxton's go-between) – VOL 1
Caxton, William (née Shuttleworth, Ronald, politician/entrepreneur) – VOL 1, 2, 3
Chambi, Martin (Peruvian photographer) – VOL 2, 3
Chaplin, Charlie (US film actor/director) – VOL 1, 2
Chintz (nurse) – VOL 1, 2, 3
Choolee (prostitute) – VOL 1
Chowdhury, Tommy (IFSD official) – VOL 2
Corazon, Neco (Brazilian president: 2030-40) – VOL 1, 2, 3
Costa, Luigi (Italian prime minister:2043-47, 2049-52, 2055-59) – VOL 3
Courret brothers (Peruvian photographers) – VOL 2, 3
Cowerbridge, Arnold (museum director) – VOL 3
Czyzewski, Walenty (Polish prime minister: 2020-28) – VOL 1

D
Davidson, Augusta (Diana Oostlander's friend) – VOL 2
Davidson, Ike (journalist) – VOL 2
Delors, Jacques (European Commission president: 1985-1995) – VOL 1, 3
Delvreux, Kolin (Anglo-Dutch poet) – VOL 3
de Roo, Arnout (son of Rudy) – VOL 1, 3
de Roo, Livia (Peter's wife) – VOL 1, 2, 3
de Roo, Peter (Kip's friend) – VOL 1, 2, 3
de Roo, Rudy (son of Peter and Livia) – VOL 1, 2, 3
de Roo, Ulla (daughter of Livia and Peter) – VOL 2, 3
Derwent, Julia (US author) – VOL 1
Donna (Crystal Fenn's friend) – VOL 2
Duck, Alexander (British civil servant) – VOL 1
Dufkova, Giselle (museum director) – VOL 3
Dumas, Alexander (French author) – VOL 3
Durring, Lindsay (school pupil) – VOL 3

E
Elly (childminder) – VOL 2
Engelhard, Karl (Diana Oostlander's friend) – VOL 2, 3

F
Fenn, Barry (Tom's father) – VOL 2, 3
Fenn, Crystal (daughter of Gillian and Kip) – VOL 1, 2, 3

Fenn, Evvie (Tom's mother) – VOL 1, 2

Fenn, Gillian (née Tilson, Kip's wife) – VOL 1, 2, 3

Fenn, Julie (née Hapgood, Kip's mother) – VOL 1, 2, 3

Fenn, Tom (Kip's father) – VOL 1, 2, 3

Ferrer i Germa, Joaquima (Catalan film maker) – VOL 2

Ferrera Magalhães, Conceição (Kip's friend) – VOL 1, 2, 3

Ferrez, Marc (Brazilian photographer) – VOL 1, 2, 3

Fortune, Matt (British politician) – VOL 2, 3

Fragrance (Tom Fenn's second wife) – VOL 2, 3

Fuller, Garth (British prime minister: 2037-45) – VOL 1, 2

G

Gabriella (bus passenger) – VOL 1, 3

Gagarin, Yuri (Russian astronaut) – VOL 1, 2

Garibaldi, Giuseppi (Italian military leader) – VOL 3

Gemma (Alfred Ajose's girlfriend) – VOL 1, 2

Gonçalves, Alicia (née Magalhães, daughter of Arturo) – VOL 2, 3

Gonçalves, João (Alicia's husband) – VOL 3

Gregory, Crispin (British historian) – VOL 1, 2, 3

H

Hapgood, Alan (Kip's uncle) – VOL 1, 2, 3

Hapgood, Eileen (Julie Fenn's mother) – VOL 1, 3

Hapgood, Oswald (Julie Fenn's father) – VOL 1

Harris, Chuck (US author) – VOL 3

Hilde (Wood Junior's secretary) – VOL 1

Hitler (German dictator: 1933-45) – VOL 1, 3

Hoop, Vi (Canadian singer) – VOL 1, 2

Horeva, Ninel (IFSD official) – VOL 2, 3

I

Imogen (Rob's friend) – VOL 2

Inti (son of Guido Oostlander-Fenn and Mireille) – VOL 3

J

Jackmann-Ives, Rhoda (Lizette Sanderson's friend) – VOL 3

Jensen, Sydney (British materials science professor) – VOL 3

Jespersen, Bobby (journalist) – VOL 2, 3

Jessop, William (doctor) – VOL 1, 2

Johns, Unwin (British poet) – VOL 1, 3

Johnson, Wilma (British history professor) – VOL 1, 2
Jones, Adam (UK prime minister: 2022-32) – VOL 1, 2

K

Kallström, Ingrid (Swedish environmental campaigner) – VOL 1
Karel (son of Tamara) – VOL 3
Kingston (Crystal Fenn's friend) – VOL 3
Kiselev, Boris (IFSD official) – VOL 2
Koper, Melanie (Phil Rumble's wife) – VOL 1
Krishnamurty, Pravit (IFSD official) – VOL 2, 3

L

Lambert, Aaron (British film director) – VOL 2
Le Gray, Gustave (French photographer) – VOL 2, 3
Liphook, Philip (aka Flip, teacher) – VOL 1, 2, 3
Lipman, Rupert (doctor) – VOL 1, 3
Lobo, Se (Brazilian journalist) – VOL 3
Lock, Josephine (née Shuttleworth, daughter of William Caxton) – VOL 2, 3
Lola (net madam) – VOL 1, 2
Lomax, Lorraine (technical director) – VOL 3
Luz (Arturo Magalhães's friend) – VOL 3
Lyndquist, John (UK prime minister: 2032-37) – VOL 1, 2

M

Madan, Triti (Indian international politics professor) – VOL 1, 2, 3
Magalhães, Arturo Fenn (son of Kip and Conceição) – VOL 1, 2, 3
Magalhães, Edna (Arturo's first wife) – VOL 2, 3
Magalhães, Eliane (née Silva, Juliano's wife) – VOL 2
Magalhães, Fatima (Arturo's second wife) – VOL 2, 3
Magalhães, Ignacio (son of Arturo and Fatima) – VOL 2, 3
Magalhães, Juliano (son of Arturo and Fatima) – VOL 2, 3
Magalhães, Tina (daughter of Fatima and Arturo) – VOL 2, 3
Magalhães Silva, Maria (daughter of Eliane and Juliano) – VOL 2, 3
Mallow, Vincent (aka Mush, British actor) – VOL 1, 3
Marcella (Olive Norrington's partner) – VOL 3
Maria (Pope: 2052-74) – VOL 3
MarySue (secretary) – VOL 2, 3
Mastepanov, Anna (Alan Hapgood's partner) – VOL 2, 3
May (Mercurio Sanderson's friend) – VOL 3
McFeather, Andrew (US president: 2017-21) – VOL 1
Meijer, Dominique (née Oostlander, Diana's sister) – VOL 2, 3

Meijer, Jurian (son of Waltar and Dominique) – VOL 2, 3

Meijer, Lukas (son of Waltar and Dominique) – VOL 2, 3

Meijer, Waltar (Dominique's husband) – VOL 2, 3

Melissa (Kip's girlfriend) – VOL 1, 2, 3

Merriweather, Horace (Kip's friend) – VOL 1, 2, 3

Merriweather Tim (Horace's brother) – VOL 1, 2, 3

Mistral, Amy (British film/theatre director) – VOL 2, 3

Monique (Alan Hapgood's girlfriend) – VOL 1, 2, 3

Monroe, Marilyn (US film actress) – VOL 1

Montechristo, Felix Rico (Ecuadorian entrepreneur) – VOL 3

Movie Martyr (US film director) – VOL 1, 2

N

Naiambana, Chidi (IFSD official) – VOL 2, 3

Nash, Liam (Diana Oostlander's cousin) – VOL 2, 3

Nolan brothers (US astronauts) – VOL 1, 2

Norrington, Olive (Lizette Sanderson's colleague) – VOL 3

O

Oakley, Finbar (British playwright) – VOL 1, 2, 3

Ojoru (Nigerian president: 2027-35, 2037-47) – VOL 1, 2, 3

Olivier, Jean-Michele (REACH official) – VOL 3

Oosterhuis, Pieter (Dutch photographer) – VOL 1

Oostlander, Anders (Diana's brother) – VOL 2

Oostlander, Dana (Diana's sister) – VOL 2

Oostlander, Demeter (aka Dimi, Diana's sister) – VOL 2, 3

Oostlander, Diana (Kip's partner) – VOL 1, 2, 3

Oostlander, Neeltje (née van der Klein, Diana's mother) – VOL 2

Oostlander, Powles (Diana's father) – VOL 2

Oostlander-Fenn, Guido Tom (son of Kip and Diana) – VOL 1, 2, 3

P

Pacciotti (Italian film director) – VOL 1, 3

Paride Bernabo, Hector Julio (aka Caybe, Brazilian artist) – VOL 1, 3

Pattison, Flora (Kip's friend) – VOL 1, 2, 3

Pedrosa, Maria (Brazilian actress) – VOL 3

Popsicle (Kip's girlfriend) – VOL 1, 3

Pouille, Henri (photograph curator) – VOL 3

Q

Quant, Lucretia (British author) – VOL 1, 3

Quasim (Angela's partner) – VOL 3

R
Rachel (Julie Fenn's friend) – VOL 1, 2
Raisa (Clarity Sampson's friend) – VOL 3
Renato (son of Angela) – VOL 3
Rob (Melissa's brother) – VOL 1, 2
Robinson, Henry Peach (British photographer) – VOL 1
Rocard, Didier (Diana Oostlander's friend) – VOL 2, 3
Rocard, Helene (née Chastrain, Didier's wife) – VOL 2, 3
Rocard, Mireille (daughter of Helene and Didier) – VOL 2, 3
Rocard, Veronique (daughter of Helene and Didier) – VOL 2, 3
Rumble, Phil (British civil servant) – VOL 1

S
Sampson, Clarity (Pete's wife) – VOL 2, 3
Sampson, Joan (daughter of Clarity and Pete) – VOL 2, 3
Sampson, Pete (Kip's friend) – VOL 1, 2, 3
Sanderson, Esos (son of Mercurio and Andrasta) – VOL 3
Sanderson, Irene (daughter of Lynn and Samuel) – VOL 2, 3
Sanderson, Jay (son of Lizette, and Kip) – VOL 1, 2, 3
Sanderson, Lizette (Kip's partner) – VOL 1, 2, 3
Sanderson, Lynn (Samuel's wife) – VOL 3
Sanderson, Mahonia (daughter of Lynn and Samuel) – VOL 3
Sanderson, Mercurio (aka Rio, Lizette's brother) – VOL 3
Sanderson, Mervyn (Lizette's father) – VOL 3
Sanderson, Samuel (Lizette's brother) – VOL 3
Sanderson, Saul (son of Samuel and Lynn) – VOL 3
Sanderson, Wendy (Lizette's mother) – VOL 3
Sanfrancissisi (aka Sanfry, Nigerian volleyball player) – VOL 2, 3
Shakespeare (English playwright) – VOL 1, 2
Singleton, Jude (British civil servant) – VOL 1, 2, 3
Spoon, Terrance (British prime minister: 2045-48) – VOL 1, 2, 3
Stalin (Russian dictator: 1929-53) – VOL 1, 3
Stockmann, Angelika (German playwright) – VOL 2, 3
Subramani (teacher) – VOL 1
Sumani, Leona (public relations specialist) – VOL 3

T
Tamara (Alan Hapgood's girlfriend) – VOL 1, 3
Tarbuck, Steve (US president: 2051-59) – VOL 2, 3

Thomas, Rike (British civil servant) – VOL 2
Tilson, Bronze (son of Kip and Gillian) – VOL 1, 2, 3
Tilson, Constance (Gillian's mother) – VOL 1
Tilson, John (Gillian's grandfather) – VOL 1
Tindle (British politician) – VOL 1, 3
Tuohy, Clint (Lizette Sanderson's husband) – VOL 3
Turnbull, Doug (Kip's friend) – VOL 2, 3
Turnbull, Lucy (daughter of Miriam and Doug) – VOL 2, 3
Turnbull, Miriam (Doug's wife) – VOL 2, 3
Turnbull, Susannah (daughter of Miriam and Doug) – VOL 2, 3

V
van der Klein, Anders (Diana's grandfather) – VOL 2
van der Klein, Betje (Diana's aunt) – VOL 2
van der Klein, Kaatje (Diana's aunt) – VOL 2
Vaughn, Leo (photograph curator) – VOL 3
Vetch, Brian (British political adviser) – VOL 1, 2
Vidrio (Crystal Fenn's boyfriend) – VOL 2, 3
Villalonga, Eduardo (IFSD official) – VOL 3
Voll, Max (Argentinian billionaire) – VOL 3

W
Wells, Vince (Jay Sanderson's partner) – VOL 1, 2, 3
Wilcox, Lionel (aka Firey, British politician) – VOL 1, 2
Williams, Cos (media producer) – VOL 3
Wood Junior, Sterling (oil executive) – VOL 1
Worcester, Paulina (British prime minister: 2056-59) – VOL 2
Worthington, Pearl (teenager) – VOL 1, 2
Worthington, Xanthe (Pearl's mother) – VOL 2

X
Xiangjun, Liu (IFSD official) – VOL 3

Y
Yewla (daughter of May and Mercurio) – VOL 2, 3
Yvonne (Gillian Fenn's friend) – VOL 1

Z
Zanichelli (Italian composer) – VOL 2, 3
Zimmerman, Jeff (Kip's friend) – VOL 1, 2, 3

FAMILY RELATIONSHIPS

BACKGROUND

Evvie+Barry Fenn   Eileen (+Oswald Hapgood)   Percival

Tom Fenn+Julie   Alan (+Anna Mastepanov)

Neil (aka Kip) Fenn

PARTNERS AND CHILDREN

CONCEIÇÃO

Kip Fenn+Conceição Magalhães

Arturo Magalhães (+Edna)   + Fatima
|(cloned)
Alicia (+João Gonçalves)   Tina Juliano (+Eliane) Ignacio

Angela+Quasim   Maria

Renato

GILLIAN

John Tilson

Constance Tilson

Kip Fenn+Gillian

Crystal Fenn   *Bronze Tilson*

DIANA

Claudine+Anders van der Klein   Maartje+Eduwart Oostlander

Betje   Kaatje   Neeltje + Powles   Saartje +Anthony Nash

Kip Fenn+Diana Demeter Dana Dominique+Waltar Meijer   Liam

Guido Oostlander-Fenn+Mireille Rocard   Jurian Lukas

Inti

LIZETTE

Wendy+Mervyn Sanderson

Kip Fenn+Lizette (+Clint Tuohy) Samuel (+Lynn) Mercurio+May +Andrasta

Jay Sanderson   Saul   Irene   Mahonia   Yewla   Esos

www.ingramcontent.com/pod-product-compliance
Lightning Source LLC
Chambersburg PA
CBHW061955170626
46813CB00006B/2654